GARTH MARENGHI'S

TerrorTome

Garth Marenghi was born in the past, graduated from his local comprehensive (now bulldozed) with some O levels in subjects. He taught for nine years at his local library reading group before becoming a full-time horror writer. He has published numerous novels of terror (too numerous to list, nay count), over five hundred short stories, and has edited thirty anthologies of his own work, which have all received the Grand Master of Darkdom Award. He wrote, directed and starred in *Garth Marenghi's Darkplace* for the Peruvian market, which subsequently aired on Channel 4 and has not been repeated due to its radical and polemic content. He commenced work on *Terror Tome* during the late 1980s, continued on it alone and unaided by editors throughout the 1990s, and on into the early 2000s, then the mid-2000s, and has only now found a publisher brave enough to unleash its chilling portendings. He is an honorary fellow.

GARTH MARENGHI'S
TerrorTome

HODDERstudio

First published in Great Britain in 2022 by Hodder Studio
An imprint of Hodder & Stoughton
An Hachette UK company

5

A CIP catalogue record for this title is available from the British Library

Hardback ISBN 9781529399400
eBook ISBN 9781399713443

Typeset in Bembo by Hewer Text UK Ltd, Edinburgh
Printed and bound in Great Britain by Clays Ltd, Elcograf S.p.A.

Hodder & Stoughton policy is to use papers that are natural, renewable and recyclable
products and made from wood grown in sustainable forests. The logging and manufacturing
processes are expected to conform to the environmental regulations of the country of origin.

Hodder & Stoughton Ltd
Carmelite House
50 Victoria Embankment
London EC4Y 0DZ

CONTENTS

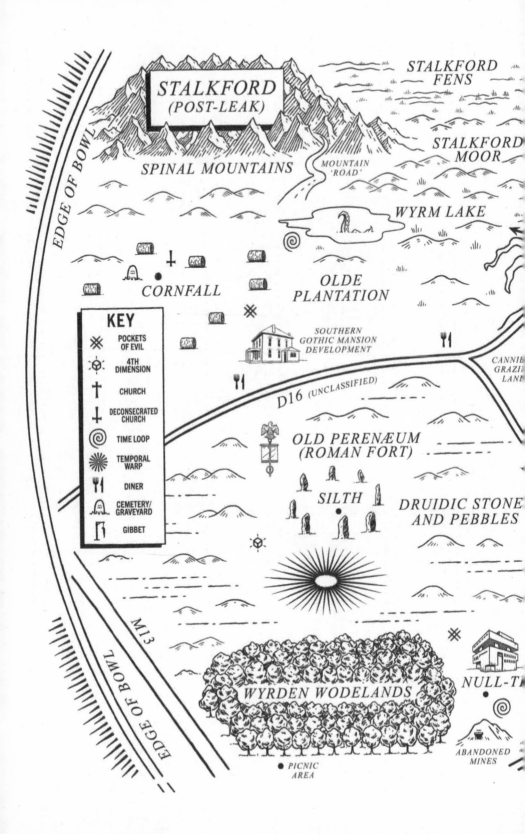

INTRODUCTION

The End Times.

They're here, pilgrim. Look around you. Whoa, easy, big guy (or girl). Just a peek. Or you'll go crazy. Only take it from me. *They're here.*

As I write this, sweating and fever-addled in my pleather sickbed, laid low by a lethal virus I foresaw – and would have foretold if I'd had a publishing deal at the time (more on that anon) – I can't help but note with sombre irkdom that my lifelong gift for presagement has been summarily spurned by an ungrateful species soon to reap its own sorry whirlwind.

Unchecked despotisms, spiralling virtuality, New Pestilence (like this one I'm sweating from), the Nether Web, thrashnalism, fearache, paranoiativity – you name it. All of it's happened on my writer's watch.*

So where the hell have I been?

The short answer is: writing the longest and most terrifying epic fictive of my career, three instalments of which you currently hold in your mortal hand/hands (I'm aware this sentence won't make sense for the audiobook version, but that's your fault for reading me 'on the go' and no doubt wishing this was a podcast instead – which, incidentally, *isn't* an art form).

The long answer is the same as above, only with extraneous detail added, which I have omitted.

---

* Figurative authorial responsibility, i.e. not a mechanical device. I defy Time on ideological grounds.

I began writing *TerrorTome* in the late 1980s, continued through-out the 1990s and carried on deep into the early and mid-2000s.

My grim vision of a world in which a horror writer's imagination *literally leaks out of his head* to wage supernatural war against unsus-pecting Mankind was not just wildly visionary for the time, but is now judderingly prescient. Who knew then that a reality would soon be upon us in which every crazy thought or theory dreamed up by untold doomscribes (Them) would possess enough potency and power in the minds of the terrified masses (You) to emerge, breath-ing and seething, as grim, hard fact (IT).

Sure, it was a simpler world back then, but the seeds of doom were already sown. By decade's end, I'd lost my publishing contract (having assaulted my then-editor with his company pager), my closest friends (who were, actually, it turns out, all arseholes) the love of my own wife and daughters (possibly *partly* my fault), a significant proportion of my sanity (nothing remotely sexual), all hope in a brighter future, and – perhaps worst of all – my beloved Jenson Interceptor (impounded on the streets of Hemel Hempstead following a view-ing of several one-bedroom apartments that ultimately were too expensive).

In my youth (though technically late middle-age), I ventured forth into the darkness on a personal odyssey of pain, to bring forth from the hell of my own brain a book of Darkdom befitting this age of ruin.

Read with extreme caution.

'The TerrorTome'.

– Garth Marenghi, Cosmic Veil-Render, Twixt-Dimensional Visionary and former Grand Duke of Darkness (now Archduke)

TYPE-FACE

(Dark Lord of the Prolix)

'The mind is its own place, and in itself can make a Heaven of Hell, a Hell of Heaven.'

– The Big Bumper Book of Quotations, *p. 319*

CHAPTER ONE

So it *did* exist.

I stood alone in the pouring rain, peering in through the window of 'Uniquities Inc., plus Eels', at a machine supposedly invented by Christopher Latham Sholes in 1867, but constructed, according to the price tag slung from its golden carriage-return lever, by a Chinese magician in the latter half of the Tang Dynasty.

I smiled, shaking my head. A bold claim . . .

Yet true. For my own research had revealed that Eastern antiquity had achieved, in its long-lost past, a level of technological advancement surpassing even Currys. Yes, the Chinese had invented paper and, thank the lord, gunpowder. But, finally, here was proof beyond all doubt that those ancient sorcerers had also created the humble typewriter.

I turned my face from the glass display and looked around me. This lonely side street off Stalkford's town centre, which I'd never noticed before today, seemed to be perpetually empty. Maybe a small second-hand shop specialising in offbeat mysterious oddities didn't attract major footfall. That or the eels were an issue.

Nick Steen's the name. Perhaps you've heard of me? Yeah, that's right. The horror guy. The insanely rich, multiple best-selling, dark and dangerous-to-know paperback visionary of the dark arts. *That* Nick Steen. If not, you soon will (in fact, you do now). But maybe not in quite the way you imagine. An apposite word, that – *imagine* – and not just because words (like *apposite*) are my trade, or *profession*. For *imagination*, which is the root noun of that previous word

– *imagine* – has everything to do with the real-life horrors that were about to unfold.

Imagination . . .

<u>*My*</u> *imagination . . .*

Let me explicate.

In my own time.

I turned down the collar of my charcoal tweed blazer over my black polo-neck sweater, smoothed back my full and flowing mane of smoky-topaz hair, then removed the buff-tinted shades of my chopper-pilot days to get a better look.

To the casual observer, the typewriter sitting in the shop window before me resembled a conventional model. Aside from its gold-plated exterior, the only difference appeared to be a set of extra keys surrounding the conventional QWERTYs, depicting obscure archaic letterings and bizarre runic symbols. These stood out, I noticed, at insane psycho-geometric angles only Carl Sagan and myself could have perceived.

But if the rumours I'd heard were true, and this *was* the very type-writer I was seeking, then this bizarre, ancient contraption also possessed certain unique powers entirely its own. For, by some unknown spiritual process long since lost to Man, this machine's original creator had supposedly instilled in it the ability to commune psychically with its owner, allowing him or her (but mainly him) access to hitherto unreachable depths of the subconscious mind, freeing, from the murky swamps of their internal id, the darkest parts of their suppressed imagination.

As a best-selling horror writer, I had to have it. (Also, there was currently thirty per cent off.)

Although I was still the hot news in horror, crafting non-stop the darkest, most terrifying novels of supernatural terror known to civilisation, sizzling on the publishing plate for nigh-on twenty years and counting, it wasn't enough.

I had too many ideas. Too many tales untold. Too much darkness left untapped.

If I was lucky, I had around forty years of life left. Fifty if I gave up red meat, which wasn't an option. And yet I hadn't even begun to explore the *true* horrors of human existence. Hadn't got anywhere near probing the deeper darkness that exists *beneath* Mankind's basest nature. Hadn't yet drawn upon the horror *beyond* horror, shall we say? That snarling, predatory *hellbeast* lying dormant in our supposedly civilised minds. If I could unleash *that*, thereby teaching Mankind (or Ladykind, if that's important to you) to live *alongside* their own particular corresponding hellbeast, then just maybe I could save all of us from ultimate self-destruction.

Endarken our world for the greater Bad.

(And make more money.)

Which is why I was here now, staring at this damned typewriter.

BUY ME.

I jumped at the sudden sound and looked around me, wondering if the owner had leaned briefly out of his shop doorway. But there was no one there. The street, too, was still completely deserted.

Then who'd spoken?

BUY ME.

There it was again. Coming from somewhere close by, it seemed, yet also immeasurable distances away. A deep voice, devoid of expression, yet possessing an undeniable tone of command.

I SAID, BUY ME.

Again. Was it originating from somewhere in my own head, perhaps? Was I, after twenty solid years at the top of my game, crafting inimitable works of challenging, visionary horror, in fact going *mad?*

I looked down at the typewriter again. If I hadn't known better, I'd assume it had shifted forwards slightly on its mock-velvet display, moving closer to the glass pane separating us.

BUY ME.

In an effort to get away from the strange voice in my head, I made my way over to the door and stepped inside. The interior of the shop was dark and gloomy. An old man in a grubby rubber apron stood behind a dusty counter on the far side of the room. He looked familiar.

'Eel?' he asked me, offering up a lidless plastic container clutched in his hand. I walked towards him and glanced inside it. It was an old ice-cream box half-filled with dirty water, with a writhing cluster of black, slimy snake-fish wriggling within.

I looked back up and stared deeply into his cataract-covered eyes. 'I know you from somewhere, old-timer.'

'I'm Moses Unique,' he rasped, chewing on an eel's head. 'I sell ... *uniquities*.' He let the eel slide inside him, swallowing the creature whole. 'Plus eels.'

'I'm interested in that typewriter you have on display in your front window.'

'This one?' he replied, lifting up a large tea cosy on the counter to reveal an identical-looking machine immediately below it.

'So they're a pair, are they?' I asked.

'A *pair*?' he echoed, confused. 'This is the only machine of its kind in existence.'

I glanced back behind me at the window display. A Victorian sex chair now stood in the space where the typewriter had been.

'An exquisite machine,' the old man continued, his oily hands hovering over the contraption's keys. 'Tang Dynasty, no less. Look at that gleaming return lever. This resplendent feed roller. Do your fingers not yearn to hammer hard upon those golden keys? Do you not hunger for the touch of its jewel-emblazoned ribbon reverse knob? The soft kiss of its diamond-adorned ribbon spool? Do you not dream of feeding your soft paper sheetage through its hard, studded platen?'

'I'm more interested in its *mind*,' I said, curious to see whether or not he understood me. The old man examined me for a moment, a spark of recognition crossing his half-blind eyes.

'Steen ...' he said, nodding to himself. 'Nick Steen ... The horror writer?'

'Correct,' I replied. 'But you're not Moses Unique.'

He grinned nervously then, his milky-white orbs darting furtively from left to right. Hell, I *knew* him, alright. But where from?

BUY ME.

That voice again. Whatever it was, wherever it was coming from, it seemed to be reading my innermost thoughts. It too, wanted me to buy the typewriter. And the strange thing was, I now felt like I was being forced. Ordered. *Compelled.* (Not tautologous, as there is a subtle difference between all three.)

I quickly did the math. Despite my fame, I knew I'd be unable to claim ancient antiquities against tax (I've tried several times, but no joy), meaning I'd need to make my savings elsewhere. If I ceased all alimony payments and sent my ex-wife to live in rented accommodation at her own expense, selling all my daughter's non-transportable toys, I might just be able to afford it without dipping into any of my own money.

Given that Jacinta had yet to forgive me for press-ganging our daughter into an early proofreading career, it would hardly come as a surprise to her if I suddenly recommenced hostilities out of the blue. And I wouldn't need to worry about any legal challenge, either. Early on in my career, I'd refused to co-write anything with another human being, including my marriage certificate, for which I'd employed several pseudonyms. So any potential ex-wife would need to descend all nine Circles of Hell in order to extract a single penny from my mounting fortunes. And, if this typewriter really was the one I'd been seeking, those fortunes would soon be mounting even higher.

Soon I'd be writing darker, more terrifying novels than any I'd dared write before. Famed the whole world over as the greatest horror writer who'd ever lived. Then finally, Roz Bloom, my editor at Clackett Publishing, would realise, once and for all, that I *don't need an editor*.

If this typewriter was the one.

The old man swallowed another eel and tapped his finger against the discount sticker.

Was the thing *truly* magical, like I'd been told?

I AM INDEED.

Dammit, that voice *again*. Either I *was* going mad, or some presence, some *force*, seemed to be communicating with me from deep within my own mind. Plumbing the murkiest depths of my subconscious.

And then it hit me.

Maybe the typewriter *itself* was already trying to communicate with me.

YES.

If that was true, there could no longer be any doubt in my mind. The machine perched in front of me truly *had* to be the one I'd been seeking. The key to unlocking my deepest, darkest nightmares.

THAT'S RIGHT. I AM.

I froze. That voice ... That voice in my head ... It was the *typewriter's* voice! As unbelievable as it might seem, the *typewriter itself* was *speaking to me*.

EUREKA.

Then this really was it, beyond all doubt. After an endless, painstaking search of several hours, the hunt was finally over. The machine I had sought was finally in my grasp.

'And will you be purchasing?' asked the old man, with the hint of a sly grin.

'I will,' I replied, pulling out my credit card. 'But I'll need a VAT receipt.'

'Oh,' he said, hands fumbling uselessly in both pockets. 'We only take cash.'

'Then put it on my slate, having first set me up with said slate,' I said, reaching for the typewriter. But somehow it was already there, in my arms.

'Ouch,' I snapped suddenly, feeling my right index finger snag sharply against part of its mechanism.

The old man chuckled, tucking into another eel. 'You have just felt, sir, the delicious, castigating pinch of its dormant ribbon vibrator.'

'Go easy on those eels,' I said. He winked at me.

'Does your rod not harden at the coy wink of its sparkling typebar?'

I ignored him and walked back over to the door, and my Honda Civic parked beyond. Then turned again in a final attempt to place the man's features.

But his face was now masked by the plastic container, which he'd tipped upwards at one corner to gulp down what remained. I stepped outside, yanked open my car door and placed the typewriter down on the passenger seat. Then found myself attaching the seatbelt across its front.

THANKS.

'You're welcome,' I said, getting in beside it and keying the ignition. Before pulling out, I turned to address it directly, realising I would look stir-crazy to anyone passing by. Fortunately, the street was still entirely empty.

'Let me make one thing perfectly clear,' I said, leaning over towards it. 'Yes, you may be ancient. Yes, you may possess untold powers beyond the ken of Man, but from this moment on, you work for me, *capiche*? I'm the master, and you do *my* bidding.'

SURE. WHATEVER YOU SAY.

I grinned, pleased we'd reached an early understanding, and keyed the engine.

COWBOY.

I glanced back for a second, confused, then pulled out on to the main road.

Sucking the blood from my injured finger.

One year later . . .

CHAPTER TWO

I woke, hot and sweaty in my bed. By the number of fresh salt rings accrued on my pleather sheet, I could tell it was mid-afternoon. I rose up, peeled back the soiled rubber underlining and unclamped my nipples from the typewriter's tab plates.

Hell, if Roz could see me now.

I extracted what little remained of my leather briefs, which the machine had ordered me to wear. This pair had finally taken the ultimate battering, obliterated by the typewriter's frenzied all-night hammering.

I drew the last sheet of paper from my master the platen and perused the results of our nocturnal labours. Five paragraphs of runic symbols and a swarm of ellipses. Plus, the font had swollen from twelve-point to twenty-four, and was quietly throbbing.

A hard night's work, indeed.

I breathed a sigh of relief that day had finally dawned, albeit with the sun already waning, and prayed that the timer on my filter machine had kicked in. Every orifice and appendage I possessed had been either probed or thrashed into oblivion nightly for the past twelve months by what was, in essence, a mechanical keyboard, and now even brewing the morning coffee was a physical trial.

It had all begun so beautifully. That magical evening, I'd pulled back my sheets to find it lying there in my bed, outer casing entirely removed, with a single red rose placed provocatively over the keypad, alongside other necessities from the Boots family planning aisle.

15

I tried to reassure myself that what followed that night, and the nights after, was natural. Romantic, even. That our frenzied thrashing was born of a mutual understanding. That as long as the prose I produced with it was good, then it could have me anyway, anyhow, anywhere. Not anytime, as I had a book-signing tour scheduled for the last two weeks in June, but July and August were currently free and ripe for intense creative frottage.

And as far as I knew, I was now writing sophisticated horror, as promised – the darkest, sickest, dare I say *sexiest* writing of my career. I wouldn't call my new work perverted, certainly when compared to what the typewriter and I were getting up to *outside* office hours, but my books were radical, polemical and apparently already evolving Mankind (if reports from the Institute of Zoology were anything to go by and squirrel monkeys really *were* learning to wipe their backsides with my discarded proofs).

Yes, the content was heavily erotic, but as the typewriter had explained, weren't writing and making love both acts of *creation*? Then why *not* combine them? After all, wasn't this merely that repressed, subconscious darkness I'd been seeking? Hadn't the typewriter simply tapped into a long-repressed love for my own mind? A deep, passionate lusting after my own *creativity*? Wasn't all this mechanical slap and tickle simply the potent, primal roaring of Nick Steen's own particular form of *hellbeast*? Sure, I was tired. Spent. Soiled. Invariably humiliated. But finally I was learning to live with my internal monster.

There was just one small problem.

My books were no longer selling.

As I caught the faint aroma of brewing coffee drifting through from the kitchen, the phone on my bedside table rang. I gave the typewriter's platen knob a playful squeeze to let it know I was still up for more, and picked up the receiver.

'Nick Steen,' I announced. 'Horror author and visionary doomscribe.'

'It's me, Nick.'

I knew who it was.

'Who's this?' I said.

'It's *me*, Nick.'

'Wrong. I'm Nick. You're a stranger.'

'It's *Roz*.'

'Like I said. A stranger.'

'I know you're being brave, Nick. That deep down you're still angry I fired you. But at the end of the day, you're the one partaking in kinky liaisons with an ancient typewriter. Not me.'

At least she was finally accepting the thing was sentient. I'd never expected Roz to embrace the notion wholesale when I first mentioned this new 'tool' in my writing arsenal, but I'd presumed, being an editor, she'd be interested at the literary level, if nothing else. But the very thought of my own physical debasement via the prongs of a sadistic typing machine, dispensing total and unrelenting physical punishment, had somehow left her cold.

So she'd fired me.

'You're a fool, Roz. Last night that machine and I plumbed untold depths of forbidden pleasure. Explored uncharted ecstasies of physical suffering. Achieved obscene and frankly unacceptable levels of pain-wracked pleasure, though I do have to have a quiet word with it about the nipple-twisting. That's delicate tissue and can cause long-term damage.'

'I'm not interested in your sordid trysts, Nick. I called to tell you that I've now fulfilled my final contractual obligations and submitted your latest manuscript to Clackett Publishing, like you asked. *Without* my recommended changes.'

Well, well, well. So, Roz did have a few surprises left in her. Maybe she *was* warming to the typewriter, after all.

'Not a single edit?' I said, wanting to ensure things were *precisely* as I'd demanded.

'Nothing. I submitted it exactly as you instructed.'

'All twelve thousand pages?'

'Actually, I took out one ankh.'

I snarled inwardly. 'Which ankh?'

'It may have been a pentacle.'

'Was it an ankh or a pentacle?'

'It was a pentacle.'

'Put the pentacle back in.'

'If you insist.'

The platen whipped back suddenly, hammering my left ball.

'And add an extra ankh.'

'Whatever you say.'

'That's more like it, Roz,' I said, tending my bruised conker. 'Not hard, is it?'

'I suppose not.'

'Sorry, Roz? I was thinking aloud.' I clenched my teeth and tried to savour the dull, aching throb emanating from down below, like the typewriter had told me to. But if I'm honest, I wasn't quite feeling it this morning.

'So what did Clackett say?'

'They passed.'

'*Passed?*' The platen retracted violently the other way, ripping free a generous thatch of my densest pubery. I shrieked.

'It's no good getting upset, Nick. They're hugely concerned about the financial implications of these new manuscripts you're delivering. And they have my sympathy, given that each one requires a significant amount of industrial scaffolding to support its multiple volumes and mini-library of appendices, plus a custom-built house-crane to turn the pages.'

Productivity *had* been an issue, it was true. According to the type-writer's manual, the machine worked by tapping directly into the user's brain, enabling them to channel their visions directly through its own internal mechanism. Which meant that my words – and more importantly my thoughts – could be harnessed *instantly* and produced at 5,000 times my usual rate. Potentially, that number might even reach infinity (again, according to the manual, though most of it was in Chinese).

'And more importantly, with your current productivity rate of one multi-volume tome each half-day,' Roz continued, 'serious environmental questions are now being raised at head office.'

'Such as?'

'Such as, should Clackett be responsible for decimating the natural resources of several developing nations in order to manufacture your *Daemonica Flagellatum Quindecimology*, which has yet to earn back a single percentage of its investment, or even make it out of the factory gate. At this current rate of deforestation, Nick, you're likely to go down in history as the man who single-handedly destroyed our natural world.'

'Did they say anything else?'

'Just that it was cack.'

I nodded, sensing this had been coming for a while now. Clackett still hadn't delivered me my author's copies, and had instead given me some bull about the book potentially compromising the structural integrity of my apartment block.

'Look, Roz,' I said, deciding to switch on the charm, 'we've known each other a long time. You were there at the very beginning of my career, when I first started out with *Hives*, a semi-autobiographical horror-thriller about a sentient skin disease. Thanks to your slight help, I soon became the pioneering voice of "Rasher" fiction, a violent sub-genre of flesh-ailment-related horror novels. Within months, we'd published *The Itching, Sunburner, Woebetigo, The Shingler, Night of the Eczeman, Eczeman 2: Derma-die-sis, Rosacea's Baby, The Swelling, The Burning, The Flaking, The Crusting, A Scab in the Dark (Scabman 1), Scabman 2: Return of the Scabman, Scabman 3: No Pickin',*

Psychoriasis (The Bleeder 1), Psychoriasis 2 (The Bleeder 2), Psychoriasis 3: Revenge of the Flesh Heads (aka Bleeder vs Scabman). Jeez, Roz, in just over a year, we'd each earned over four hundred pounds.'

'Of course, Nick. How could I forget?'

I heard it in her voice. A softening. I was getting there. Stoking memories of times past. Memories of us. Of that skin disease I'd inadvertently spread throughout Clackett with an ill-advised hand-shake upon signing my initial contract, which only brought us closer (we were in the same ward).

'We used to understand each other, Roz. We used to click. First through the overwhelming local success of my "Rasher" series, then via a genuine shared interest in our persistent skin conditions. Who knows where we might have ended up one day? Maybe we'd have spent long, hazily romantic afternoons at some dermatological clinic, followed by late-night, booze-fuelled erotic sessions of mutual-examination fantasy and "itch play".'

'Nick, I have to go.'

'Apologies, that's the typewriter speaking. It has me looking for the erotic in pretty much everything I do, these days. Look, I know you respected my writing back then, Roz. Believed in my visions, however terrifyingly provocative or socially unacceptable they might have been. Yet now, when I'm breaking down genre boundaries, challenging conventional logic, evolving Mankind, forcing it to face and ultimately conquer its deepest, darkest fears, you're pulling out on me for the sake of some trees.'

'No company we've contacted can replant at a sustainable rate, Nick.'

'Not my problem, Roz. And to be frank, I think the real issue here is that you're upset because I told you I was getting increasingly fresh with my typing implement.'

'Because you've changed, Nick,' she said, wiping away tears. (And yes, I could hear her doing that.) 'Ever since you bought that damned typewriter. Your work's become more intense, more crazed, more . . .'

'Radical?' I asked, interrupting, because Roz did have a tendency to bang on.

'No, Nick. *Rubbish.*'

She spat out the word, and if there hadn't been a phone between us, and a cable, and walls, plus several streets, lines of traffic, etc., I'd have copped it full in the eye.

'Your books are now incomprehensible. Confused. Meaningless. An insane collection of bizarre runic signs and jumbled, wordless nonsense, which you somehow think contains some shred of meaning. If I didn't know better, I'd say you were either raving mad, Nick, or that typewriter you bought is *cursed.*'

I looked over at the machine. It was no longer on my bed, but had somehow managed to manoeuvre itself into my en suite, where it was now busy taking a shower.

'I think you could be right, Roz.'

'Whatever it is, Clackett want nothing more to do with you. And neither do I, Nick. Neither do I.'

'I heard you the first time, Roz. Goodbye, then. Only let me tell you something before I go. I'm writing the best horror fiction of my career, and there's plenty more of it to come. And if Clackett don't publish it, someone will.'

'No, Nick, they won't. Because we'll all be dead before then.'

'You can't stop visionary horror, Roz. I won't be shackled or censored by the frightened, primitive pagans who run today's publishing industry. So go tell Tony Clackett to shove my manuscript up his arse, where it can fester and consume his sorry behind from deep within his eternally-ulcerated intestinal wall. Because the world might well be a dark place, Roz, but my fiction is *darker*. And if you think I'm going to go down without spreading a little of that darkness into people's lives – people who *need* a little ray of darkness, Roz – then you're wrong, and you'd best have another think.'

I slammed the phone down, aggrieved that Roz had already slammed down hers halfway through my speech.

It was over, then. My writing career was dead.

I heard the typewriter sluicing out its mechanism inside the shower cubicle. Sighing, I stood up, prepared as usual to go and scrub clean my master the platen, when I stumbled across the sheet of paper it had left on the floor by my feet.

BUY MORE RIBBON.

I got dressed and obeyed.

CHAPTER THREE

On my way back from the stationer's, I detoured via that lonely side street off Stalkford's town centre, which I'd never noticed before that day a year ago, hoping that the typewriter's 14,000-year warranty, which had run out the night before, might still be honoured. But the street, when I reached it, was even emptier than before.

Because Uniquities Inc., plus Eels wasn't there.

In its place stood a derelict shoe smith's, due for demolition, according to an official notice nailed to its door. In fact, the entire street was condemned in order to make way for a new department store, scheduled for construction in the coming months. I cast my eyes over the numerous boarded-up windows and torn refuse sacks scattered across the road and pavement. Had this place ever been populated? The shoe smith's itself looked as if it had been established centuries ago. So why had it resembled a mysterious-looking curiosity shop the last time I'd visited?

My mind began to wander, and as it did, an image flashed suddenly into my brain. The shop-owner . . . That old man in the rubber apron who drank down eels. Moses Unique. I suddenly remembered where I'd seen his face before. But it couldn't be him, surely? It just couldn't.

Could it?

I cast my mind back to a memory I'd hoped would remain buried deep in my subconscious. A guilty secret I'd never once revealed to any other human being. A minor incident really, in the grand scheme of things. As a boy, I used to deliver newspapers by hand to an elderly retired writer of occult supernatural fiction by the name of Algernon Tench. I often found him trapped on his lounge commode, so one day took the opportunity to read him one of my own fledgling efforts in the genre. That may sound presumptuous, but I looked upon it as a kindness. An act of charity. A gentle reminder, shall we say, that time had moved on, horror fiction had changed irrevocably since his day, and he shouldn't keep wasting everyone's time trying to stave off the inevitable.

It did the trick, as the particular story I read him was so gruesome, so shocking, so violently visceral, that he literally suffered a cardiac arrest as I was reading it to him, having first begun to weep bitterly about the decline of Western civilisation.

But that wasn't what troubled me. Nor was it the fact that, in my youthful arrogance, I'd torn up one of his own books in front of his face in an effort to shift him from the commode, hoping the spiritual agony of seeing his life's work being shredded with such radical and anarchic courage might somehow break the vacuum trapping both cheeks.

No, it was a minor detail that bothered me. Something I might easily have remedied, but had refused to – with a smile on my face, too, if I remember. Call it arrogance, call it the usual dose of professional jealousy, call it demonstrating once and for all that the old dinosaur's era was extinctified. But the truth was that as I left that old boy lying there on the floor in a pool of his own effluence, I'd taken the only toilet roll he had left.

And I'd never forgotten that look on his face as he'd mopped himself dry with his own Victorian triple-decker Gothic novel.

That's why I recognised the old bastard.

Yet how *could* it be him? That doddering old crock was *dead*.*

Whatever the reality, it looked like I was now stuck with the damned typewriter, after all. If Uniquities Inc., plus Eels could no

---

* Or *was* he?

longer refund me what I hadn't paid, I guessed I'd have to get rid of the thing myself. But somehow, I didn't think it would be too happy about that.

I stopped off at the newsagent opposite to check how my latest book was selling. *Diaballos Apocalypsicum Penetratio* was still there in the corner of the shop, standing on one end and towering over the neighbouring rack of conventional-sized paperbacks. Despite a width (or height, depending on the angle from which you looked) exceeding nine feet, I saw it was priced significantly lower than it had been the previous week.

'Not selling, Gavin?' I asked the proprietor, whose name was Gavin.

'No one can see the cover,' Gavin replied, surlily. 'Plus it's mainly asterisks.'

He was wrong there. The back-cover blurb contained more parentheses than asterisks. But no one could read that, either. The novel's rear end sat hard against the shop floor, imprisoned by the sheer weight of the pages stacked above it. Browsing the book's contents would require strong arms and a portable stepladder. Even then, the book would most likely destroy a supporting wall if toppled.

I moved to the paperback rack beside it and picked up one of my earlier novels. Clackett had reissued *The Slothman Prophecies*, my novel about the sinister Slothman, a mythical yet sedentary furred figure prophesying apocalyptic catastrophes *after* the event. Admittedly, the book hadn't sold well on its initial run, let alone the reprint, but I'd grown tired of debating the supposed 'plot hole' with critics who had no grasp of reverse-inter-dimensional time-warp-barrier-theory. Yet part of me was beginning to wish someone had prewarned me about the *Diaballos Apocalypsicum Penetratio* problem.

It was all very well penning oblique and unfathomable scrolls of cosmic doom writ in the hieroglyphical parlance of fictional elder gods, but if no one possessed the ability to read them . . .

I stepped away from the dark, imposing shadow my latest novel was casting over the shop's interior and reflected on the practicalities of penning literally ground-breaking works. If I continued at my current rate, all the world's newsagents and remainder outlets might require racks the size of the Giza pyramid complex to store even a fraction of my continued output.

Despairing, I grabbed *Slothman* from the rack and was preparing to harangue Gavin for failing to refresh its price stamp (after several years, removing a 'reduced' sticker can potentially rip away the gloss lining of a paperback, so it must be replaced regularly – Gavin *knew* this) when a hand grabbed my wrist.

I was about to grab it back with my remaining hand when I saw that the hand grabbing my hand was different from the standard human hand, containing an index finger thrice the length of a conventional digit. Suspicious, my eyes followed the hand to its wrist and saw that the arm it belonged to protruded from the sleeve of a clerical cassock. I smiled knowingly to myself. There was only one clergyman in all of Stalkford that suffered from the advanced stages of Phalangic Stalk Syndrome, and that was the Reverend Kenny Marmon, Dean of Vampton, whom I'd met last year at the skin clinic.

'Morning, Kenny,' I said.

'Beware, Nick Steen,' he replied. 'Beware!'

'I heard you the first time, Kenny.' I stepped back from him. 'Let go of my arm.'

His finger, which had remained wrapped around my wrist despite the rest of his hand letting go, finally uncurled, releasing me. For a moment, I felt a strange burning sensation there, as if the grasp of God Himself had seized my flesh, found my soul wanting, and passed judgement upon me. That, or Kenny had recently applied Deep Heat.

'You're doomed, Nick,' Kenny said, thrusting his prehensile protuberance upwards into the air, beside his head. No wonder church attendance was down. '*Doomed!*'

'Again, I heard you the first time.'

'This morning, I received a letter,' he continued, ignoring me. 'Typed in squalid detail were the most foul, unholy and *blasphemous* accounts of thy hellish coupling.'

Kenny had been doing that a lot, lately. Talking like a crazed Puritan elder. It was probably a by-product of the finger issue, but it always seemed specifically directed at me.

'Is this about me sleeping with a typewriter?' I asked, masking my private annoyance at Roz. Trust her to have spilled the beans, no doubt deciding, in her editorial wisdom, that my so-called 'perversions' required Divine intervention.

Kenny stared grimly at me, still holding up the finger.

'Nine Circles of Hell there be, Nick Steen . . .'

'*Are*,' I said, as he jabbed his finger upwards even further, perilously close to the ceiling fan.

'Nine!' he continued, ignoring my correction, even though *I* was the writer here. 'Yet the Brethren and I have prayed, in light of your unforgivable sin of fornicating with a typing machine, for a *tenth*. You have set yourself against God, Nick Steen. You are destroying His world. Decimating His glorious Temple of Creation. Bringing the whole edifice down on our worthy heads through your blasphemous sins. For thou hast signed a pact, Nick Steen. A Faustian pact, with Satan, the Dark Lord of Misrulery.'

'I know who he is, Kenny.'

But he had a point. Thinking about it, the deal I'd struck with the typewriter did indeed resemble a Faustian pact. I'd signed my real name enough times on the sheets of paper it spooled, which was presumably binding from a pact perspective. But as far as I understood it, the chief lure of a Faustian pact is that the recipient is supposed to enjoy the fruits of a doomed covenant for decades before the inevitable demonic bailiffs come clawing, yet mine were already swarming about me with no discernible evidence of worldly success beyond what I'd already achieved for myself without them. Instead of the endless nubile wenches I might have been picking from, I was instead drawing all earthly physical ecstasies from an outdated metallic appliance.

'Some pact,' I said, aloud.

'A confession!' Kenny screamed. 'The witch hath confessed!'

'Calm down,' I said, aware his finger was rising higher all the time, ever closer to the whirring fan blades above us. 'If I *have* signed a Faustian pact, then I no longer retain any statutory rights in the matter, so there's not much I can do about it. Incidentally, your finger ...'

'*What about my finger?*' Kenny screamed, suddenly enraged. But instead of heeding the warning I was about to give him, he raised the digit even higher, intending to preach me a full sermon.

Its tip struck the rotating fan blades overhead, shearing the distal phalanx clean off.

The severed lump flew off in the direction of the tills, striking Gavin in the left eye, while the cheap fan blades splintered, tilting upwards with the sudden impact. Kenny shrieked and flailed below them, blood pumping violently in large spurts from his sliced joint.

My head swam amid an explosion of horror. Blood rained from the upended blades on to my unsold books, instantly devaluing them, while the dark shadow of *Diaballos Apocalypsicum Penetratio* now seemed to be moving of its own accord, looming over us both, smothering Kenny's screams amid a cloud of darkness.

I realised that the vast tome was leaning at a slant. Air from the fan's tilted blades was blasting into its piled pages, flipping and fluttering them apart in their thousands, until the sheer force of shifting weight teetered the vast spine backwards, sending my latest masterwork toppling.

A burst of thunder exploded somewhere above us. Kenny stared in terror, frozen to the spot, as, with a colossal and terrifying creak, *Diaballos Apocalypsicum Penetratio* collapsed.

TYPE-FACE

'Curse ye, Nick Steen!' Kenny yelled under the fast-approaching monolith, and was immediately crushed flat.

All I could see of him when the dust cleared were his legs and arms sticking out either side of my toppled masterpiece. The remnants of his deformed index finger curled upwards from the impromptu grave, twitching like the crooked limb of a dying insect, each slowing death-spasm flipping another page of the book under which he lay buried.

At least they could see the cover now.

Maybe Faustian pacts weren't so bad, after all.

★

Except that they were. Of course they were. And if I needed any proof, the heavens tore open as I headed back home, pelting me with torrential rain and blinding shafts of ethereal light. Clearly, God was seriously hacked off about me destroying His natural world with my dangerously increased productivity rate. I guess I was effectively ousting His career, running roughshod over His glorious Creation, exactly in the way I'd done to that old author I'd refused to wipe clean, years before.

The celestial maelstrom appeared to hover directly over me alone, even following me into the underpass. Yet, drenched as I was, I still paused, as I always did, on the forecourt before Hellview Heights, the imposing executive apartment block I'd made my permanent home, in order to reflect upon the astounding treasures my mind had gifted me up until now.

Yet today was different. As I watched the storm clouds massed above the imposing concrete tower, its grim edifice lit frequently by great flashes of purple lightning, I realised that the heady thrill of basking in my own literary glow was now gone; in its place existed the grim dawning realisation that things no longer quite added up.

29

Kenny's mention of a Faustian pact had truly set me thinking. Those earlier novels I'd penned had earned me enough to move into Stalkford's most affluent district, with a fiercely-contested top-floor executive apartment-suite overlooking the distant cosmos and also outer Stalkford. But since I'd bought the typewriter, sales had plummeted, I'd been fired by my publisher and no one appeared to understand a single word of the complex prose I was churning out. Worse still, I was deemed an environmental menace. The Dark Duke of Deforestation. According to the typewriter's manual, I was meant to have secured access to the deepest, darkest abyss of my subconscious mind, yet all I really had to show for my efforts was a fetishistic, sado-masochist interest in the thing itself.

Which was becoming increasingly temperamental.

Things were changing for the worse, and not just in the bedroom department.

Against the heavy rumble of thunder overhead came a sharp, proclamatory fanfare of trumpets. I saw His angels gathering in a flock far above me, their long, styled manes swept back over vinyl trench coats as they prepared to carry me off to some form of distant Divine punishment.

Unperturbed, I gave His angelic host the finger, boldly crossed the forecourt of Hellview Heights and strode through into its main entrance lobby. There was another priest on the visitors' couch, and two more blocking the parcel lockers, all warning my soul to jump ship from this mortal frame. Kenny's Brethren, I realised. I barged past them to retrieve my mail (which included a replacement platen knob I couldn't recall ordering), and walked back round to the elevators.

There was another priest inside the lift, which explained why it hadn't been working for the last few months. He'd barricaded himself within and plastered the walls, ceiling and floor with pages from the Bible (plus a few good-time nun pics) and had apparently only just rediscovered where the emergency button was. Now that the

30

interior had been flushed out by a team of janitors, the lift had once more resumed business.

He continued to yell dire warnings at me all the way to the top floor. My blind and deaf neighbour Mrs Brown rode with us the entire way, oblivious to the noise, grinning inanely as the lift's swift ascension tickled her ancient and barely functional tummy. With her advanced age and state of bodily decrepitude, I guessed she got her kicks where she could.

As I moved through the parting doors, a blast of sudden lightning hit the outer building, frying the lift's cheaply manufactured electrical circuits. As the elevator plunged violently downwards to the lower floors, the priest's shriek echoing back up the shaft alongside Mrs Brown's final bout of soft chuckling, things finally grew quiet again.

Something seemed to be protecting *me alone* from God's wrath.

I approached the door to my apartment and let myself in. I moved through the entrance hallway, which was adorned with framed paintings of my various book cover illustrations (a canny investment, as I now owned the copyright as well and could potentially sue each artist for selling prints), plus medical photographs of assorted brain X-rays. These were mainly of my own, but I'd also requested those of Paul McKenna for comparison.

Moving through into the lounge, I saw that there was a freshly brewed mug of coffee awaiting me on my desk, steam rising from its gold-plated rim. I crossed over to the typewriter and placed the new ink ribbon down on the desk beside it, along with the replacement platen knob. There was a blank page already spooled through the machine. I picked up my mug, sniffed the subtle aromas of the recently ground beans, blew steam from the surface and closed my eyes, preparing to savour my initial sip. When I opened them again, a freshly typed message awaited me on the spooled page.

EVENING.

'Evening,' I replied.

The keys began to hammer.

Of their own accord.

I could hardly believe what I was seeing. I say hardly, because I *had* been having sex with the thing, after all. And though at times I'd tried to fool myself that it was just me role-playing the entire sordid escapade, deep down I'd always known that my hammer-hard lover had a genuine personality. Perhaps not feelings as such, but here at last was proof that the thing had a fully functioning mind.

HAVE YOU EATEN?

'I bought a pork pie from the Spar. You?'

More hammering.

I WAS WAITING FOR YOU.

'Sorry, I got held up.'

More hammering.

WHO IS SHE?

'Nobody.'

More hammering.

LIAR.

'I'm telling you the truth. I got waylaid at the newsagent.'

More hammering.

YOU BOUGHT MY RIBBON?

'Right here.'

I attached it delicately, trying not to get too aroused. It was shameful to admit it, but essential typing maintenance now caused me colossal throbbing.

'I see you managed to order a replacement platen knob easily enough by yourself, though?' I asked, pointedly.

More hammering. (Look, I'm going to stop adding 'more hammering'. You get the idea.)

YOU'LL FIND I'M FULL OF SURPRISES.

'You're not wrong,' I said, suddenly detecting a freshly completed manuscript on my 'out' pile. 'What the hell is that?'

YOUR NEXT NOVEL.

I picked it up, perusing the contents. A cold feeling shot through me. I hadn't written a word of it.

IT'S ONLY THE PROLOGUE.

'Look,' I said, sternly. 'Let's get one thing straight. My books are *my* books. I don't co-write.'

YOU DO NOW.

'No, I do not.'

YOUR BOOKS ARE MINE, BITCH.

'Excuse me?' I snapped. '*No one* writes my books except me alone. Now, I paid good money for you to do one job, which was to help free my subconscious imagination and unleash its hellish visions.'

PLUS BONK.

'That wasn't a stipulation I was aware of until you ravished me in that first session. And while we're on the subject,' I said, getting cross now – hell, it looked like it was *all* going to come out – 'I'm getting just a little bit tired with you always wanting my body, day and night. I'm an individual with feelings and sensitivities, and I have a right to ...'

COME HERE NOW AND DO ME, COWBOY.

And dammit, if I didn't do just that. Was I compelled? Was it really the pursuit of insane sexual oblivion I craved deep down? Did I imagine the thing loved me, somehow? Or did I think, with its newfound desire to write my books without me even being present, that instead it loved my *writing*? Yes, that was it, wasn't it? I believed it was in love with my writing. Despite all evidence to the contrary, I somehow convinced myself at that mad, insane moment that it loved and respected my *words* – those hellish visions forever swimming around in the primordial swamp of my inner psyche.

I tugged on the pair of fresh leather pants it flung at me (Japanese Wagyu leather for extra give), stood before it and waited.

And waited.

And waited.

Until, teasingly, the tender message came through.

KISS GOODBYE TO YOUR BALLS.

Then an explosion of light and sound. The typewriter suddenly went all crackly, like a sparkler, and a mighty tornado blew the pants clean from my body in one rip as several long, blood-flecked chains shot out from both tabular keys and pierced my chest nipples. These dragged me violently, limbs flailing, towards the space bar, catapulting me upwards over the keys to face my master the platen. I continued typing, despite myself, as the cylindrical shaft rolled lecherously around, sucking me in, winding my exposed rod deep between the mashing mangle.

Then it was back to business. Another deeply sordid and socially unacceptable act of literary *creation*. Yet one infinitely more potent, painful and punishing than any I'd conducted before.

Now I really *was* the typewriter's bitch.

As my member meshed with metal, and the body and brain I'd surrendered finally fused with the machine's mechanical, metallic clutches, I thought suddenly of Roz, and how she'd really dodged a bullet by firing me.

Howling with delirious agony, my brain's pummelled thoughts melting like hot butter between the typewriter's probing keys, I glanced down, insensate, at the mounting sheets of paper piled beside us.

And the words typed upon them.

YOUR WORLD WILL BE MINE.

CHAPTER FOUR

I placed another pile of completed manuscript in each corner of the kitchen floor, attempting to distribute the weight as evenly as possible. I'd awoken to the ominous sound of crumbling cement and a sudden shifting of the bedroom floor, realising, as I frantically scrubbed grains of interrupted sleep from my eyes, that if the giant tome we'd completed overnight remained in its current position for one moment longer, we might well be moving production to the lower floors.

'I've just had these tiles redone,' I moaned, observing fresh cracks in the grouting. There was no audible response from the machine. Which didn't surprise me. There'd been no coffee awaiting me this morning, either.

I mopped my sweating brow and moved back through to my study to tackle the remaining sections, which I'd already spent two hours desperately rearranging into safer piles around the lounge. Unfortunately, my entire apartment was now creaking like an old ship. The wall nearest my bookshelf had formed a visible slant and, according to the paramedic who knocked on my door an hour later, several sections of ceiling plaster had fallen on to the tenant living immediately below, braining him. Fortunately, his injuries, while severe, were unlikely to affect the structural integrity of my own flat.

I picked up yet another pile – around 1,000 pages, I estimated – and wondered where the hell I was going to put it all.

'We're out of space,' I said.

A clatter of keys. Then I looked down at the typewriter's freshly spooled page.

SO PUT IT IN THE FRIDGE.

'Fridge is full. Bath's full. Shower's reserved.'

DAMN RIGHT, SCRUBBER.

I thought now was as good a time as any to raise the sensitive subject of nipple-tweaking.

'You do realise teats are tender areas for men?'

YOU LOVE IT.

'I don't, actually. Exquisite pain's one thing. Teat-twisting is quite another.'

NIPPLE-PIERCING?

'That's okay, as long as you respect my safe word.'

'"FUCKING STOP"?'

'That's the one.' Technically, it was two words. But it had changed from 'living metaphor', at least, which didn't exactly trip off the tongue in the heat of battle.

I slammed the pile on the desk beside the machine and sat down, casually leafing through the manuscript we'd supposedly completed together. I say 'supposedly completed together', because there was no way on earth I'd written a single word of this garbage.

It was all symbols. Asterisks, ampersands, hyphens, glyphs, hiero-glyphs, logograms, that German-looking skull thing you get in *Asterix* books when someone's swearing. Total nonsense. A vast and impenetrable collection of elliptical symbols, conveying no meaning whatsoever. How the hell hadn't I realised it before?

What had *really* been happening? Ever since I'd seen those pages the typewriter had produced without me being there, it was as if a veil had fallen suddenly from my eyes. No longer could I pretend that there had been any meaning in the novels I'd been churning out for over a year now. No more could I continue lying to myself that the complexity of the prose I'd been producing was somehow so advanced that Mankind itself needed to evolve further in order to comprehend it. No wonder no one was buying my books. Because no amount of internal plot-sense and narrative know-how could hide the fact that not a single word of this stuff had *ever* been mine. For the past year, I'd been producing nothing but bollocks.

'This is bollocks,' I said.

SHOW ME YOUR BOLLOCKS.

'Will you take bloody five?' I snapped, getting shirty. I'd just about had enough of being its sex toy. There was no way Clackett would ever publish a book like this, I realised, even if they hadn't already refused to. And even if I sent it to Roz anyway, she'd take one look at the proportions alone and immediately start suggesting cuts, which, even though I didn't understand a word of what I'd written, I would instinctively oppose. Things had ground to a complete halt for me, creatively. Unless, of course, what the typewriter had written last night without my input was *so* visionary, *so* damned radical, that even *I* couldn't understand it.

The typewriter clacked again.

BUY ME THESE.

I drew out the sheet and looked down at another list of items. There was no way I'd find these in a stationery shop.

'What are "two black miracles of mortal clay?"'

YOU AND ONE OTHER.

I didn't know what the typewriter had in mind, but its demands were growing increasingly strange.

'Who's the other?'

The reply, when it came, chilled me to the bone.

ROZ.

Damn, the thing was after my editor now.

'Leave Roz out of this.'

THEN YOU *ARE* SEEING HER.

'I'm *not* seeing anybody. As you well know, Roz sacked me when she discovered you and I were having a torrid physical affair, and I respect that decision. Even if I don't respect her editorial judgement, I *do* respect her willingness to condemn the sadomasochistic practices of a former professional client and his supernatural writing implement.'

BRING ME ROZ.

'No way.'

OR YOUR NIPPLES *REALLY* GET IT.

I stood there in silence, defiant. Then shuddered involuntarily.

What the *hell* did it want with my erstwhile editor?

*

We arranged to meet, for old times' sake, at the dermatological clinic. Roz had an appointment there for her psoriasis and had reserved an extra hour for us in one of the powder rooms. I took her a pot of E45 as a peace-offering, and she, unexpectedly, and rather movingly, given our recent falling-out, gifted me a fresh tube of hydrocortisone cream.

'Mind if I spread here?' I asked.

'Go ahead,' she replied, tucking the pot of E45 into her handbag.

'You can apply some too, Roz,' I said. 'I won't peek.'

'It's okay; I'm freshly lathered from my appointment.'

'How is it at the moment?' I asked, unbuckling my slacks and applying a generous layer to my flanks and haunches.

'Knees and elbows still rough, but the scalp's improving.'

'Good, I'm pleased,' I said, lifting my left leg upwards to smooth the reddened area under my groin. 'You don't mind?' I said, checking again.

This time, she averted her eyes. 'I picked the brand especially,' she said, transferring her gaze to an information poster outlining the potential risks of excessive talc application. 'It calms the body's immune response in order to reduce pain, itching and inflammation.'

'That's swelling, right?' I said, generating some initial small talk.

'Yes,' she replied. 'It's also a hormone replacement for those who don't produce enough cortisol. Yours is mixed with antimicrobials, incidentally. I didn't know if you were still treating a bacterial or fungal infection.'

'You chose right,' I said, smiling softly as I stripped and moved on to my top half. 'I appreciate that, Roz. I really do.'

'What did you want to see me about?'

'All in good time,' I said, feeling more relaxed than I had done in over a year. This was top-grade hydrocortisone. Maybe Roz was softening towards me. 'Must have cost you more than a basic prescription?'

'It's on repeat.'

'Repeat?' I repeated, suddenly suspicious. 'For you?'

No, it can't have been for her. Roz's infections were never predominantly fungal, as far as I recalled. I noted she hadn't replied. Hell, I should have seen this coming.

'Met him at a psoriasis clinic as well, did you?' I said, coldly. 'Soon as we're through, you hire some other flaking writer, probably half my age and twice as scaled. All the while ordering more items than you actually need on *his* prescription so you can hawk the surplus to score petty points with me.'

'I haven't hired *anyone*, Nick.'

'Really, Roz?' I said, swinging my legs over the side of the bed and sitting up to face her. 'I'm not sure I believe you.'

'Look, Nick. What do you *want*?'

I saw tears forming in her eyes. She was right. Her scalp *had* improved.

'I'll level with you, Roz. I want you back. As my editor.'

'That's not going to happen.'

'I want another book deal.'

'That's not going to happen, either.'

'Look,' I said, exasperated. 'I can prove the rubbish I've been writing this year is entirely the work of my typewriter.'

'That's it, Nick. I'm leaving.'

'Wait, Roz,' I said, screwing the lid back on the hydrocortisone tube. 'I admit I bought that typewriter to access the darkest depths of my subconscious psyche, and thus restrict your editing influence to grammar alone.'

'Please, Nick.'

'But the truth is, Roz, you're right. I *have* changed since buying that typewriter. I'd never have considered fornicating with a writing machine before then, and for the life of me, I can't see how or why I get off on it now. I think the thing *is* cursed, like you said. I think I've unwittingly signed some kind of Faustian pact with a haunted writing implement. It *talks* to me, Roz. And this morning it gave me *this*.'

I handed her the typed list, which she quickly read.

'What are these "two black miracles of mortal clay"?'

'According to the typewriter, that's you and me, Roz. For some reason, it wants us both.'

'Why?'

'I don't know. All I know is that I'm no longer writing my own books, and what *is* being written makes no sense whatsoever. Maybe it needs an editor.'

She walked across the room, continuing to examine the list in her hand. 'What's a "dark key of dreams"?'

'I've got no idea. Neither did Timpson.'

She turned back to face me, her expression deadly serious. 'I think this is black magic, Nick. I think you're right about a Faustian pact. These look like ingredients for some kind of ritual. A terrifying satanic rite.'

'Relax, Roz. I doubt it's planning anything crazy like that. A mechanical typewriter organising some form of blasphemous secret ritual? With me, its owner and sexual plaything, blissfully unaware the entire time, until at last something catastrophically deadly occurs when I least expect it? Really, Roz, that's like something out of one of my books.'

'Nevertheless, I'm convinced that machine's up to something, Nick. Something involving you, that you as yet have no idea about. And – if it has its way – something involving *me*, too.'

Suddenly, I remembered the letter.

'Incidentally, Roz. What were you doing discussing my sordid bedroom habits with Kenny Marmon?'

She shook her head, confused.

'Don't play dumb, Roz. Kenny Marmon, the Dean of Vampton – now *deceased*.'

'Who?'

'You sent him that letter, didn't you?'

'I've never heard of him before now, Nick. Let alone sent him any letter.'

Then I twigged. Kenny hadn't specified *who'd* sent him a letter. Just that a letter had been sent. A *typed* letter . . .

'Dammit. The *typewriter* sent it, Roz. Told Kenny Marmon, the Dean of Vampton, about our frenzied bouts of abhorrent lust-making. And then Kenny told *me* that God and the Church had renounced my soul. That I was eternally damned . . . He was crushed to death before my very eyes, Roz. By my *own* book. That means I'm now expelled, Roz. Expelled from Heaven. Like Satan before me. And it's all this typewriter's fault.'

'Then you have to get rid of it, Nick,' she said. 'It's clearly after you and me for some as-yet-undisclosed nefarious purpose. You're dabbling with satanic forces, Nick. Dark powers beyond your control.'

'What do I do, Roz?'

41

'Is it still under warranty?'

I sighed, shaking my head. 'Ran out the day before yesterday. Plus, the shop I bought it from has since mysteriously disappeared.'

'You mean you've been hoodwinked into signing a Faustian pact about which you knew nothing, and consumer rights no longer apply?'

'It *is* the Devil, Roz,' I said, giving the Dark One his due. Then suddenly, I had an idea. If the Devil, Lord of Misrulery, routinely went back on his word, then why wouldn't he do so again? Maybe I could negotiate a fresh pact with Satan to undo my current pact with Satan.

'Roz, I'm going to renegotiate my current pact with Satan. Though he's evidently a tricky customer, I'm better schooled than most in the malevolent machinations of the Infernal, and therefore confident I can come away with a good deal.'

'You fool, Nick. You're playing with infernal fire. I want nothing to do with it.'

I glared at her, hardly able to believe my ears.

'I understand, Roz,' I said, coldly. 'Farewell, then, fair-weather friend. Thanks for the hydrocortisone.' I crossed over to the door. 'If you need any help applying yours, you'd best ask someone else.'

'*Nick*,' she said, longingly. I stopped, kept looking ahead of me for a moment, as if I couldn't bear to hear what she was about to say, then turned around to face her again.

'Yes, Roz?'

'What will you do? When it finds out I'm not joining you? Won't it punish you even *more*?'

We stood there, gazing at each other from opposite ends of the powder room. The floating grains of talc made everything soft-focused and dustily romantic. For what was dust really, after all, but lovers' skin? Dead, and yet also sort of alive? Not that we were lovers, of course, but the science still applied.

'The cream will help,' I said, bravely. Then turned and departed via the main door.

She may well have whispered, 'I'll miss you,' once I'd gone, but I couldn't hear that from where I was, and as this is first-person narration and therefore not omniscient, we just won't know.

CHAPTER FIVE

'Can I get you a coffee or tea?' I asked off-handedly, preferring not to encourage conversation with tradesmen.

'Do you have any chicken blood?'

'As a matter of fact, I do.' I'd been trying my hand at augury to see if I could foretell any changes to my future with Clackett, but so far the bird's liver had failed to speak. Ditto the entrails.

'Mug or goblet?'

'Goblet, if you have one.'

I went to the fridge and poured him a large helping from the carcass.

'Giblets?'

'Please.'

'One lump or two?'

'Two, please. Do you have any cartilage spare?'

'No cartilage, but I do have some sinew?'

'Sinew would be great, thanks.'

I scraped him some out and closed the door, tutting again at the large scratch still visible on my newly-tiled floor. I'd installed the fridge unit six months back, but the instructions had specified two heavy-lifters and neither Roz nor her ageing mother had been anywhere near strong enough. Though they *had* finally stumped up compensation for the damaged floor.

'So you've been cursed, have you?'

I checked again that the door of the lounge was shut, praying (to whom I wasn't sure) that the typewriter couldn't hear us.

'More of a satanic pact, really,' I whispered, handing him the goblet. 'But one conducted illegally, under false pretences. Essentially, I was tricked into entering into a contract with the Dark One, and now he's reneging on the deal.'

'Sounds about right,' the man said, sipping his drink.

'So I want you to draft a new satanic pact to undo my current satanic pact. I have leverage, courtesy of one unwilling female soul called Roz.'

That was harsh of me, I'll admit, but I *was* dealing with the Devil. Plus, Roz had properly hacked me off.

He plucked a shard of poultry bone from his beard and flicked it back into his drink. I grimaced inwardly. Though I was aware I'd hired a satanist, I had no idea he'd be *this* far along the left-hand path.

'And you're a horror writer, are you?'

I hated the telepathy thing, too. This guy knew everything I was thinking. I'd barely even considered phoning the local coven before he was there outside my door, buzzing himself in. I'd asked if we could reconvene at his deconsecrated church, but it was apparently being hosed out after a particularly heavy night.

'We seek doomed souls telepathically,' he explained, reading my mind again. 'Then once we're attuned to your aura, we aim to materialise in your mortal plane within twenty-four hours.'

I nodded as something screamed from behind the fridge.

'Sounds like you've got a portal,' he said, looking past me.

'Portal?'

'We use them in sacrificial rites. Demons or dark angels generally materialise via portal, or cloud if a ritual's conducted in the open. That's trickier these days, of course, orgy-wise.' He moved over to the fridge and peered around the back. 'Yep, there's one right here.'

There was another disembodied scream. Close, yet distant at the same time.

'From beyond the veil, I reckon,' he said, tapping at a dark patch on the wall I'd assumed was mildew. 'Hear that disembodied wailing?'

I listened again. The effect was impressive.

'Immeasurable distances away, if I'm not mistaken. You'll have to move this fridge.'

'Move it?'

'To open up the portal.'

'I'm not opening up any portal – and I'm not moving the fridge again. It needs at least two people, or it scrapes the tiles.' I manoeuvred him back into the middle of the room. 'Can we just get back to the contract?'

'You're the boss. Are you a successful author?'

'I *was* . . .'

'Pact's over, then. Your side of it, anyway.'

'I hadn't signed a pact, then. Now that I *have* signed one, my books aren't selling. Aren't I supposed to enjoy certain additional "fruits" before minions come to collect my soul?'

He took another swig from the goblet, chewed on the contents for a moment, then raised an eyebrow suggestively. 'Have you experienced any sensuous erotic delights?'

I thought about that for a moment.

'Again, *technically* . . .'

'Pact's over, then.'

'Yes, but it's sex with a . . . it isn't sex you'd expect.'

'I doubt it,' he said, draining the last of his poultry blood. 'We're pretty hard to shock.'

I lowered my voice to a whisper, keeping one eye on the lounge door. 'Look, I'll level with you. I'm in a highly destructive and damaging psycho-sexual relationship with my typewriter.'

'Then it *is* a cursed artefact?'

'You tell me,' I said, exasperated. 'You're the one reading minds.'

He stared at me for a moment, doing just that. 'I see you have a subconscious urge to do it with typebars.'

'Yes, I know that. It's all to do with a socially unacceptable love for my own writing. But now it's become something else entirely.'

I pulled the typewriter's list from my back pocket and handed it over. 'These are its demands.'

He ran his eye briefly over the typewriter's words, rolling his tongue quizzically against his cheek. 'Who owned it before you?'

'No idea. It's aeons old.'

'*Aeons*?' he said, looking up suddenly.

'Tang Dynasty, according to the manual. Though the English translation's appalling.'

'And where is it now?' he asked.

'I thought you could read minds.'

He paused for a moment, thinking, then shook his head. 'For some reason, I can't pick up its own thoughts . . .'

I pointed conspiratorially at the lounge door behind us. 'In there.'

He glanced over at the door, the expression building on his face quite unusual for a satanist. He looked . . . *scared*.

'Who are the "pupils of pain"?' he asked, examining the list again.

'I assume I'm one of them,' I said. 'But it's also after my editor, Roz. Luckily, she still has dignity and a moral compass.'

'You do realise "blank page of unknown suffering" refers to your own soul?'

'Really? I presumed that was already taken.'

He looked at me, his expression grave. 'This is referring to a plane of suffering *beyond* Hell.'

'*Beyond* Hell?' I repeated. What on earth would suffering be like *beyond* Hell?

The lounge door burst open, swinging back hard against the kitchen wall. Fortunately, I'd attached stoppers when I'd moved in.

In the room beyond us, motionless upon my writing desk, sat the typewriter.

Glaring.

The satanist dropped the sheet of paper. 'It's been eavesdropping,' he said.

'Yeah, it channels the subconscious, I'm afraid,' I said, 'which does erode privacy. It also goes crackly like a sparkler and shoots barbed hooks through my nipple-teats.'

'That's a thing of evil!' he yelled out, suddenly. 'An evil *beyond* Lucifer! An evil beyond Hell!'

With that, he fled from my kitchen and hurled himself through the front door, satanic robe flapping wildly as he ran off down the stairwell.

I saw he'd done one on my tiles.

As I made a pretence of reaching for the Ajax and some J-cloths, I heard the words I'd been dreading, deep inside my head.

OH DEAR.

'Morning,' I said, and began whistling.

OH DEAR, OH DEAR, OH DEAR.

I sprinkled some Ajax on the offending tile.

'What's wrong? Out of ribbon again?'

TURN AROUND.

'Beg your pardon?' I said, commencing to scrub at the tile. Never had cleaning a soiled stain seemed more alluring.

I SAID TURN AROUND. <u>NOW</u>.

I realised there was no way of avoiding it. No way at all. I turned around.

PUNISHMENT TIME.

And what, really, had I expected? I'd failed to bring it Roz. So now I'd have to pay.

TOO RIGHT YOU'LL HAVE TO PAY.

'I'm sorry for ruining your ritual,' I said, desperately.

TYPE-FACE

I'M SORRY FOR RUINING <u>YOUR ARSEHOLE</u>.

And with that, punishment commenced. Hooks and chains sprang out at me, drawing my bodily flesh and taut sinews apart, flinging me once again into that cursed machinery, mincing my organic parts into stew like the macerator toilet in my previous house (which needed regular servicing despite the claims, so I would personally avoid them).

Desperately, I fought to grasp on to what was left of my disintegrating particulars as that damned typewriter flung more barbed hooks at me, spearing my nipples through and through, dragging me into it again and again, sucking my brain towards its whirring rubber platen. And I began to laugh, to scream, to explode in a heady ecstasy of exquisite psychic agony as I dashed my mind and physical bits hither and thither against those hellish keys and yes ... Yes ... *YES*, I began to sing! To sing the song of myself. The melancholy yet anthemically-catchy song of Mankind's eternal, cosmic agony. And as I sang, I was joined by Tanita Tikaram for the chorus sections, and the heavens thundered above me and within me, and the typewriter began to fizz and crackle, and then I was inside the machine itself and outside it too, body parts drained of my essence as my soul poured like melting butter once more into its internal rotor system (Tanita had left by this stage), with my brains mashed to pulp as the rubber platen ground me up, and I beheld a host of strange planets spinning on their axes inside what was left of my head, and found myself cast upon a mighty wind blasting from an arse I could no longer feel, and at last I rode the typewriter.

Yes, *I* rode the typewriter, and I rode it hard, tapping and hammering and telling my tale as I raced through the cosmos, then fell from the heavens like a broken marionette (yet still muscular), to emerge from the Hell of my own head, feeling again the limbs and appendages I feared had been lost for all eternity, or at least mangled beyond practical use.

I sensed familiar ground below, and slowly, gently, willing my eyes to adjust themselves to the surrounding darkness, opened them at last to find the ancient typewriter in pieces all around me, smashed into a million shards, with slips and strips of A4 floating about me like paper rain, lit up by slanting shards of thin, blue light that speared the shadows through unseen walls.

And then I heard a deep, sinister chuckling, and knew that some Keeper of the Chaos, some great Swirler of Confusion, was close by; realised in one split second of mental clarity that whatever had been trapped inside that haunted machine, biding its time throughout the centuries, had at last been freed by me, unleashed to assume its proper physical form.

And it spake.

I WILL TEAR YOUR BOOKS APART.

CHAPTER SIX

I lay, disorientated, in the darkness. How long had I been out of it? Hours? Minutes? Days? Weeks? Months? Years? *Decades? Centuries? Millennia? Decamillenniums? Megaannums? Ten megaannums (possibly 'decamegaannum' or 'megamegaannum')?* Hell, maybe it was even *tempus immemorial*, i.e. Latin for 'always' or 'beyond the scope of time'? Trying not to panic, I checked my watch. Just over two hours. Though I daren't breathe a sigh of relief just yet. While a watch could tell me *when* I was, it couldn't tell me *where* I was.

I looked around, waiting for my eyes to adjust to the gloom. Slowly, I made out what looked like a closed door ahead of me. There was a written sign upon it, though I couldn't make out what it said from here.

I walked over, but the lettering remained blurred, as if buried under a bank of fog. Giving up, I passed through it into another darkened room, identical to the one I'd just left. Another door stood opposite me, sporting another indecipherable sign.

I couldn't make out what this word was, either. It looked like lettering, but the word remained hazy as I approached, despite my proximity. I clutched the handle and moved through into another room, dark and featureless as before. There was *another* closed door opposite. And hung upon this one, yet another familiar-looking sign. But this time, the lettering was clear as day and I was finally able to make out the word I'd been missing.

PERCEPTION.

So I was moving through Huxley's infamous doors, was I? Maybe he'd owned the typewriter before me? Maybe I'd meet even him somewhere nearby.*

Steeling myself against whatever lay beyond, I opened the third door and found myself in a room that looked uncannily like the entrance lobby of Clackett Publishing. It even contained the same red bubble sofa and courtesy table, upon which had been arranged an identical treasure chest of stale Celebrations and an urn of tepid water flavoured with sliced cucumber.

Yet something was *very* different. Adorning each wall were numerous enlarged prints of my official author's publicity photograph. That might sound impressive to you, but you'd be wrong. Because all of these pictures were defaced in various ways. Several bore comedy moustaches, a few others had elaborate punk mohawks, but the majority depicted massive erect penises rising from my forehead, alongside bold speech-bubbled obscenities ridiculing my writing.

I looked away, transferring my irate gaze to a large desk, behind which perched a twenty-something female redhead with confrontational glasses and tardy attitude to match. The sign in front of her said 'PERCEPTIONIST'.

I strode up to her.

'Where am I, Missy?'

'The Prolix,' she replied, failing to look up.

'What's the Prolix?'

She smiled to herself, then pointed to the area behind me with her pen. 'Take a seat, please. Type-Face will see you shortly.'

'Type-Face? Who's Type-Face?'

But '*Take a seat, please. Type-Face will see you shortly,*' was all I could get from her. Tutting loudly, I crossed over to the bubble sofa, hoping against hope I might retain some semblance of feeling in my blasted

---

* I didn't.

derriere, fearing deep down that hope might be all I had left. I sat down gently.

And felt nothing.

Forcing back tears, I glanced over at the perceptionist, who was now busy scrawling obscene doodles on a pile of my promotional eight-by-twelves.

'What are you doing?' I asked, even though I could see perfectly well.

'Defacing you.'

'I see.'

Two minutes later, I'd thought of a pithy retort, but was cut short by the telephone ringing on her desk. As she reached over and picked it up, I turned my attention to the coffee table in front of me and picked up a copy of Clackett's latest catalogue. The cover showed a picture of my face with the word '*Knobber*' stamped across my forehead in Baskerville font (my least favourite). What was going *on* here? Evidently in this nightmarish parallel world in which I now found myself, I was not considered the innovative literary genius my own reality recognised.

I opened up the catalogue and something slimy and blue flopped off the page into my lap. It looked like an emaciated eel.

'What in hell?' I barked, struggling as it wriggled violently about in my lap.

'Ahh, you've found a Tome-Wyrrm,' said the perceptionist, momentarily lowering the phone from her ear.

'What's a Tome-Wyrrm?' I shouted as the thing squirmed past my nether regions and up on to my stomach.

'A primeval book worm,' she said, covering the receiver with one hand, 'though they do look a bit like eels. Except they're deadly. That one's after your brain.'

I tried to bat the thing aside, shuddering as the dark-blue gelatinous grub stuck fast to my hand. I flicked my wrist in vain, flapped and flailed in futile attempts to dash the mucoid succubus against a nearby wall. Yet the greased, inky-hued Wyrrm merely sucked itself closer, slithering further up my arm, towards my shoulder.

My neck, I thought in sudden panic. It's almost at my neck.

Then it'll get my head.

Then my *brain* . . .

'Of course, I'll let him know,' the perceptionist said into her receiver, then hung up. She finally glanced over in my direction.

'Type-Face, Lord of the Prolix, will see you now.'

She flipped a switch on her desk and the bubble sofa sprung backwards violently, propelling both me and the hideous Tome-Wyrrm down through parting floorboards, hurtling us into an endless cylindrical shaft extending vertically downwards beneath the Earth's crust (although I hesitate to call it the Earth's crust, as technically it wasn't Earth-based, which I will reveal imminently.)

I fell. Oh, how far I fell. Far, far into the very depths of Hell (again, not technically official Hell, despite my use of the word 'very' – see above parenthesis note, and pay close attention because I won't be explaining things a third time). And with me fell that monstrous, cartridge-coloured parasite. For forty minutes and forty seconds, we fell and fought, and fought and fell, and fell and fought and rinse and repeat, etc., ad infinitum diabolicatum.

And when at that point, both exhausted from the fray, we paused for a much-needed comfort break, we fell yet further still, but I was at least able to examine my immediate surroundings and get my bearings.

Despite the speed at which I passed them by, I saw that the walls of the shaft were formed from densely piled wads of dried papier-mâché. I caught an occasional glimpse of random letters, scattered words and phrases and assorted mystical runes, many of which looked vaguely familiar. I began to suspect that this tattered wall of rushing prose, part resembling the interior lining of a gigantic wasp's nest,* might well be constructed from torn-up strips of my very own rejected manuscripts.

Before I had a chance to panic at the horrendous implication – that my sacred words were now nothing more than pulp passing before my very eyes – the hideous Wyrrm reappeared (having decided he no longer needed a number two), and thus we resumed our titanic battle. Yet now I saw that the beast had neglected to remove a small pair of miniature glasses it presumably applied for bouts of gentle toilet-reading, and gasped in abject horror. Those were *my* brown shades it was wearing. Precise copies of them. The thing was *taunting* me . . .

As it launched itself at me again and attempted to slide up my right nostril, I screamed wildly, flipping myself backwards while kicking out with the tacked toe of my Texan boot (which I never take off, even when intimate). The sharp metallic tip pierced its flesh, sinking my foot half in before the sheer force of the blow catapulted the Wyrrm's grotesque body against the passing shaft wall.

I continued to plunge downwards, eventually crashing arse-first (not that I felt anything) into a giant stack of shredded paper, which finally broke my fall.

I barely had time to gather my wits before realising I was still sinking downwards, slowly submerging into a tangled nest of scattered A4. It felt damp below as my toes and ankles brushed against soft tissue, and I realised my body was caught in some sort of current; a flowing underground river of torn, mulched prose. I clutched at the ragged strips around me, dangling a handful in front of my eyes to peruse their content. From the immediate element of profundity evident in the words and phrases I beheld, I quickly recognised that

---

* It isn't a wasp's nest, but if you are interested in wasp horror, may I recommend *Stingpregnators*, my cosmic parasitic space-wasp quintology.

my greatest fear had indeed been realised – this ocean of forlorn, abandoned work was my *own*.

Sensing I might soon be drowning in the foul waters passing below me, I flailed wildly among the drifting detritus, shedding tears at the words I'd once held so dear now floating in ruin about me.

I fought against the relentless flow, lunging myself forwards through the massed mulch, grabbing for what looked like a rock jutting outwards from the nearby bank. With luck and both hands I grasped it, dragging myself upwards on to the rocky verge. I caught my breath, smoothed sodden strips of lost words from my drenched limbs, and glanced behind me. The river of mind-waste flowed away into the distance, plunging at length into a tunnel of blackened rock, journeying unseen beyond the cavern wall towards some distant, unknown region.

I'd been deposited in what appeared to be a vast, subterranean chamber. Far above, thin luminescent shafts of bright blue light shone from slatted openings in what might have once formed the walls of an ancient prehistoric temple. But on closer inspection, I perceived large patches of organic material, slowly throbbing and oozing at intervals through the surface of the rock. These areas of pale, blood-veined matter resembled, to my eyes, the spongy tissued lining of some colossal human brain. Was that where I was? Drifting on a pile of my life's shredded prose within a vast psycho-geographical mani-festation of my internal mind?

YES, said a familiar voice.

I flinched, terrified. I'd heard the word alright, but not aloud. I'd heard it from deep inside my own brain. Which, in this place, was technically the same thing.

EXACTLY. THIS IS YOUR BRAIN. THE HELL OF YOUR OWN HEAD.

YOUR ... *HELL HEAD.*

HEH HEH HEH.

'I thought it was called the Prolix,' I yelled back.

IT IS CALLED THE PROLIX TOO. ALL THINGS IN THE REALM OF THE PROLIX HAVE TOO MANY WORDS, NAMES, APPELLATIONS, MONIKERS AND SIGNIFIERS.

SEE? UNDERSTAND? COMPREHEND? ARE ABLE TO PROCESS?

'Show yourself!' I demanded. Instantly, the shafts of light above were extinguished and I was cast once more into total darkness. I realised then the true horror of my situation. Not only had highest Heaven and deepest Hell *both* rejected me, but now my own head was subjecting me to eternal torments of the soul.

PRECISELY. EXACTLY. AN ACCURATE APPRAISAL OF THE SITUATION. PREDICAMENT. QUANDARY OR PICKLE.

So this was a realm of suffering *beyond* Hell. A realm *beyond* the beyond . . .

OR THE BEYONDER. THAT'S ANOTHER NAME WE USE. EMPLOY. IMPLEMENT.

'I said show yourself!' I cried again. 'Show me who you are!'

I peered into the shadows. At length, I glimpsed a shape moving towards me from the darkness. It was no longer pitch black, by the way, as the slatted windows in the walls above had opened up again, illuminating the area with rays of otherworldly light. I later discovered these were dimmable, hence me not immediately noticing.

The thing from the darkness slowly emerged, silhouetted against the shadows. It was tall and thin, sporting a long leather trench coat (of which I approved) covered with open sores (which I was less keen on). Lost souls dangled from both pockets, and the thing's face, I saw, once I'd put on my driving shades, was spiked all over like hedgehog skin.

Pins . . .

Pins . . .

Oh God, the *PINS* ...

The *DAMNED PINS* ...

Except these weren't pins.

Not even close to being pins.

Oh, that they *were* pins ...

But they *weren't* ...

Not *pins* at all ...

Oh no.

These pins all ended in ...

Typebars.

A *typewriter's TYPEBARS*.

The face skewered with *TYPEWRITER'S <u>TYPEBARS</u>* opened its mouth (not easy under the circumstances), and rows of rusting, metallic teeth commenced to clatter like the hellish hammering of a thousand typewriter keys.

Then it spake:

I AM TYPE-FACE, LORD OF THE PROLIX.

AND I HAVE TORN YOUR BOOKS APART.

CHAPTER SEVEN

'*Why* have you torn my books apart?'

SO THAT YOU MAY SUFFER AS YOUR READERS SUFFER. FROM A SURFEIT, A GLUT, AN OVER-EXCESSIVE LITANY OF PROSE. WORDS. LANGUAGE. NARRATIVE.

'Are you my typewriter?'

YES. IN ITS ULTIMATE FORM. I AM TYPE-FACE, LORD OF THE PROLIX. AND YOU, NICK STEEN, ARE MY ...

It raised its arm towards me, pointing an elongated finger.

... BITCH.

'I know that already.'

So this was what I'd been sleeping with. This *thing*. This monster. This grotesque parody of the human form. This hideous human-typewriter hybrid is what had been having its wicked way with me for the past twelve months. A living keyboard possessed by some cosmic demon from another dimension. But *why*?

BEHOLD. LOOK. SEE.

Type-Face swept his extended arm sideways, and as he did so, the black cavern walls behind crumpled and rolled back like scrolling parchment, to reveal, beyond us, a terrifying vista. Another world. An alien realm ...

THIS IS THE PROLIX. A REALM OF TOTAL AND ULTIMATE CHAOS. OF SUFFERING BEYOND THE BEYOND. A PLACE WITHOUT MEANING. A PLACE OF DEATH.

I stared out into Hell (again, not technically Biblical Hell), my eyes barely able to take in the myriad horrors afore me. Everywhere I looked, there were strips of torn paper, abandoned children's letter blocks lying higgledy-piggledy, roads and paths leading nowhere and more often than not ending in unexpected cul-de-sacs. Signs pointed upwards when they should be pointing downwards. Arms indicated left when they should be indicating right. This was a world where in was out and out was in. Dictionary-factories spewed wrongly spelled words into the air to form new, meaningless words, which floated directionless into the ether, losing themselves in the never-ending chaos. And all the while, a chorus of tuneless jazz saxophones blew discordant, cacophonous physical notation towards my extremities. The result was an unholy, meaningless din.

YOU HAVE FAILED US, NICK STEEN.

'Failed?' I cried, sick to my stomach. 'This place is total chaos. There's no way a writer like myself could ever concentrate in an environment like this. Writing and reading would be a complete nightmare. I want nothing to do with it.'

AH, BUT LOOK. YEA, BUT OBSERVE. NAY, PAY CLOSE ATTENTION. BUT SOFT, ATTEND.

As Type-Face spoke, a shadow fell across the land and I craned my neck upwards, seeking its source. There, towering above everything like a sick parody of my novel *Diaballos Apocalypsicum Penetratio*, loomed a vast mountain of ever-accumulating paper. A colossal and endless work-in-progress, an ever-growing proto-novel branching upwards through the black thunderous clouds gathering overhead.

BEHOLD THE ENDLESS BOOK. THE UNFINISHED TOME. THE OPUS WITHOUT END. IT WAS INTENDED FOR YOUR WORLD, NICK STEEN.

BEHOLD . . . OUR CHILD.

So *that's* what we'd been doing. Suddenly, it all began to make sense. Those thrashing acts of vile procreation had been an attempt to conceive the ultimate book. Evidently, Type-Face had been using me, body and mind, as an unwitting conduit in order to invade and take over the world. Using me to produce, via demeaning acts of bodily subjugation, colossal works of total nonsense that would eventually destroy the planet's natural resources, confuse humanity and allow Type-Face to spread the realm of the Prolix into our own, like some form of vile cosmic disease.

What an arsehole. As I watched, sheets of paper blew hither and thither, floating upwards through the air into the dark heavens, to land, I assumed, atop the book that would never end.

NOW THAT YOU HAVE DISOBEYED ME, NICK STEEN, SPURNED ME, OPPOSED MY WILL, I HAVE BROUGHT YOU HERE TO THE PROLIX TO AWAIT YOUR DOOM. YOUR SUFFERING. YOUR TRUE PUNISHMENT. LIKE SISYPHUS, YOU SHALL REMAIN HERE IN THE PROLIX FOR ALL ETERNITY, YOUR ENDLESS TASK NEVER DONE.

'Sisyphus is here, too, is he?'

FIGURATIVELY SPEAKING. METAPHORICALLY SO. NOT LITERALLY.

I had to get out of here, somehow. But that somehow was a big somehow, given I was in a parallel dimension formed partly from the inner workings and trappings of my own mind.

And given that I was incarcerated here with a foul being from some race of dark cosmic gods hailing from another dimension, poised to infiltrate our reality, it didn't look like it was going to be easy.

AND NOW ...

He waved his hand the other way and the cavern wall scrolled back to black, obliterating my vision of the Prolix.

... THE SUFFERING.

'Before we get started,' I said, affecting an air of nonchalance. 'Can we dispense with the excess words? Because I do get the point.'

FINE. OKAY. SURE.

'I *said* ...'

JOKING.

'Fine.'

MOCKING. RIBBING.

'Will you stop that?'

HA HA HA.

'*Will* you stop?'

HEH HEH HEH.

'Christ ali ...'

HO HO.

I waited.

HO.

I continued to wait, prepared to string out my silence all night if I had to. After four hours, Type-Face spoke again.

FINE. GO AHEAD.

'What do you ...'

PROCEED.

Forget it. What was the bloody point?

ENOUGH TIME-WASTING. PREPARE FOR SOME <u>REAL</u> PUNISHMENT.

Type-Face held up his bony hand. From the sleeve of the long leather coat emerged a cloud of minuscule black forms, like tiny midges. Only these were a mixture of distorted shapes; small, squiggled lines like stray falling hairs; jagged dots of black, like burned oven scrapings, all swarming and darting about the air in my line of vision, everywhere and anywhere I cared or dared to stare.

'Jesus H.,' I said, realising what was now materialising before my very eyes. A writer's worst fear. '*Floaters* ...'

Before I knew where to run, they were upon me, flashing and darting over the surface of my eyes like a swarm of flying insects.

Desperately, ultimately in vain, I attempted to fight them off, knowing that they were indeed not only a writer's worst enemy, able to distort and distract one's train of thought from the unsullied whiteness of the blank page, but a reader's, too, whose mental suffering at this relentless, annoying squiggling might spell the end of their reading habit for ever, thus condemning my (and potentially other authors') work to the charity shop shelf, where it would ultimately fail to earn additional royalties.

'Get them off me!' I screamed. 'They burn! They bite!' They actually did neither, but I was getting frustrated. Yet Type-Face merely laughed at my suffering, his teeth continuing to chatter as the dreaded floaters filled my irises, swarming in and around me like a plague of locusts,* breaking my concentration and irritating my vision.

'Enough!' I cried, crying tears in an effort to rid myself of these bloody floaters. 'Enough, damn you! I've suffered enough!'

NO, NICK STEEN, YOU HAVE NOT SUFFERED ENOUGH. NOT NEARLY ENOUGH. NOT NEARLY ENOUGH BY HALF.

'Look, I know you had plans for me. I know you were using me as a means to invade our universe. But I won't let you destroy me here, either, Type-Face. Whatever you do to me, I'll resist. And I'll survive. I'll escape the Prolix and then I'll come back to get you in particular. I'm your bitch *no more*.'

APOLOGIES, I WASN'T LISTENING.

Like I said, an *arsehole*.

NOW, LET THE *REAL* SUFFERING COMMENCE.

All at once, I heard music again. No longer jazz saxophone, but instead the brash, swaggering brass trumpery of a late-night Soho sleaze-band.

* And I've written nineteen locust novels, so this is no idle comparison.

63

STEP FORTH, SOUL STRIPPER.

I looked up, trying to sneak a peek of what was now approaching slowly from the darkest corner of the cavern, but what eventually appeared was no foot-lit, suspender-strung nymphette of the scantily clad variety.

It lacked breasts and buttocks and sported knives for hands. Long, black, rusting blades of the catering-school variety. Grim realisation slowly dawned. I'd seen those blades before. They were the ones I'd used to shred that old writer's manuscript in front of his very eyes. The man whose face I'd subsequently recognised in Moses Unique, that strange, rubber-aproned owner of Uniquities Inc., Plus Eels.

I recalled how gleefully I'd gripped those black steel blades (a childhood keepsake, or so he'd screamed) in both hands to slash the pages from his life's work with impunity and without mercy, howling in raucous, victorious laughter as he struggled to squeeze himself free. What approached me now, then, was evidently some form of unjust punishment for my supposed crime. For the dreaded Soul Stripper, Arch-Ripper of the Prolix, was about to tear me a new one.

I tried to turn, hoping I might dive back into the river of pulped prose, but instead felt myself yanked backwards in sudden pain on to a waiting surgeon's trolley. Before I knew what was happening, I was lying prostrate upon the metallic bed, shrieking in pain as a second volley of chained hooks shot from the darkness and speared me in my front side, jerking me forwards violently, forcing my helpless body upwards into a sitting position.

I screamed again as the chains dashed me brutally back and forth, sitting me up then slamming me down as the Soul Stripper approached, whirling those immense rusting blades of blackened steel.

NOW STRIP HIS SOUL.

And lo, I was stripped.

FRIGHT BREAK

The following passage has been flagged on grounds of good taste by the publisher. For those of a stronger disposition, who aren't human cowards, the passage is available to read in full on page 281. Meaning for those of you who are craven cowards, do not read page 281. For avoidance of any doubt, neither the author nor the publisher will be held responsible for any offence or psychological injury sustained by reading page 281. You have been warned . . .

Having flayed me,* the Soul Stripper tossed my spent face-wrapper to the slavering floaters, walked over to a nearby cupboard that had just appeared and took out a giant salt-shaker.

Before I could formally object, the Soul Stripper tipped the shaker upside down and commenced pouring salt on my wounds, both literally and figuratively (i.e. doubly bad).

The pain was beyond description, therefore won't be described.

WELL FLAYED, said Type-Face, as the Soul Stripper finished pouring the salt and began to rub it into my exposed flesh with both hands, which were still carving knives, remember. I just couldn't believe it. This was heaping indignity upon indignity. Pouring further salt on my wounds by first pouring salt on my wounds, then rubbing additional salt on said wounds. I was livid.

'Okay, you've flayed me,' I said. 'Big deal. What else you got?'

Type-Face walked over to me and leaned down to leer and hiss in my ear. He was so close to me that I could have reached out to strike one of the typebars on his damned face if I'd wanted to. But I was beginning to feel like I'd had enough of writing, if I'm honest.

Had enough of everything.

---

* This is explained in detail on page 281, so if you haven't read page 281 (see above warning) you are completely missing out.

But Type-Face hadn't. That was all too apparent by the way he leered at me and laughed and looked like he was gearing up for something else entirely. No way had he had enough.

NOW ... he said, the typebars on his face hammering away furiously with each word he spoke.

... REMAINDER HIM.

CHAPTER EIGHT

They flipped me over on to my front. I realised I was dripping body juice all over the floor, but they didn't seem to care about the mess I was making, although I'd have been absolutely livid if it was my flat. I'd gone mad enough about that lone crack in my kitchen tiles, after all. I guess I was delirious, but I was inside my own mind, and it was sure as hell working in mysterious ways. I forced what was left of my neck upwards and glimpsed another figure emerging from the shadows. It was a tiny woman in a tweed suit resembling a mousy-looking librarian I'd once berated for failing to enforce overdue fines on my books, thereby reducing my personal PLR income over a ten-year period by nine pounds and seventeen pence. She dangled a black marker pen in her right hand, and as she drew close to me, held it out against my benumbed derriere and drew a thick black line across my skinless buttocks. I felt *that*, alright.

But the old hag wasn't finished.

ADDITIONAL FRIGHT BREAK

Yet again, the following passage has been excised on grounds of good taste by the publisher. For those of a mature disposition, who aren't abject failures of human beings, the passage is available to read in full on page 285. Meaning for those of you who still require reins to engage in what I deem to be your pathetic excuse for an existence, do not read page 285. For avoidance of doubt, neither the author nor the publisher will be held responsible for any offence or devastating psychological injuries sustained by reading PAGE 285. You have again been warned.

'Do your worst, you old bag. You won't break me.'

YES, WE WILL.

'Like hell,' I screamed. 'I'm all that stands between you and a demonic invasion of our mortal realm by cosmic beings from another plane of reality, and there's no way I'll let being completely flayed from top to toe and cruelly remaindered prevent me fighting off a legion of black angels hellbent on vanquishing the existence of Mankind!'

SORRY, WE WEREN'T LISTENING TO YOU.

He would in time. Though I'd been flayed, balded and un-shouldered* in this parallel dimension of eternal physical and psychological torture, I began to wonder what else Type-Face could possibly do to me that would make my situation any worse.

THIS.

Yet another Hell-Priest of bodily horror emerged from the shadows, scuttling towards me like a giant spider. I saw it had two gigantic thumbs, which rubbed together periodically like feelers. The thing was a grotesque parody of the human hand, haired and greasy; a hand so large and distorted it could only have belonged to a particularly low-grade type of worker. Perhaps a door-to-door tradesman or overweight trucker. The creature moved upon what looked to me like a spread of fat, knobbled fingers. A knuckular beast then, resembling the hand of those particular readers I loathed at book-signings. The sort who would take a brand-new copy of your latest book, seize it twixt both hands, then bend the pages so far

---

* See page 285 which, remember, you have been legally warned against reading, even if comprehension of the main text will be severely compromised as a result. You do the math.

backwards they practically formed a rounded cylinder which they then expected you to sign.

BEHOLD . . . THE SPINE-CRACKER.

'I'm beholding him already.'

Rubbing its large thumbs together so hard they began to generate smoke, the hideous form reared its mighty thumbs skyward, raising itself over my prone body. Without warning, it scurried speedily on to my back.

Pausing for a moment to perform its strange ritual, caressing both thumbs together like an insect preparing to mate, the creature then slammed either one hard across my opposite ends, imprisoning my feet and head as its bed of knuckles underneath locked me in place, clamping my body tight as if in an ironmonger's vice. I screamed again, quite hoarse now, as the thing proceeded to force my spine backwards, with the intention, I presumed, of making me meet myself in the middle.

To crack said spine, in other words.

EXACTLY. PRECISELY. YOU GOT IT.

I felt it going. Sensed the balls of my feet approaching the back of my head. Felt the calloused skin of the creature's thumbs against the front of what used to be my forehead as it bent me round and into myself, forcing the bones outwards, towards breaking point. I could almost hear the mighty split approaching; a slow but steady cracking of my spinal shaft, like the settling of a rented wooden log house in a summer heatwave, with all the attendant sanitary issues. I heard the steaming hiss of bubbling spinal fluid, threatening to erupt into a terrible life-draining geyser of my . . .

THIRD AND FINAL FRIGHT BREAK

The next two words have been excised by the publisher on grounds of good taste, although they are available to read immediately on page 287. Previous warnings apply.

★   ★   ★

I didn't care anymore. I felt myself slipping into painless (though still hugely painful, tbh) oblivion as my numbed, mangled frame gave way to the natural process of death, even though this particular death was anything but natural (I was currently bent backwards between two giant disembodied thumbs, remember).

Was I dead, or only dreaming now? For I thought I could sense via what used to be my nose the sweet scent of summer flowers. Then a strange calmness swam over me.

Was I now so divorced from my mangled nerves that complete detachment from insufferable agonies had finally been granted by whatever power ruled this realm of complete and total pain?

Was that sweet smell I sensed the mystical scentage of my own spurting spinal fluid, that blessed internal tincture wrought by merciful Nature to spirit its owner loftily oblivion-wards on soft clouds of numbing back-vapour during one's final seconds? Or was it but the calming breeze from yonder sward, seeking a route through the darkness 'twixt life and death, in an effort most nobleth, to comfort this poor, nayfaring wayfarer?

Or was it Shalimar, by Guerlain?

I sniffed hard, struggling to draw something in via the twin sunken craters of my mashed nasal cartilage.

Yes, it was definitely Shalimar, by Guerlain.

Mustering what little strength remained in my flayed and salted body, I forced my eyes open (which actually wasn't hard, as my lids had completely gone and they were permanently open anyway) and I saw, like a miracle before me, the silhouette of a delectable female form I knew all too well. For Shalimar, by Guerlain was Roz's perfume of choice, and here she was, an angel standing before me in the Hell of my own head, staring down Type-Face and his demonic horde.

'You leave Roz out of this!' I yelled, spluttering on my own juices.

LEAVE HER? EDITORS ARE A THREAT TO OUR VERY EXISTENCE. WHY, EVEN HERE, ROZ MAY ATTEMPT TO

TYPE-FACE

TIDY UP THE PROLIX. TRIM, CLARIFY AND ERASE EXCESS WORDAGE. SHE MIGHT EVEN ATTEMPT TO TIDY THE PLACE UP AND MAKE IT MORE PRESENT-ABLE. VACUUM MY ENTIRE REALM AND DUST IT. REARRANGE MY BOOK CUPBOARDS SO THAT THE LOUNGE AREA LOOKS MORE SYMMETRICAL. FOR THAT REASON, SHE TOO MUST BE DESTROYED.

I watched, helpless, as the demons started moving towards her.

'Roz!' I yelled. 'I don't know how you got down here, but I feel it's fair to warn you that if you attempt to edit this place, these guys *will* flay you.'

My voice must have snapped her out of it. She shook her head and turned towards me.

'God, Nick,' she yelled, tears forming in her eyes. 'What have they *done* to you?'

'Flayed me, Roz. Plus remaindered me and cracked my spine. It's literally a bloody nightmare.'

GET HER.

As the horde advanced upon Roz, all I could do was watch help-lessly. I considered looking away to give her some dignity, but as her arms dug into her handbag, I realised what they were clasping. A small white bottle. Roz lifted up the object in her hands, twisted off the lid, then flung the contents into the faces of her demonic tormentors.

NO! NEVER! NO WAY!

The demons shook and shrunk into themselves, curling up like sprayed insects. Meanwhile, Type-Face shrieked as another white stream of correcting fluid struck him directly between his typebars.

AAARRGGHHH! CORRECTION FLUID! HOW IT BURNS! HOW IT STINGS! HOW IT SMARTS! HOW IT NEGATES MY SENSE OF SELF BY ERASING MY OWN THOUGHTS AS I TYPE!

71

'Run, Nick!' Roz yelled. 'We have to get out of here!'

'But there is no way out, Roz! The place keeps changing form, and right now it's essentially an oubliette. Then again, given that it *has* changed before now, it could theoretically change again. Maybe we should just run into a small area of darkened shadow? There might actually prove to be a tunnel or similar corridor-type affair somewhere close by? Perhaps mere centimetres beyond the furthest scope of my vision, which is impaired anyway given the current state of my flayed eyes,' I screamed.

'Then let's try and find one, Nick,' she yelled back, grabbing what remained of my hand before immediately letting go of it and retching.

'You look like one of those illustrations in old medical journals,' she gasped.

'You mean, not quite skeletal but as good as? All red and white musculature with a mass of exposed tendons?'

'That's it, exactly. *Look . . .*'

She pulled a small lady's mirror out of her lady's handbag and flashed it at me. The mirror immediately cracked, exploding in her hands, but I'd already seen enough. Now *I* was retching.

'Listen, Roz, I've only been flayed,' I said, between heaves. 'It's still *me.*'

'Nick, we don't have time to retch. Any second now, Type-Face is going to wipe that Tippex off, and I only have a few drops left. We need to run away from here, like I said a minute or so ago.'

'What about the area of complete darkness we're fleeing into for safety, Roz?' I asked, despairing. 'How will we see in front of us?'

'Luckily, I have a torch,' she said, producing a small lady's flashlight from her lady's handbag. 'I stopped by your house on my way home, so I had all my work stuff with me. Including my trusty bottle of correction fluid.'

'Thank God for that,' I said as she flicked on the torch. Nothing happened.

'Out of batteries!' she cried.

'Dammit, Roz, don't you keep a spare?' I shouted, aware that Type-Face had now wiped off most of the correction fluid, although a couple of keys had gone a bit stiff and crusty.

'Hold on,' she said, scrabbling about in her lady's handbag again.

'Be quick about it, Roz!' I yelled. 'He's picking bits off with his nails!'

'Here!' she shouted, producing a fresh new pack of double-As.

'Quick, Roz! Change the torch batteries!'

'Dammit, Nick, I can't!' she yelled, starting to lose control of herself. 'I forgot, this torch takes D-batteries!'

'I don't believe it, Roz!' I screamed. 'I really don't. Of all the times to find that out, this must be the absolute worst.'

If Roz didn't locate the right pack of batteries soon and change them at record speed, Type-Face would soon have removed all remaining crusts of correction fluid from those stiffened typebars I mentioned, and would once more be able to concentrate his efforts on attacking us.

'Here they are!' Roz exclaimed, pulling out a brand-new pack of D-batteries.

'Are they rechargeable?' I asked. 'Because we have no time at all to recharge.'

'They come fully charged when you buy them, Nick,' she cried. 'But dammit, these ones went off six months ago!'

'For crying out loud, Roz!' I yelled. 'Why do you girls never keep up-to-date batteries in your handbags?'

She looked as if she was about to cry, then rallied suddenly. 'I've found them, Nick! I've *found* them!'

She unzipped a side pocket on the bag and pulled out another pack, holding them up so I could see them. 'And they're in date

– just!' She was crying hysterically now, the stress of the situation finally getting to her, too, it seemed.

'And they're D–batteries, not double-As?'

'D–batteries. It says right here. Look.'

I looked and confirmed that they were indeed D-batteries, and the pack was in date, like she claimed.

'Great, Roz,' I said, knowing I'd have to coax her a bit now, having snapped at her for endangering my life and hers. 'Now change them pronto, babe.'

She began to do as I commanded, then nicked one of her nails on the torch's battery compartment and winced.

'Just give the thing to me, for God's sake,' I said, grabbing the torch from her. Within ten minutes, I had the battery compartment open and was just starting to change them over when Type-Face at last shifted the final clogs of correction fluid from his face and began approaching us again, teeth chattering like a row of clacking type-writer keys. 'Hold him off, Roz!' I yelled.

She flung the last few remaining drops at our attacker. The leather-coated monstrosity hissed as the fluid once more splashed his face. He bent over, slapping at his head with both hands, trying in vain to remove the stain.

Roz screamed, in tears again. 'There's no more correction fluid left.'

'One more minute,' I said, swapping the batteries back round, having been unable to physically locate the + and - symbols in this dimly lit space.

'Quick, Nick! He's coming for us!'

After two more goes, I finally had them changed back round. I slid back the cover, resealing it with the small Phillips screwdriver I kept on me for emergencies, and had previously employed to open the battery compartment in the first place. I flicked the on switch to 'on' but realised there was still no light emerging from the bulbed end, so banged it against the ground a couple of times until the thing finally lit up.

'Now, Roz! Run!'

I'LL GET YOU BOTH.

Dammit, Type-Face was right behind us.

YOU JUST SEE IF I DON'T. AND WHEN I DO, YOU'RE BOTH <u>REALLY</u> FOR IT.

'God, Nick, I'm so frightened by Type-Face!'

I grabbed Roz's hand in mine, which made her retch again, but to be honest, I was getting used to the gagging. Then together we fled into the darkness, which, as we ran, ceased to be darkness owing to the light emanating from the torch I was holding, and for which I'd fought so dearly and bravely against overwhelming odds. It began to flicker, and soon I realised that my blood was seeping into its mechanism via the sealed grooving, so I reluctantly handed it to Roz.

'Look, Nick,' she said, shining the torch at the walls of the tunnel we were now fleeing down. 'You were absolutely right about the darkness being a tunnel or some sort of corridor-type affair, and it having been concealed from our view in that confined area of darkness, which has since been exposed by the beams of torchlight. Good thinking.'

'Thanks,' I said.

'If I'm not mistaken, these walls seem to be formed from some kind of papier-mâché. Look, there are occasional sections of typed print visible, exposing assorted words and phrases.'

'I know all that already, Roz,' I said. 'They're shreds of my life's work, now hellishly and fiendishly strewn hither and thither in an effort to torment and ridicule my very sense of self. We're in the Prolix, Roz – a realm of total suffering and excess wordage. Type-Face was using me as a psychic portal into our own reality so that he could commence an invasion of Earth.'

'God, Nick, that's *awful*.'

'Sshh ...' I said, suddenly. I could hear Type-Face behind. Gaining on us. Sniffing out our whereabouts.

'Where do we run to?' asked Roz.

'I don't know,' I said, staring at a million different signposts, all pointing nowhere. 'There must be over a million different signposts in here, all pointing nowhere. We're lost, Roz. In the Prolix. With Type-Face right behind us. And time running out. Trapped. Maybe forever. In the Prolix. A realm of eternal chaos and suffering. The Prolix.'

'Oh God,' she whispered.

'He won't help us,' I said. 'God, that is. We're truly doomed, Roz.'

And she couldn't even hold me tight for fear of retching again.

The poor cow.

CHAPTER NINE

If I hadn't been flayed to within an inch of my life, I wouldn't have felt it. Small mercy, but mercy nonetheless, that my nerve-endings were completely exposed and thus able to pick up the minuscule change in air pressure.

'There, Roz,' I said, aiming the torch at the ceiling above our head. 'Another tunnel, I think. Running crossways just over us and causing a minute alteration in air pressure via this slight crack here. I literally felt it in my bones.'

We traced the hairline fracture along the tunnel's ceiling, which widened slowly, eventually forming a small hole leading to an opening above.

'We need to crack that open,' I said. 'Unfortunately, I have no nails any more, just nubs of raw flesh, so you'll have to stand on my shoulders, Roz, and hack at it with your lady-nails. Be quick about it.'

It took longer than I'd hoped, initially because Roz kept sliding from my wet, mucoid rotator cuffs each time I hoisted her up. Eventually, we used some paper torn from the surrounding walls to pad them out a bit, and though still damp, Roz was finally able to find some purchase and scrape the hole above us into a bigger shape. Minutes later, she was able to pull herself upwards into the tunnel above. She reached down with one hand to lift me up after her.

'This isn't going to work,' I said, sliding free from her grip for a fifth time.

'Wait,' she said finally, tossing down a pack of Kleenex she'd drawn from her lady-bag. 'Mop up what you can with these.'

I began wiping at my exposed wrist sinew, swearing beneath my breath as the damp ooze of me kept shredding the cheap, pound-shop-quality fibres. I started to panic, hearing Type-Face again, getting nearer all the time.

'It's no good, Roz,' I said. 'These are too abrasive. You should have bought Balsam or Ultra Soft.'

'Here,' she said, throwing down a square of cotton-fibre cloth.

'Where's this from?' I asked, warily.

'It's my personal cleaning cloth. I always carry one with me, in case I'm ever hit by the urge to polish chrome when I'm out and about.'

I did my best to wind it round my hand, holding it up to Roz so she could tie a decent knot in it. Then she grabbed my hand again and yanked me upwards. That part was easier than we'd anticipated, as I'd lost a significant amount of body weight during my recent flaying. Once up, we switched off the torch and waited there in the darkness for Type-Face to pass in the tunnel below. We froze as he drew near, then mutually thawed once he'd finally passed by. Roz snapped the torch back on and I began the monumental task of picking stray specks of lint from my dripping limbs.

'You should have bought a lint-free cloth, Roz,' I said. 'This one's tantamount to terry-towelling.'

'Sorry, Nick,' she said, observing the delicate if ultimately pointless labour of my seeping fingers. 'Does it hurt?'

'Yes, but it's the dripping I can't stand. Bits of me eventually dry over and get crusty, but then I start bleeding again underneath, and that then breaks through and suddenly I'm all drippy again. Then, by the time that bit's crusted over ...'

'Thanks, Nick,' said Roz, pale-faced and interrupting again. 'I get the idea.'

'Well, correct me if I'm wrong, but you *did* ask.'

'I know I did,' she said. 'And I'm sorry.'

'I forgive you. I just wish I knew how to get us out of this place, Roz. But if I'm honest, I'm not sure I'd be accepted back into polite society anyway, looking like I do.'

'I think you look cute. *Sensitive* . . .' Roz said, cracking a smile I hadn't seen in months. Was she softening at last, or openly taunting my shame? There was no trace of irony on her face – just pieces of me that were coming away with each shred of lint I flicked off. So I guess she was *technically* softening. And she was *here*, after all. How and why had she come after me? With all the commotion of my daring escape and rescuing of her, I'd forgotten to ask.

'How did you get here anyway, Roz?' I asked. 'How did you enter the Prolix? And why?'

She blushed.

'I . . . I guess I had second thoughts, Nick. About everything. About your writing. About *us*. When Clackett Publishing fired you, I realised I still had a job. But I didn't have *you* – my favourite writer. I felt bad we'd parted that way in the dermatological clinic, and then when I put on your E45 cream . . .' She looked up at me and smiled. Wiped a strand of dripping flesh from my cheek. 'That night, I stopped by your flat. To see if I could make things up to you, somehow. But you were nowhere to be found, Nick. I knew it was the typewriter that had torn us apart, so I wondered whether there was a way of destroying it myself, without you knowing. Perhaps throwing it down the rubbish chute, or detonating it with some high explosive. Then I saw it on your desk. It was *looking* at me, Nick. Though it didn't have eyes, I knew it was looking at me. And I hated it. Oh, how I hated it. And, hating it, I recalled the good times you and I had had together, Nick. Before the damned typewriter came between us. And I realised I still respected you, Nick. Emotionally and . . . and yes, intellectually. Despite you wearing those pants out in public, and telling me dirty anecdotes about clacking keys, I knew I wanted to publish you again. And as I started to cry, realising what a fool I'd been to let you walk right out of my life, I saw that message you'd left me.'

'Message?' I asked, repeating one of her words.

'On the page spooled through the typewriter,' she continued. 'The message addressed to me. The message that said, "Roz, I wish you were my publisher again, but I guess you'll never read this message, by Nick Steen.""

I hadn't left her any message . . .

'Then, as I leaned over to draw the paper out, that massive spiked rubber platen thing reached out and drew in *me*.'

'The damned irony,' I cursed.

'Well, Nick, what do you say? Would you be happy to come back to Clackett?'

'Well, Roz, let me show you the ways,' I said. And despite my rancid form, Roz and I made sweet love, right there in the shredded psychological refuse of my colossal tormented brain.

HORROTICA SECTION

The following passage of hot erotica has been excised by the publisher on 'moral' grounds. Despite the advice and counsel of a MASTER OF HORROR, explaining in numerous emails and fraught agent-based exchanges that the finest fright fiction should always contain at least one major scene of hard spice (preferably two, plus a liberal hotting up of any overtly pedestrian passages), it would appear that the editorial prerequisite today is for 'restraint' and 'public decency'. For those of a more liberated bent, the near-censored passage of artistically justified white-hot sleaze is available to read immediately – in FULL – and without any unexpected charges, on page 289.

– Garth Marenghi

'That isn't like your typewriter does it, I'll bet,' Roz said, lighting a weak menthol cigarette from her lady's handbag.

'No, Roz. It really, really wasn't.'

I sighed. She looked up at me, worried.

I cracked a smile. 'It was *better*, Roz. *Much* better.'

'Again, Nick,' she whispered eagerly, yanking my starter rope with both hands. 'I want it *twice*.'

'Steady, tiger,' I said. 'I'm damaged goods, remember?'

Then I snapped out of it. Because none of the physical intimacy between Roz and myself as described above* had actually happened. Yet the experience I'd imagined had been so vivid, so sensual, so damned *potent*, that I realised my fecund, provocative imagination had almost escaped my own mind. Maybe it was because my cranial flesh was no longer there to contain my brain and its contents, but somehow I suspected that for one split second, my own imagination had *escaped* . . .†

Unfortunately, I had no time to discuss this with Roz (probably just as well) as a voice interrupted us suddenly in the darkness.

'Eel?'

I looked round and shone the torch on a figure in the far corner of this paper cave. It was Moses Unique, the shop-owner from Uniquities Inc., Plus Eels.

'You,' I said. 'Moses Unique. The shop-owner from Uniquities Inc., Plus Eels.'

'Technically they're Tome Wyrrms, not eels,' he replied, swallowing. 'And technically I'm not the shop-owner of Uniquities Inc., Plus Eels.'

'No, you're that old writer guy I used to deliver papers to,' I said. 'The one whose story I shredded in front of your own eyes.'

* i.e. The Horrotica Section censored against my will but still available to read *IN FULL, RAW, NO-HOLDS-BARRED DETAIL* on *PAGE 289*. GM
† This is foreshadowing what will later be of crucial narrative import, so do remember this section.

'Too late for apologies.'

'I'm not apologising. It freed you from that commode, didn't it?'

'Will you please excuse me for a moment?'

The man's eyes closed as he reached upwards with one hand towards his head. I shone the torch a little wider and saw another figure perched beside him, baring its arse at us. It was some sort of medieval demon, and the two appeared to be engaged in a form of bizarre repetitive ritual.

The action began with the old man dipping a feathered quill into a large hole that I now saw formed the top section of his head. He then proceeded to compose an entire page of prose upon a scrap of parchment, using his own blood as ink, before handing the finished page to the demon, who then wiped his behind with it and flushed the man's work down an adjacent toilet.

This went on repeatedly, and while disgusting, was ultimately quite soothing.

'I, too, was like you, Nick Steen,' the man said as he dipped the quill once more into his brain. 'A best-selling writer convinced that the fruit of my labours, my precious words, meant something to humanity. Little did I know it was all bollocks. I, like you, dared to challenge the gods, raise Mankind (not Ladykind) above the level of beastdom through the conquest of Knowledge. But then I, too, was captured by Type-Face, Lord of the Prolix, and imprisoned here, my own precious words smeared on the bared arse of a demonic entity for all eternity. One who cannot even read, though he does respond to the occasional picture book.

'Then one day, I was promised my freedom if I could locate the soul of another writer in order to facilitate Type-Face's invasion of our world. Who better, I thought, than that vile, hard-nosed little ragamuffin who tore up my work, threw it back in my face and told me to make myself presentable for the ambulance crew?'

'That was just punkdom.'

'So I agreed, and was cast back into your reality, armed with a dimension-portal disguised as an ancient typewriter, hoping to entice your colossal ego through the promise of supposed literary immortality. Except that now, having absorbed your soul into the Prolix alongside my own, Type-Face has reneged on our deal – he is a *real* arsehole – and I am back where I began, dipping quills into my own, useless brain for all eternity.'

'Is there a way out of here?' I asked, getting somewhat bored, if I'm honest.

'There is,' he said. 'A single portal leading back to your world, but finding it will not be easy. For I resolutely refuse to tell you where it is.'

'But you *know* where it is?' I asked.

'I do indeed. I've just come from there, remember?'

'And yet you won't show us the way?'

'No, I won't.'

'Would you show Roz the way?'

'Wait a moment.'

We waited another moment as he finished scrawling out a fresh page and handed it to the demon beside him, who duly soiled the man's words on its scaly behind again and flushed them down the toilet. Sighing deeply, he turned back to us.

'What was the question again?'

'Would you show Roz the way?'

'No.'

Before he could taunt us any more, the floor below him burst apart and up through the hole rose a terrifying creature. The familiar-looking inky-blue form roared up from below, clasping the old man between its jaws. The creature's vast body was dark and slimy, and at one end I made out a familiar-looking pair of reading shades, stretched almost to breaking point over its massively bloated face.

83

The *Tome-Wyrrm* ... Only now it had grown to monstrous size, having feasted on a million discarded words since last we'd fought. Before the old man had a chance to notify us where the portal back to our own reality lay, the giant bookworm had sucked out his exposed brain and swallowed him whole, spewing out his desiccated remains from its far end almost immediately. Even I gagged at the sight. All that now remained of Moses Unique was a steaming pile of digested flesh and a knotted tassel from his former robe. As the bum-demon scooped up what was left of him and proceeded to wipe its backside yet again, Roz screamed in my ear.

'Nick! It's coming for us!'

Despite her screaming in my ear, she was right.

It *was* coming for us.

The Tome-Wyrrm was coming for *us*.

CHAPTER TEN

'The portal must be *somewhere* round here, Roz!' I yelled. 'Why not start by going down that corridor there? I'll follow and try and hold off the Tome-Wyrrm.'

But Roz couldn't move, so transfixed by fear had she become. Maybe it had all finally got to her. Our initial falling-out, the sentient and overly horny typewriter that had then become Type-Face, Lord of the Prolix, the Prolix itself, then the Soul Stripper, the old lady with the giant hole-punch, the Knuckle-Beast, my flaying, our subsequent bout of imaginary nookdom, a man dipping quills in his head beside a brain-dead arse-demon, and now a gigantic book-worm consuming old-age pensioners with head injuries. It was enough to write a book about.*

'Roz, I *need* you to do this,' I said, although I didn't, in actual fact – that's just a lazy phrase which helps steer a lost narrative back on course when readers are giving up in droves, and is, ironically, a major sign of *bad* writing. But I knew Roz would have encountered that a lot in her career as editor of books by authors other than me, and would no doubt have employed it herself to fix failing narratives in desperate situations, and thus I used it here to snap her attention back from her own internal abyss.

'It's you, Nick!' she said suddenly, one hand rising to cover her mouth in horror. 'Your ... Your face!'

* Heh heh heh. GM

'What about my face?' I replied. I was aware it had crusted over again, but I could feel *something* oozing back through the holes where my nose had once been. 'Tell me, Roz. And be quick about it, because that giant Tome Wyrrm is coming towards us and really ramping up the tension and suspense.'

'I can see ... I can *see* ...'

'*What* can you see, Roz? *What* can you see?'

'*Letters*, Nick. Beginning to rise from your own head. Just like Type-Face himself. You're becoming ... like him! Like Type-Face. You're becoming something else, Nick ... You're becoming ... *Letter-Head*!'

Others would have gone mad with terror. But being a writer, I grew pedantic instead. 'Isn't that a little lazy, Roz? Two demons with letters coming out of their faces in the *same* realm? That's sloppy writing, Roz. That's what that is. And you know it. Sloppy writing. Really sloppy writing. Bad, bad writing. Writing that needs a *lot* of editing.'

'But don't you see, Nick? We're in the Prolix. That's what the Prolix is. Nothing here is neat. Everything's messy and open-ended. Not taut, or tight. All is overblown, overlong, over-extended, tauto-logical, tautologous ...'

'It's *my* brain, Roz.'

She looked at me strangely, and I realised we were back to the old arguments again. And all the while, our situation was getting worse. Not only were we both trapped in the Prolix (which was essentially the inside of my own head, but was also partly a parallel realm/alterna-tive cosmic dimension, remember), but everything Roz had accused me of, every rookie writer's error she'd implored me to correct throughout my writing career was here with me, surrounding me, infusing me, borne out by those damned typebars now poking through my own flayed facial muscle. I was just another Type-Face-in-waiting, perhaps doomed to ensnare, entrap and encatchen some other unwary writer, scribe or novelist on some future date, juncture or occasion.

Dammit, I was even speaking like Type-Face now. I should have listened to Roz back in the day, when the publishing world was my oyster. Shellfish. Sea mollusc. I guess I should have agreed to let her do the occasional edit. Cut. Alteration.

'This way!' shouted Roz, but I was no longer listening to her. Like I'd never listened to anything she said when she'd told me, 'This bit needs work, Nick,' or 'That's poor syntax,' or 'I would cut this bit down and lose all the offensive stuff, and you really need to leave those particular decisions regarding good and bad taste to me.'

I wasn't listening because at that precise moment, the Tome-Wyrrm barrelled into view and grabbed me in its jaws, dashing me violently around the paper cave. It smashed and dashed and battered and beat me from wall to wall, from ceiling to floor and back again, my bursting head hammering great, gaping holes in the lining of the tunnel. The Tome-Wyrrm thrashed crazily about in the swirling chaos, desperate to get at the words in my head.

'Goodbye, Roz,' I yelled as the Tome-Wyrrm tossed me upwards in its jaws to gain better purchase, then swallowed me whole, churning my mangled body through its flabby, acidic interior until I emerged, liquified, through its rear end. I was spewed out into purée as Roz screamed, unable now to see where I began or where I ended.

'Nick! *Nick!*'

'I'm here,' I wailed weakly, my eyes still able to locate two of my teeth among the foul soup of myself. Luckily, they spotted my brain as well. But that was about it.

Then I realised the Tome-Wyrrm was already moving towards Roz.

'It's coming for you, Roz,' I bellowed, as loudly as I could with only two teeth and a sloshy lung. 'I would imagine you're next.'

Roz screamed as the foul monster splashed and belly-flopped its fat way towards her. But there was nothing I could do about it now, having only soup for arms.

'Nick! Nick! Save me!'

There was no way I could, being, as I say, essentially liquid. Roz was as good as dead. But at that moment, the Tome-Wyrrm suddenly stopped (again), inches from Roz's head, sniffing once more at the air with its fattened snout. *Sensing* something . . .

'Roz!' I yelled. 'Look what it's doing!'

'What Nick? What is it doing?'

We watched as the beast's fat neck – which was essentially also its head – continued to sniff and nose hungrily at the air. It had scented something it wanted.

'It's scented something,' Roz said.

'Yes, something it wants,' I said back. 'There, Roz,' I continued, and would have pointed if I'd had anything to point with. 'The wall is weaker there, almost as if it's made of a thinner material than the other walls in this realm of the Prolix. Even though they, too, are essentially formed from paper and not particularly difficult to break through, us having proved that several times thus far in our travels through this strange subterranean world. Yet that particular wall looks especially thin. I wonder why?'

We watched as the Tome Wyrrm began to munch and eat its way through the widening hole, much like a monstrous, fat caterpillar would, until at long last the space beyond its jaws grew visible.

'Look, Nick! It's the back of your refrigeration unit.'

It couldn't be. It *couldn't* be. *Could* it? The portal the satanist had mentioned when he came round. Could it *really* be that?

'What make is it?' I yelled, hardly able to believe my ears.

'I don't know, Nick. I'm too scared to look.'

'Look, Roz, I *need* you to do this,' I cried. 'I need you to do this thing.'

Roz nodded, steeling herself, realising she needed to do this thing too, deep down for herself, and turned to look through the gap. 'It's a Zanussi.'

'Model number?'

'Hard to tell, Nick, but it's a double unit and would need two people to shift. Surely this is the one my mother and I moved?'

'Sounds like it, Roz,' I barked, ecstatic. But I had to be sure.

'What kind of floor is it standing upon?'

'A tiled floor, Nick. Umbrian grey sandstone, I think. Exactly like the one my mother and I recently paid to repair.'

A miracle. A goddamned grade-A miracle.

'That is indeed *my* floor, Roz. My kitchen floor. That's *my* fridge you're looking at. My portal home!'

She turned to face me, terrified.

'And yours,' I said, reassuringly. '*Our* portal home.'

'Can it be true, Nick? Can it really be our portal home?'

'Dammit, yes, although it *is* technically mine on paper. That satanist I hired yesterday told me there was a portal right there, just behind my fridge. For some reason, the Tome-Wyrrm is attracted to it, and I think I know what that reason might be.'

'Tell me, Nick,' said Roz, intrigued. 'Tell me what the reason is.'

'Well, Roz, it's like this. I always keep my latest manuscript inside my fridge whenever I'm out. It's simply the safest place. I don't know if you're aware, Roz, but burglars generally defecate mid-robbery, and frequently smear their effluence over the victim's walls, often in insulting patterns to boot. So I figured the last thing they'd need during a robbery at my house is anything that might theoretically exacerbate an imminent bowel movement to potentially dangerous degrees, like leftover curry, say. Therefore, I always hide my manuscript inside my fridge under a carton or two of half-eaten lamb bhuna, to ensure it's *never* stolen. I guess the Tome-Wyrrm must have smelled my words inside that very fridge and sensed there were fresh stories of mine for the taking.'

'Makes sense, Nick, but how are we going to get *through* the portal with that Tome-Wyrrm in the way, with the fridge itself blocking our exit, and you meanwhile floating in a pool of your own filth?'

'You're right, Roz. I guess we're stumped. *Unless . . .*'

She looked down at my floating teeth. 'Unless what, Nick?'

'Roz,' I said, trying hard to form a face from what was floating around me. 'Do you have a jar or anything similar in that lady's handbag of yours?'

'As a matter of fact, Nick, I have the coffee mug I use at Clackett's. I took it home because I thought I'd be out of a job when I took you back, and it's a really funny mug. It says "Edit? I'd rather shred it!"'

I laughed at that, mainly to get on her good side. After all, she was the one who'd be scooping me up. I *needed* her to do this.

'That's so true, Roz. And *so* funny.'

'Here it is!' she said, pulling it out of her lady-bag. It was even funnier in the flesh.

'Now scoop me up, Roz.'

She waded through my remains and reached downwards, filling up the mug with my eyes, teeth and brain.

'Your mind won't fit in, Nick,' she said, getting panicky.

'Just squash it down inside.' It didn't matter, after all. I was beyond pain. And maybe crushing my brain would edit out a few tautologies.

'How much juice do you want?'

'Better fill it up with as much juice as you can, Roz. That mug might well be my home from now on. Though ideally, if you could transfer me to a glass jug or vase when we get in so that I can look out, I'd be more than grateful.'

'Sure thing, Nick.'

Suddenly there was an almighty roar as the wall behind us burst in. My eyes rolled around in Roz's mug, but alas I couldn't see much over the rim.

'It's Type-Face,' screamed Roz. 'Type-Face is now here, too! He's found us at last! And I have no more correction fluid!'

GET AWAY FROM THAT PORTAL. GATEWAY. DOOR OF PERCEPTION, yelled Type-Face. GET AWAY. MOVE. SHIFT IT.

Roz informed me that the Tome-Wyrrm turned suddenly from the hole, still chewing at the words on the wall, sniffed the air for a moment, then turned to look up at Type-Face.

COME HERE, BOOKWORM. GET HITHER, TOME-LARVA. HEEL, OPUS-GRUB.

Roz informed me that the thing looked suddenly terrified, flopped back into the swamp and swam almost shame-facedly over to its waiting master.

'Roz, to prevent you having to tell me everything that's going on, and to give a potential future reader of my exploits a greater sense of excitement were I to relate these events further down the line, why not hold my eyes in one hand and point them at specific areas of interest?'

'Good idea, Nick,' she said, doing exactly as I'd recommended. Back in the flow of things again, I could see that we had very little time to get through that portal.

'Quick, Roz. Now!'

At my command, she splashed over to the half-chewed portal opening and attempted to force herself through.

'I can't fit through it, Nick. We need two people to shift that fridge, or I'll end up scraping your tiles again.'

'Dammit, Roz, there must be another way!' But if there was, I didn't know *what* it was, and now we had more problems to deal with. Both Type-Face and the Tome-Wyrrm were striding and sliding across the swamp towards us, resuming their attack.

'Let me pour you through this tiny gap, Nick,' Roz said. 'I'll flick your eyeballs through afterwards. Better one of us escapes than both of us spend all eternity in this horrifying realm of the Prolix.'

'Never!' I cried. After all, how the hell would I get off the floor without Roz there to sluice me up? My dead neighbour's cat (Mrs Brown, who crashed to her death in the lift) would probably get in and drink me *and* the milk I'd stolen.

'Just scrape the tiles, Roz,' I said, barely able to believe the depths I was sinking to.

'Are you sure, Nick?'

I saw the Tome-Wyrrm rearing upwards again, jaws agape.

'Do it, Roz. And hand me the concealed manuscript that's beneath my lamb bhuna.'

'But your *tiles*, Nick ...'

'Roz, I *need* you to do this.'

As I gazed in horror at the approaching beasts, I heard Roz force the fridge aside. The appalling sound of its scraping against my new tiles would have pierced my spine if I still had one, but I figured there probably wasn't much point in being house-proud from this moment on, given I'd be staining pretty much anything I sloshed against.

'Here,' said Roz, handing me the manuscript I'd placed under the uneaten bhuna. 'Are you sure you want to destroy it? It's a strong opening, even if it tends to overplay the theme of ...'

'Actually, you throw it, Roz,' I said. 'Because I realise I still don't have arms.'

'Sure, Nick. And sorry for scraping your floor.'

'So am I,' I said.

She tossed the manuscript as far as she could, which wasn't that far, to be honest. But it distracted the Tome-Wyrrm long enough for Roz to reach in and grab the rounded side of her mug with me in it. She clasped me close while I steamed, just like a soup advert, but before she could yank me through to safety, a dark figure rose into view from the foul waters of the pulp-swamp and reached out to grab the handle on the mug's other side.

NOT SO FAST. WAIT RIGHT THERE. EASY, TIGER.

'Quick, Roz! It's Type-Face! Hurl some more Tippex!'

'I told you, Nick. I'm all out. I used it all up rescuing you from that earlier flaying scene.'

'So you did,' I said, concurring. What the hell could I do now?

TYPE-FACE

And what was I, after all? Just a mangled collection of teeth, eyes, brain and blood-juice in a humorous mug. With typebars growing out of my frontal lobe.

And suddenly, with that, I had my answer.

'UNHAND ME,' I said. 'I AM LETTER-HEAD.'

WHO? said Type-Face.

'LETTER-HEAD, DARK DUKE OF THE PROLIX.'

I AM TYPE-FACE, LORD OF THE PROLIX.

'BUT I AM LETTER-HEAD, DARK DUKE OF THE PROLIX.'

THERE CANNOT BE TWO RULERS OF THE PROLIX. A PAIR OF RULERS OF THE PROLIX. DOUBLE RULERS OF THE PROLIX.

'AND YET THERE ARE,' I said. 'TWINS. DUPLICATES. BINARY BEINGS.'

NO. NEVER. NEIN.

'YES. AFFIRMATIVE. JA. FOR THAT IS THE PROLIX. A REALM OF EXCESS WORDAGE AND BAD WRITING. POOR SYNTAX. LEXICAL SLUDGE.'

Type-Face paused, shaking his head, confused. Then he began muttering to himself.

WHAT THE ... WHO THE ... WHY THE ...

He reached up with one hand and pressed one of the typebars on his face. The one marked 'Backspace' (essentially 'delete'). But nothing happened.

WHAT THE ... WHO THE ... WHY THE ...

'Quick, Roz, hand me your pen.'

She did so, and I gripped it hard between my scattered teeth. Mustering what strength remained, I yelled out my final orders.

'LOOK ON MY WORDS, TYPE-FACE, SLAVE OF THE PROLIX, AND DESPAIR. CRY. BEMOAN.' (This was all a bit garbled by the fact that I was holding a pen in my mouth, but it still did the trick.)

Type-face lifted up the mug I was sloshing in, staring down at what remained of me, quite unable to process the fact that this liquified mess in a mug was his successor.

'IT'S THE END FOR YOU, TYPE-FACE. THE END. FINIS. NOT TO BE CONTINUED.'

And with that I slopped myself forwards in the mug and, using the pen gripped in my teeth, splashed forwards and quickly scrawled two words across Type-Face's face.

THE END.

All at once, he began to scream, hammering at the 'Backspace' button (i.e. 'delete' again), trying to erase what I'd just typed.

'You forget, Type-Face,' I said. 'Typewriters don't have a true delete button. What you're pressing is a backspace button. What I've scribbled will always be there now, on your head. The only thing that would effectively erase it would be Tippex, which you don't have.'

He continued to scream and howl, releasing his grip on Roz's mug, thus freeing her hand to pull me in. As she whipped me back to safety through the portal into my kitchen, I averted my eyes from the double scrape now taking place on the floor as she began wrenching my refrigerator back into place.

I shouldn't have done that. Averting my eyes, that is. Because it meant that I saw Type-Face one final time. Saw the tears in his eyes.

I *DID* LOVE YOU, NICK STEEN. I REALLY DID. YOU WERE ONE HOT SOD.

I paused. Smiled. Tried to blow him a kiss, I guess. And the tears I spent at that moment meant that I never saw it coming. Never saw Type-Face's hand reach out one final time between that shortening gap, to play one last trick on me. To squeeze my writer's brain between his treacherous fingers.

Releasing all the horrors of my head into *our* world.

Yeah, he was an arsehole, alright.

EPILOGUE

Roz and I awoke, entangled together on my writing desk, the typewriter somewhere in between us.

'Did we ...?'

'No, Roz, that was just my imagination. I think ...'

We extracted ourselves from the machine and tried our best to figure out how we'd got here from the hole in the kitchen wall.

'At least you have your body back,' Roz said, after I'd brewed us both some coffee. 'And the typebars in your face have gone down, too.'

'That's a relief. I'll certainly think twice before I avoid any of your edits again, Roz.'

She smiled up at me.

'And *this* ...' I said, picking up the typewriter and moving across to the rubbish chute. 'This antiquated piece of rubbish goes straight in the bin.'

I opened up the chute and tossed the typewriter inside. I heard it drop and smash to pieces at the bottom of the shaft. I peered in to check it was completely beyond repair.

A bank of malevolent yellow eyes stared up at me from the darkness.

'Either that thing's still alive, Roz,' I said, 'or the killer hives from my debut novel have taken up residence in the basement of this building, because this is *exactly* how that book starts. Yet that couldn't be. *Could* it?'

'Nick,' Roz said worriedly, switching on the TV. 'Look at this.'

I walked over to the screen to catch a news report about a killer skin disease currently laying siege to the dermatological clinic at Stalkford Hospital.

It was the same story on every channel. The specific horrors differed from region to region, but all of them mimicked events from my numerous horror tomes.

Type-Face had worked his revenge after all.

The horrors of my mind had now been truly unleashed. Into our world. Mankind's own realm. Hellbent on destroying Stalkford, and then outer Stalkford. And then, presumably, a bit further.

The country, maybe.

*And then the world.**

'This is bad news, Nick,' said Roz. '*Really* bad news.'

'You're telling me, Roz. I've just escaped the Hell of my own head, and now I've woken up to find that a different Hell from my head has escaped.'

'What do we do about it, Nick?' Roz gasped.

'Fight them, Roz,' I said. 'Like one of my continuous multi-volume pulp-horror series come to life, from this day forth I must face wave after wave of terrifying horrors from the unholy depths of my own imaginata, and destroy them.'

'Can I help?' asked Roz.

'I'd be delighted, Roz,' I said. 'I expect I'll need some help.'

'Then you can depend on me, Nick,' said Roz. 'Apart from Wednesday afternoons.'

'That's fine,' I said, remembering that was when she got her nails done.

'But please, Nick, no more imagined hanky-panky, alright? There'll be plenty of sexual tension, I'm sure, but that typewriter thing of yours was a permanent turn-off.'

---

* This is the crucial plot development that was subtly foreshadowed earlier on. GM

'I get it, Roz.' It was going to take me a long time to get over that, too.

'Looks like the pen is indeed mightier than the sword, Roz,' I said, learning from an obscure cable news channel that my *Flesh Merchants of the Living Dead* were fast approaching my fictional coastal town of Flooden.

'To reiterate: we've woken up in a world of my own horrors, Roz. The Hell of my own head must have escaped into our world when Type-Face squeezed my brain. Now we must fight the unleashed horrors of my own books. You and I must work together, to try and find a way to defeat the horrors of . . .

'. . . *The Terror Tome*.'

BRIDE OF BONE

CHAPTER ONE

The gates to the asylum were wide open. Ahead, beyond the long, sweeping driveway, flashes of lightning exposed a towering Victorian edifice that had – until half an hour ago – housed Stalkford's innumerable Insane. As the storm continued to rage around him, Cliff Capello, burned-out 'talk' therapist from the town's disbanded twenty-four-hour counselling service, drew up before the twelve-foot-high ring of outer security fencing in his battered Peugeot 405, rolled down the driver's window and craned his neck outwards against the lashing rain to take a better look. And to air the car a bit. It had been a petrifying thirty minutes.

No one about, he concluded. Not even the crazies.

Capello ducked back inside the car, wound his window back up and wrestled once more with the radio knob, trying to recapture the lost frequency.

Several prolonged bursts of static later, the voice that had woken him abruptly from his recurring nightmare returned at last.

'... unimaginable scenes ... death in the corridors ... patients defecating with impunity ... endless, mindless gibbering ...'

The signal broke up again. Capello re-twisted the knob violently. Hell, he had to know. He had to *know*.

'... authorities are advising members of the public ...'

'Yes?' Capello snapped impatiently as another blast of static silenced the announcer. Finally, the voice returned amid an intense flurry of crackling.

'. . . must . . . avoid . . . the lunatic asylum . . . completely . . .'

'Why?' Capello yelled, punching the radio with his big fist. 'Why?'

'. . . Because deranged serial killer and former avascular necrosis research student Nelson Strain . . .'

'Yes?' Capello punched it again. The last time, he decided, as he'd skinned a knuckle.

'. . . has escaped . . .'

He didn't take in anything after that. Capello switched the radio off abruptly and covered his mouth to stifle his rising panic. So, the unthinkable had finally happened.

Strain was free.

Dammit, he'd warned them, hadn't he? Hadn't Capello told them every day for the past five years, occasionally emphasising his points with barely restrained bouts of sudden and unprovoked violence, that there was no curing a killer of such cruelty, such unholy perversions, such cold-blooded evil?

'Dammit! Dammit! Dammit!' he yelled, headbutting the steering wheel three times before biting down forcefully on its leather covering.

Keep calm . . . Mustn't break the car. Mustn't break my only means of pursuit . . . Mustn't do anything that might prevent an opportunity to kill him . . .

That's right, your honour. Kill. Why mince words? Why say 'restrict potential life options' or 'curtail breathing capacity' when I can use 'kill' instead?

Capello eased himself back into the driving seat and lit his thirtieth cigarette. Hell, talking hadn't done a damned thing, anyway. Strain had been stringing them all along. And only he, Capello, had seen it. Only he, Cliff Capello, had possessed enough foresight to warn the authorities not to move Strain's dead mother's belongings back into her son's asylum cell, so that the deranged serial killer might finally make 'peace' with her memory and that

102

of the whale-bone corsets he'd had to help her strap on each morning.

Only Cliff 'Livewire' Capello had been bold enough to state, despite endless patronising reassurances from his liberal-minded colleagues, that Strain would be cataloguing his dead mother's girdles again as soon as the lock, and their backs, were turned. It's what the Insane did, Capello had screamed at them, choking one of the orderlies half to death with his leather-gloved hands. Until he too, finally, had been restrained. Questioned. Threatened with sectioning . . .

The damned irony.

A grim smile cracked across Capello's worn, moustachioed features.

The damned double irony, in fact. Because Strain was worse – far worse – than even Capello had suspected. Feeling a familiar twinge in his heart (mostly to do with his colossal nicotine intake, but also born of an emotional trauma he'd long since given up trying to bury – more on that later), Capello forced himself to recall that dreadful day of infamy . . . That terrible scene of mind-blowing, unspeakable horror, which he'd stumbled upon as part of Stalkford East's 'talk' therapy unit's home-counselling service. That mind-shattering moment when the authorities finally cottoned on to the extra-curricular activities of Dr Nelson Strain, and burst in, unannounced, to find that the meek, butter-wouldn't-melt junior practitioner had used his dead mother's realigned bone-bodice to dress up the unpro-testing and pliable frame of his self-constructed betrothed.

Capello had seen the thing with his own eyes, propped up in Strain's bed via a system of wire pulleys and pins, the bride-to-be that Strain had always desired, yet forever been denied. An adoring yet compliant paramour, whom Strain's insane and overbearing mother had forbade him to woo on pain of intense physical emascu-lation. A female figure forged by Strain himself from blackened frag-ments of dead and dying osseous matter; the body consisting entirely of avascular necrosis-ridden* offcuts assembled meticulously into a ragged, uneven imitation of the human skeleton.

Strain's fiancée. His lover.

His Bride of Bone . . .

Something caught Capello's eye, interrupting his thoughts. A glimmer of movement ahead, beyond the asylum walls. Capello craned his neck forwards, peering through the ever-thickening squall and relentless, yet largely inadequate, repeating motion of the Peugeot's struggling wiper blades.

Figures, Capello descried. Human figures. In light blue gowns.

Crazies.

He drew his former driving instructor's Beretta 70 revolver, which he'd been given as a prize for passing, from the holster beneath his dressing gown (he'd come out in his pyjamas) and yanked open the Peugeot's door. Stepping outside the car, taking care to avoid a big puddle, Capello stared out into the rainswept darkness as a distant herd of wandering Insane shambled vaguely, bizarrely, grotesquely forth from the asylum's walls, stumbling about in random directions. Perhaps, Capello figured, they were part-dazed from opening their lunatical eyes upon a world they no longer had any right to glimpse, nor capacity to understand.

Two staggered in Capello's direction, attracted by the glare of the Peugeot's headlamps. Once upon a time, Capello might have walked towards them. Cajoled them. Reassured them with softly spoken words and – hell, he could hardly believe it now – an understanding heart. He would have talked them into a psychic haven of imagined safety and

---

* A bone disease whereby your bone dies and goes all grey and black inside you, and you really ought to have it removed. Generally caused by undiagnosed minor bone-snaps, or the blood supply being cut off, thus starving and killing your bony privates, which go all grey and black, like I just told you, making you look, feel and smell like a living corpse. If you want more info, look it up. I don't have the time. GM

half-grasped understanding that he'd once believed these crazies deserved. But he was past all that now. 'Talk' therapy achieved nothing. The world was through with 'talk' therapy. Only action therapy counted.

Capello raised his Beretta and shot them.

The first slug went wild, Capello forgetting in his white-hot rage to compensate for a strong easterly headwind. But the second bullet, which he'd aimed at the target on the right, also veered left, taking the former crazy smack-bang in the pate, exploding him.

Or her. It was hard to see a thing in this damned rain.

The surviving crazy bent down, sniffing at its fallen comrade, then tried and failed to eat its brains before dancing off again into the storm, playfully sweeping and ruffling its sodden gown to whatever mad tunes were now playing inside its head.

'Poor bastard,' Capello sighed, an unexpected rush of pity briefly clouding his judgement. He ought to have put them both out of their misery.

Instead he grabbed a flashlight (or American torch) from his jacket pocket and shone it up at the tall security watchtower looking down over the breached gates below. The machine-gun nest Capello had insisted the authorities install was now empty, its guard slumped life-lessly over a bank of raised sandbags, blood dripping slowly from a raised, crooked arm, to form a neat crimson pool at Capello's feet.

The Italian glanced sideways at the long parallel line of security towers he'd recommended they add to this one, arranged at equal distance along the entirety of the asylum's main perimeter. These were meant to have scoured the grounds day and night for any who dared mount an escape attempt.

A flash of lightning revealed what Capello feared most. All those who'd volunteered to man these towers – that thin, green-capped line that had stood alone between the defenders of Sanity and the forces of Brain Chaos, including their Scout Leader – were dead. So what had happened?

Nelson Strain had happened.

Evil had been unleashed here, Capello knew. Evil now stalked the land. He reloaded his Beretta and moved forwards, advancing across the outer grounds in the direction of the asylum's vast sprung doors.

Then stopped.

Despite relentless bursts of clashing thunder and an incessant howling wind, Capello could sense an eerie quietness about the place as he approached. Where were the rattling echoes of the howling inmates, he wondered, whom the authorities still insisted on referring to as 'patients'? Where was the regular, distinctive crack of the commandant's whip? The raucous clash of mingled screams and insane laughter as the wardens went to work on their programme of 'rehabilitation'?

All that would have to wait now, Capello reflected, bitterly. One day, when people finally woke up to the grim reality he alone understood, society would hopefully change. But he doubted it. More likely, it would be up to Capello himself to keep Stalkford sane. Even if he had to do it in his pyjamas.

But first, he must nail Strain.

Capello heard a shriek. A blood-chilling sound – half snarl, half yell – coming from the vicinity of the asylum's inner courtyard.

Another crazy? No, this shriek hadn't sounded human. An animal, then. Perhaps one of the vicious Dobermans Capello had recommended patrol each wing, day and night, until a subsequent mass mauling had put paid to the notion. Maybe one or two of those dogs had escaped into the depths of the building and bred.

But no. That didn't explain the dead Scouts in the towers. Dobermans couldn't climb ladders, could they? But then, thought Capello, there were many deeply strange things happening in the town of Stalkford in recent weeks. Unnatural things.

Frightening things . . .

The shriek sounded again. No way was it a human cry. No human vocal cord could produce such a bowel-shatteringly terrifying cacophony as that. An explosion of cracking, snapping and clacking, like some sinister breakfast cereal. Why, it sounded like two diseased and disintegrating bones rubbing against each other in an attempt to produce hellfire.

Capello caught a flash of movement between the main gates ahead. He raised the Beretta as a group of five inmates hurled themselves through the freshly flung-open doors. But these crazies no longer looked insane, Capello realised. These dumb bastards were clearly terrified.

Of what? As they fled past him, Capello resisted the urge to mow them all down, distracted by the thought that whatever these lunatics had seen up ahead had terrified each one back into some semblance of sanity.

He peered harder into the gloom. Nothing in front of him but incessant rain and darkness.

Then he saw it. A flash of whirling grey. Coming fast towards him among that horrendous clattering of inhuman sound. A demonic din hammering inside Capello's ears, like the hideous clack-snapping of dead and discarded matter come to sudden life, pounding his canals.

Inexplicably terrified, Capello turned and fled back across the muddy, rain-drenched grass, over the outer grounds, back past the abandoned towers and broken gates. The lights of his Peugeot created long, eerie shadows upon the drenched path, formed by the fleeing, terrified patients ahead. No doubt his own shadow cast a contorted shape behind him as he sprinted wildly in the direction of the car, desperate to escape whatever was now pursuing him at speed.

He dived into the vehicle and slammed the door shut, striking down the locks. The wiper blades still raced to clear pounding rain from the windscreen, and as Capello looked out into the howling maelstrom beyond, his vision became obscured once more, as whatever had been following him dissolved into a vague and rain-blurred distortion.

Capello smeared beads of water-sweat from his brow and blinked frantically to get a better view. Useless. He'd have to wait until the thing was close up before he could get any idea of what was after him.

Could it really be Strain, he wondered? For when he'd last seen the killer, the doctor had still resembled the same pathetic-looking creep who'd been arrested inside his mother's house, arm in arm with the half-formed, half-human plaything he'd created. A little older, perhaps, but still the same thin, odious-looking product of his warped mother's rage.

Yet now, Capello wondered? What in God's name had caused Strain to scream in such a hellish fashion? What fresh horror had asylum life inflicted on this pathetic excuse for a junior bone specialist?

Then Capello saw it, directly ahead of him as it raced briefly through the beams of his Peugeot's headlamps. It was wearing a doctor's lab coat, he noticed, but before he could discern anything else, the thing had leaped with an unpleasant snap of clacking limbs on to the roof of Capello's car.

The Italian held the Beretta close by his cheek, ears and eyes trained on the hammering dents pounding downwards, just above his head. Hell, the thing was scratching the bloody paintwork too.

'Show yourself, Strain!' Capello yelled, jabbing the Beretta's stubbed barrel hard against the fabric headliner. 'Show yourself, you deranged, insane, sonofa—'

His words were cut short by the sudden slam of a fist striking the driver's window.

Flinching violently, Capello turned to face the splayed, hideous form hanging downwards from the vehicle's roof. Protruding from the white, sodden lab-coat sleeve was a grotesque, emaciated parody of the human hand. Whatever the thing inside that clothing was, it couldn't be alive. *Could it?* No hand so distorted, so thin, so grotesquely blackened, so malformed as the one that stretched across Capello's driver's window, could possibly move and flex like a living, breathing thing. Could it? Could it? What in hell's name was up there?

'What in hell's name is up there?' Capello yelled angrily, attempting to hide his mounting fear.

The hand on the window turned over obligingly, allowing Capello a more detailed examination.

It was bone.

Bent, blackened bone.

The hand – though Capello couldn't quite believe it – of a living skeleton ...

'Okay, I have some idea of what you are now.'

Immediately, the hand that was not a hand whipped upwards, dragging its bony fingers over the pane, scratching the glass and presumably more of the paintwork above. Then Capello heard a light bump, as if whatever had been crouching on the roof of the Peugeot had sprung off in a single bound.

He caught a murky glimpse of the white lab coat in his car's rear-view mirror as the thing raced off into the darkness of the storm-filled night.

Capello leaped out, avoiding the large puddle by the side of his door again, and squeezed off several rounds. It was useless. The thing was long gone, having already vanished into the darkness of the surrounding moorland.

The authorities were right about one thing, at least, Capello reflected as he reloaded the gun and lit his thirty-first cigarette of the hour.

Nelson Strain, or what was left of him, had indeed escaped.

CHAPTER TWO

'Quick, Nick, there's another one!'

'Where?'

'Right there! On the wall.'

Former horror paperback-writer Nick Steen, whose dark and terrifying imagination had escaped into Stalkford when his mind was squeezed by a cosmic demon after he was sucked into another dimension having unwittingly engaged in kinky sexual relations with a cursed typewriter, levelled his flame-thrower and prepared to propel a fresh burst of flammable petroleum into the smoking lumber yard of Stalkford's larger branch of B&Q in an effort to engulf the terrifying swarm of giant mutated stick insects currently concealing themselves in rows of unsold and now largely unsellable timber planking.

'Where, Roz? I can't bloody see it.'

'That's because it's petrified, Nick,' Roz replied, keeping her voice calm. She'd learned to do that in the years she'd spent as Nick's editor. Not because Clackett Publishing's star novelist had a temper, although he certainly did. More that every book Nick 'The Cardinal o' Chill' Steen wrote was a masterpiece of literate visionary horror, and Roz's suggestions, frequently driven by commercial imperatives and not through any worthwhile or intelligent understanding of the dark artistry inherent in his work, occasionally rubbed Nick up the wrong way.

'It's keeping completely still, Nick,' Roz continued, wondering if she could at least save one of the doomed creatures. 'It's praying you'll leave it alone.'

'Tell that to the poor store operative it unnerved.'

'Nick, phasmids are peace-loving vegetarians. The hippies of the insect world. Admittedly, they've grown to gargantuan size since your imagination escaped and leaked the contents of your giant insect-themed novel *The Stealth-Hive Parallax* across outer Stalkford, but these creatures are still completely harmless. I did point that out when you first sent me the manuscript, remember?'

'And I told you it was shudder fiction, Roz,' Nick replied, with a loud, exasperated sigh. 'A subtler form of the classic horror text. One that builds up a gradual atmosphere of increasing dread until the enveloping wave of mild anxiety creates a subtle frisson. A knowing chill. The aforementioned shudder. That book sold, Roz, as you well know, because people fear the phasmid's natural ability to disguise itself in wooden and leafy environments, like this lumber yard and adjacent garden-plant-slash-summer-furniture display.'

Nick squeezed the trigger, shooting an indiscriminate burst of liquid fire across the entire wall, engulfing the area completely in a roaring torrent of scorching, white-hot flame.

Now it was bloody moving.

'Was that really necessary, Nick?' asked Roz, once the bank of toxic smoke had finally dissipated through the charred remains of the warehouse ceiling.

'No time for niceties, Roz,' Nick replied sternly, driving one of the reduced garden hoes he'd had his eye on through the still-twitch-ing thorax of the felled insect. Yeah, the handle was weak, he decided, hammering down on the tool a fourth time, still failing to fully sever the creature's grilled mesothorax from its smoking metathorax. He chucked the hoe away. No wonder they were reduced.

'Come on, Roz. We have two more DIY stores and nine garden centres to raze to the ground by morning. Then we'll need to flame that petting zoo up by the dual carriageway, as well. That's where they emerged from, remember?'

Roz remembered, alright. Nick's book had featured the site as the central source of the mutating insects. In Nick's story, an unseen batch had escaped from a glass tank and gorged upon the abandoned leftovers of the zoo cafeteria's brand-new and much-vaunted veggie burger meal, with cataclysmic results. Before Mankind had known what was happening to it, the sated insects had swollen to gigantic proportions, then literally branched outwards into Stalkford town centre, mildly intimidating every-thing in their wake.

'I still can't understand it all, Nick,' Roz said as the store's staff members slowly emerged from their own hiding places to quell the smouldering flames. 'Last week, that petting zoo was just a scene from your original book. A brilliant and memorable scene, I admit, but fiction all the same. Yet now it's here for real, operating the exact same insect-petting business from a disused warehouse on the A78 that previously wasn't there, all the while selling the same radioactive vegetarian burgers you dreamed up from the dark, swirl-ing abyss of your subconscious mind. It's horrifying, Nick. Brilliant, yet horrifying.'

'Which is why, ultimately, we need to flame the place, Roz. And it's also why we should be eating more meat as a species. Each new vegetarian recipe Mankind allows is a *recipe* for disaster.'

'That sentence would be brilliantly funny, Nick. If it weren't also terrifyingly true.'

'I know, Roz. If only I could allow myself to appreciate the stark humour of it. Yet the reality is, these vegetarian fast-food outlets are the wild west of the modern convenience snack. And we've only just begun to realise the full implications of messing about with suppos-edly "healthy" ingredients that Mankind can neither taste nor understand.'

The store's overhead speaker system snapped on. No doubt an attempt by the manager to reassure and encourage his terrified night staff. But the newsreader that began speaking across the airwaves was already reporting on other supernatural calamities now plaguing inner and outer Stalkford. And it had been like this for weeks. Though fictional in origin, all of the horrors created in Nick's subconscious mind were suddenly, terrifyingly real. Dark, destructive elements of Nick's unfettered imagination, now released into our world by forces of supernatural chaos beyond human comprehension. Warping reality in their wake. Turning Stalkford into the terrifying contents of Nick's collected and yet-to-be-completed oeuvre.

'More killer hives,' said Roz, listening closely to the newsreader's increasingly sombre announcements. 'Plus a plague of killer storks pecking the shit out of a local orphanage.'

'That's already been handled,' Nick said, screwing one of the stick insect's torched hindlegs to his discarded hoe blade. 'The babies they think they're carrying in those beak-handkerchiefs are actually grenades put there by the local militia I advised. Things should hopefully play out by the book. A damned good book, if I don't mind saying so myself,' he added, chuckling. 'I.e., my book.'

'Again, that would be funny, Nick. If that weren't so terrifyingly true. Your book was damned good. But damned in a literal sense, too.'

'I know, Roz. Besides visionary horror, I also possess a natural knack for wordplay and the pithy statement. I only hope my instincts for plotting are correct.'

They heard the distant crump of heavy explosions, followed by panicked cawing as the flock of killer storks began their final downward spiral into the hands of Stalkford's waiting kindergarten militia.

'At least that's one adversary we no longer need to worry about,' Nick said, swinging his modified hoe, assessing its combat effectiveness. Satisfied that the stick insect's roasted thorax had improved the blade tenfold, he tucked the pole into his tool-belt and prepared to head out again into the night. It would feel good to use their own damned legs against them.

'Come on, Roz,' he said. 'There's no time to lose.'

'Hold on, Nick,' Roz said, grabbing his arm. 'There's something I have to tell you.'

'What is it, Roz?' Nick turned slowly to face her. 'That you realise I'm right, after all? That the sordid trysts I engaged in while under the influence of Type-Face, Lord of the Prolix, were in fact a necessary precursor to the awakening of a superior intelligence you've long been refuting all those years you deigned to "edit" me at Clackett Publishing? Is that what you want to say to me, Roz?'

'No, Nick. I was going to say that I think you should go back to your wife and daughter.'

'Not that again.'

'Yes, that again, Nick. That, and . . .'

'That and what, Roz? What that and?'

'That, and I can't come along to kill more massive stick insects with you.'

She turned away, embarrassed. Nick turned away too, hardly able to believe that Roz had turned away first. Mankind might flee from the horrors, but not Roz. Surely not Roz? Nick's attention was momentarily distracted by another news bulletin coming through the overhead speakers. Something about a violent commotion in the vicinity of the town asylum . . .

However, realising Roz might soon start feigning tears if he didn't respond adequately to her theatrics, he switched off the radio entirely; luckily, the switch was located in the lumber-yard area of this particular branch of B&Q, just inches from Nick's hand.

'Why not, Roz? Tell me. Why can't you come with me to destroy another nest of giant mutated stick insects?'

'Because I have a prearranged pedicure appointment in an hour's time.'

Nick could hardly believe what he was hearing. 'Now?' he spluttered, checking his wristwatch. 'At one o'clock in the morning?'

'They have a late licence, Nick. Plus a mini bar. And their own overhead hi-fi system with fully paid-up PPL. With better surround than this one, too, Nick. I'd invite you along, but . . .'

'I get it, Roz. Deep down, you think a combination of newly painted toenails and two large Babychams will ultimately aid in our fight against the supernatural?'

'Something like that, Nick.'

'Fine. Well, guess I'll see you around.'

'Bye, Nick,' Roz said, hobbling off towards the exit.

Nick watched her go, trying not to laugh. Actually, it was high time he said something. 'Roz, why don't you grab some work-boots from the tool aisle? Those high heels are way too tight for your feet. You look like you've had six Babychams already.'

'These are the correct size, Nick,' Roz snapped testily, attempting in vain to correct her stride. 'They just feel two sizes too small.'

'There's no shame in wearing male work-boots, Roz,' Nick offered, placatingly. 'They're comfortable, durable and dependable.'

'But these slingbacks are perfect,' Roz snarled, her wild feminine instinct turning suddenly against a perceived aggressor. Then, just as quickly, she softened, embarrassed by the temporary madness. 'Though they do cut off my circulation to worrying extremes.'

'Hey, I'm not saying another thing,' Nick joked, holding both hands upwards in mock-submission.

Ignoring him, Roz shuffled her way moodily through the exit doors with increasing difficulty, then stumbled outside towards a waiting taxi.

Nick watched her go, pitying her Achilles' vanity, before strapping a fresh tank of liquid paraffin fuel on to his back.

'Mind if I put the radio back on?' asked the lowliest of aisle-stockers.

'Be my guest, amigo.'

The radio announcer's voice resounded once again through the burned-out warehouse.

'... whose violent escape from Stalkford's secure unit within the town asylum has been confirmed at last by the authorities.'

Though Nick's keen instincts were briefly piqued, the item that followed instead secured his fuller attention. 'In other news, former horror novelist Nick Steen continues to wage his courageous war against swarms of giant immobile phasmids now threatening to destroy our way of life and timber yards as we know them ...'

The cleaner looked up at Nick, hardly believing his unskilled eyes. 'You?' he asked.

'Me, *sir*,' Nick corrected. Then winked wryly at the pock-faced squit and left without saying another word. The night wasn't over yet, he reflected. Not now that Roz had deserted him.

And it was about to get longer still.

Longer than even the visionary mind of Nick Steen could imagine ...

★

Barely sheltered from the drumming rain, Capello stood impatiently in the soiled phone box, studying the bizarre dents and elaborate scratching adorning his Peugeot's roof as he continued to wait for the authorities to run the information he'd provided through their central databank system, which they assured him was connected directly to an information cable at Stalkford Library's brand-new computer room.

'What do you mean, no record?' he snapped as the voice of the authorities finally came back on the line.

'Precisely what we say,' the authorities replied. 'Dr Nelson Strain has never been incarcerated at Stalkford Asylum. Not in the last five years, nor since our records began, back in 1897. Furthermore, there is no account of him attending any of our local medical schools nor educational establishments, and no record of any courtroom appearances, police incidents or even a legal birth certificate. Nelson Strain, quite simply, does not exist.'

'Of course he exists,' Capello snapped. 'I was there when they arrested him, dammit! He fashioned a female soulmate from chunks of dead and dying bone matter he'd culled from the diseased joints of his victims! I watched them lock him in the slammer myself! I was part of his "talk" therapy team. God forbid, I even tried to cure him! And now he's escaped, you hear? Escaped to kill again. To kidnap innocent ladies with avascular necrosis issues and expropriate their dying parts for his own warped desires!'

'Sorry, who is this?' asked the authorities.

Capello could hardly believe his ears. 'Me? I'm Cliff Capello, dammit! Brother of Dwayne Capello. We're both therapists!'

Another lengthy pause. Capello could hear the tell-tale sound of information being sucked mechanically along the connecting telephone wires.

'Hello?' he barked, holding the receiver away from his ear while yelling into the mouthpiece. He put it back again. There was no way he'd hear anything that way.

'I'm afraid we have no record of you, either,' said the authorities.

'No record? Of me?'

'None at all. As far as Stalkford's central computer can tell, nobody called Cliff Capello, brother of Dwayne, has ever lived in this town.'

'Then your computer's bloody nuts!' Capello yelled, slamming the phone down hard on the hook. He was about to storm outside into the pounding rain when it began to ring. Stifling his rage, Capello picked it up. It was the authorities again.

'We hadn't finished speaking. We found one mention of Nelson Strain, a junior doctor specialising in avascular necrosis research, but he is only a fictional character.'

'A fictional character?'

'That's what we said. A fictional character. He appears in a pulp-horror paperback penned by local writer, Nick Steen.'

'And is *he* fictional?'

'No, Nick Steen is real. He writes fiction, like we said. Including a fictional book featuring a fictional character called Dr Nelson Strain.'

'And what's the book called?' Capello asked.

'*Bone Death (A Sextology)*.'

Nick Steen, thought Capello. The same initials as Nelson Strain. Either this Nick Steen was a poor writer with insufficient imagination to vary the initials of his central character, or there was more to Nick Steen's imagination than initially met the eye. Maybe far more.

'Is that everything, then?' asked the authorities.

'I guess so,' Capello replied.

'Okay, bye.' The authorities hung up.

Capello replaced the receiver and lit his fifty-ninth cigarette. Was he going mad here? How could the authorities have no record of a lunatic they'd been holding under maximum security for the past five years?

And how come there was no record of either him or his brother Dwayne? Why was the fictional Strain now part-skeleton, for that matter? Jesus, was he, Cliff Capello, also going crazy? Was he now close to being the maddest man in Stalkford?

One thing was certain, at least. Something truly strange was happening round here. Something truly strange and deadly frightening.

Because either the authorities' own database was now completely kaput, or reality itself was no longer quite what it seemed.

Hell, he had to find Nick Steen. But where?

The phone rang again. Capello picked it up.

'By the way, Nick Steen's on the news,' said the authorities. It was them again. 'He's currently slaying a swarm of giant stick insects rampaging through inner and outer Stalkford.'

'Thanks,' said Capello.

'Okay, bye again,' said the authorities.

'Giant stick insects?' Capello said, hardly believing the sound of his own voice as he hung up the receiver.

Well, either I'm mad, or the whole damned world is.

Time to find this Nick Strain, Capello decided. Time to find him, and if it turned out he was the one behind all this madness …

Kill him.

Not recalibrate his life's trajectory for the worse.

Not freeze his conventional lung mobility and replace all the oxygen.

No.

One word, your honour. One simple word.

Kill him.

CHAPTER THREE

'Need some help getting out, miss?'

Roz glanced up at the rear-view mirror and fixed the cabbie's eyes with a determined look. 'I can manage perfectly well, thank you.'

She lifted both feet and winced inwardly as a sharp, stabbing pain shot up from her compressed toes, into her soles and ankles. Masking her pain, Roz swung both legs free of the car and planted her treasured crimson slingbacks firmly down upon the damp, soggy earth of Stalkford Moor.

They sank down the full nine inches.

'Are you sure, miss?' the driver continued, leaning out to address Roz through the wound-down passenger window. 'It's just . . . them shoes . . . they must be agony.'

'They're perfectly comfortable,' Roz replied croakily, struggling to free both feet from the damp, sucking mud. Finally, with a violent, exasperated bellow of primal fury, which she kept in reserve for life-or-death occasions like this, Roz yanked her left shoe upwards, freeing it suddenly from the sodden earth with such force that the movement upended her, causing her to stagger and flail like one of those damned crazies up at the asylum. As Roz struggled to maintain her balance, incessant rain continuing to hammer down around her, the cabbie spoke again.

'Terrible night, miss. What with this rain, and that there shoe business there, and all this strange supernatural 'appenin's cross the land, or so they do say. What in God's name be that be about, I do wonder?'

She could tell him, Roz realised. She could tell him everything right now, but he'd never believe her. Hell, how would anyone believe her?

Except Nick, maybe. He'd been there when it happened, after all. Had caused the whole thing. Yeah, Nick might believe her. In fact, he believed her already, she remembered, as they'd been discussing this self-same explosion of supernatural happenings ever since they'd both escaped the Prolix. So scratch that thought.

'Sure you want droppin' out here in the middle o' nowhere, miss?' asked the cabbie, behind her, breaking her chain of thought. Locating her centre of gravity at last, Roz finally took control of her flailing, unbalanced body and managed to drag her remaining heel free of the sodden marsh, temporarily placing both heels firmly down on a patch of harder ground that just happened to be there. Turning round, she handed the cabbie his money.

'Of course I want dropping here. That's what I said, didn't I?'

'Sure, as an' ya did. But alone, miss? On the moor? In the dead of night?'

'This is the address I was given,' she said, hoisting up her umbrella so that she could consult her appointment letter again. 'Shadowy Former Military Research Facility, Restricted Area 3, Stalkford Down, Stalkford Moor, Stalkford, Stalkfordshire, ST13 ALK666.'

'Aye, but that place has been shut down for years, miss. There were some sort of disaster, if I recall it rightly, so they do say.'

'Well, this is the address I was given,' Roz said, neglecting to tip him, not having Nick there to remind her, and also not wanting to.

'What you be doing out here anyways, miss, if un' you don't mind as me as asking, like?'

'A pedicure,' she blurted, too quickly.

'Oh, a pedicure. Well, that's fair enough, then. Got to stop the flakin'.'

With that, the driver pulled away, winding the passenger window back up against the rain as he sped off. Leaving Roz alone on the moor, in the middle of a thunderstorm, in the dead of night.

Finally, thought Roz. By myself at last. Free from that damned yokel driver. Free to be myself and think my own thoughts without the damned men in my life laughing at me and my personal choice of punishing footwear. At least they all fell for the pedicure story. The fools! That driver, Nick bloody Steen and Mr 'do this, do that and double-quick, Roz,' Clackett, too. All of them stupid men, who neither cared nor understood the natural yet potentially lethal lure of the perfect shoe. Only ladies could truly understand such a uniquely female instinct. Only ladies risked their personal health and safety each day to sport heels that empowered as much as they impaled. Cool ladies. Tigresses.

Kick-ass lionesses.*

Except that wasn't entirely true, was it? For *he* had understood, hadn't he? *He'd* listened to her anguish. Promised her he was going to cure her ailment, so that she, Roz Bloom, might once again wear her restrictive slingback pumps without fear of physical dismemberment. *He* was going to reverse the process. Stem the dreaded wave. Halt the relentless deathly spread that threatened to creep outwards from her middle toes to engulf the entirety of her feet. And then, God forbid, the rest of her body . . .

Only *he* stood between the bodily ecstasy of a replenished trotter, and the slow, agonising death of her crushed, long-unflexible digits. Only he, the *good doctor*, the handsome, junior practitioner with whom she'd been corresponding these past few months, knew how to prevent the spread of her dreaded toe-consuming necrosis.

Dr Nelson Strain.

---

* I hereby draw your attention to this phrase as certifiable proof that I *can* be a feminist, have written a 'strong' lady character here (part cat, in fact) and staved off alienating my female readership (as 'advised'). GM

Roz stared out across the moor. The rain and wind battered against the sodden, freezing hills stretched out against the horizon, lashing down upon the splayed patches of wild grass and overflowing mud pools. The ground here was perilous, she knew. Somewhere close by, there were rumoured to lie the sodden banks of Stalkford Mire, a marsh so deep, so unsteady, that the earth below it housed an entire cemetery's worth of doomed, unwary ramblers.

Therefore, she couldn't risk her heels sinking again. She'd need to remove both shoes and walk across the moor in her bare feet. That was easier said than done, however. Painfully, Roz sat down upon a nearby wooden stump that just happened to be there and drew each shoe gradually from her feet.

Roz winced as she pulled the vamps forwards over her blistered appendages, gagging at the thick red welts curving neatly across her skin where the toplines had choked mercilessly. Traces of blood trailed upwards, she noticed, reaching both insoles, though no one would ever see those. Plus, they blended quite well with the colour scheme.

Her feet able to breathe at last, Roz rose from the wooden stump and made her way across the long stretch of muddy grass, shoes clasped together in her free hand. According to Strain's letter, the private hospital she was booked into was directly ahead, housed in that disused military research facility mentioned on the address. Cheered and emboldened by the thought of an imminent cure, Roz pressed on against the elements. Then, after a vigorous bout of harsh and relentless trudging, she glimpsed a trace of eerie green light in the distance.

As Roz ambled forwards, her umbrella now dashed by the wind into a thousand flapping scraps, she found that the strange, phosphorescent glow appeared to emanate from a group of dark, nondescript buildings forming a small, self-contained complex. Roz counted five units in total, each a two-storeyed and flat-roofed construction, much like a conventional industrial warehouse, sealed off from the world with a thick mesh of security fencing, which now leaned and sagged in neglected heaps around the perimeter. The strange green light that had caught Roz's eye evidently came from somewhere inside the central building directly ahead, although its source was hard to pinpoint and appeared to be flowing through the connecting rooms like the dim and distant glare from some giant industrial lava lamp.

A fresh gust of wind caught what remained of Roz's umbrella and yanked it clean out of her hand. She watched helplessly as it bounced over the grass and came to a halt a short distance away, upon what looked to her like a solid, wide bank of mud.

Then sank.

Roz could hardly believe her eyes as its handle disappeared slowly under the surface of the ground, leaving nothing but a cluster of heavy, slow-bursting bubbles in its wake.

'Stalkford Mire . . .' she whispered to herself.

She'd have to tread carefully now. Steeling herself, Roz navigated her way around this natural obstacle, moving through a torn line of barbed-wire fencing ahead of her, then pushed herself through the abandoned security barrier and past an unmanned sentry box, before veering around what looked like a row of nuclear decontamination units. At last, she strode into what must be, Roz figured, the main reception area of the central building.

Except there was no one here. No one at all. The place was pitch dark. Apart from that strange green glowing, which seemed to come from somewhere deep inside the building, there wasn't a single light on in the place. No one to check her in. She examined the letter again. She was in the correct place, alright. On the correct date. At the correct time. So where was everyone?

'Dr Strain?' she called out, her voice echoing down the dark and lengthy corridors leading off into the main facility. 'It's Roz Bloom,' she continued. 'I have an appointment?'

She listened quietly for a moment, hearing only the continual howl of the wind outside, then gradually sensed a different noise coming from somewhere along the corridor to her left. Almost a shuffling sound, she thought, though not quite as conventional-sounding as the noise she might have expected from someone simply walking towards her along the corridor. It was a strange sound, she decided – not quite earthbound, if she had to put a label on it. Which she didn't. But did anyway. A sound like a walking pile of twigs, or a loosened bag of discarded rubble that had somehow suddenly developed the ability to move.

'Dr Strain?' she called out, again. 'Dr Nelson Strain?'

Far along the corridor ahead, a pale, thin figure finally emerged from the darkness. It seemed to stagger as it walked, shuffling towards Roz on horribly crooked legs, which appeared to be producing the bizarre clicking sounds she'd been hearing. Unnerved, Roz was considering heading home to arrange a daytime appointment instead, when the thing, in a sudden burst of frantic energy, advanced at speed towards her.

Roz had just enough time to register the lab coat it was wearing when the advancing figure crossed a ray of moonlight that was breaking through the overhead clouds, casting its unworldly rays through the parted doorway through which Roz had just entered.

The lab coat was the only visible clue to the creature's identity. Because the face Roz now gazed upon in abject horror as she began to black out, was a jagged mess of twisted, badly conjoined skull fragments.

A living, breathing *skeleton*.

★

Nick fired one final blast of liquid flame into all that remained of the petting zoo's radioactive cafeteria and ordered the few surviving customers into the parked-up meat-wagon outside.

There were always casualties, Nick reflected, consoling himself. And anyone feeding themselves from the contents of an all-night radioactive vegetarian café at two in the morning, frankly, had it coming. Not that he'd cull these human victims just yet. First, he and Stalkford's military needed to observe their slow, agonising demise while the effects of radiation poisoning took increasing hold of their systems. Then, with playtime over, the real work would commence. Endless rounds of breakfast conference meetings and lunchtime conflabs with medical experts across the world, attempting to hammer out a cure for radiation poisoning once and for all. Perhaps through a vaccine, or a medical injection.

Then, finally, he'd cull them.

'How do we get through this?' cried the café's manager, weeping forlornly into both hands.

Nick assumed it to be a rhetorical question.

'How do we go on?'

'You build,' Nick said, holding out the modified hoe with the burned stick-insect leg in place of a pole. 'With this.'

The manager looked up, wiped the tears from his eyes and clasped the hoe in both hands, a look of reverent awe slowly spreading over his features.

'Technically it's a hoe,' Nick explained, 'but it will do for the beginning. This dawn of a post-phasmid age. Then, when you can get down to B&Qs again – probably in three weeks, given the state of the ceiling – you can buy a cheap spade and keep this one for ploughing.'

'Thanks, Nick.'

'Don't mention it.'

'I already have.'

'Then don't mention it again.'

'I won't. I promise.'

Nick nodded and strode back out into the car park. As he neared Roz's orange Renault Clio, which he'd borrowed in order to prevent his own car being potentially chipped or scraped by marauding supernatural forces, he discovered he was boxed in by a blue Peugeot 405.

'You arsehole,' Nick declared loudly, striding round to challenge whoever was currently sitting in the driver's seat.

Except that the interior was empty.

'I said, you arsehole,' Nick thundered, loudly. Then froze at the distinctive click of a revolver being cocked, right beside his ear.

CHAPTER FOUR

'Nick Steen?' said a voice, the accent mostly Italian yet carrying a tinge of Stalkford estuary.

'Who wants to know?' Nick replied, cool as a proverbially compliant yet ever-ready-to-pounce cucumber.

The man pointing the Beretta at Nick's head moved round slowly to reveal himself (not in that way). He was half-Italic, half-Stalkfordian, Nick observed, and heavily moustachioed. The clothing he wore consisted of a conventional pair of crumpled pyjamas, blue-striped and collared, with a toothbrush tucked inside the chest pocket. A brown, belted dressing gown and check closed-back slippers completed the effect. Beside this unconventional choice in rugged outerwear, given the all-night monsoon, there was yet one further anomaly Nick's eagle-eyed brain was swift to note. A large, canary-coloured butterfly bow tie sprung from the man's closed neck collar, the tips kissing each end of the man's facial whiskers.

'Nice duds,' said Nick. 'But I'd lose the bow tie.'

'It's a disguise,' replied Capello, sensing the initial look of confusion on Nick's face descending swiftly into outright mockery.

Hell, Capello had meant to strike fear into Steen's heart. Not derision. He couldn't help the pyjamas – those were what he'd woken up in. But the bow tie was all he'd been able to afford from the all-night supermarket, having forgotten to grab his wallet while exploding out of the house. Now that Nelson Strain had seen him in the flesh, it was vital Capello altered his appearance, transform his look entirely,

128

if he was ever going to sneak up, unobserved, on his prey. But perhaps he should have plumped for the alternative.

'It was this or an eyepatch,' he said, concluding from Nick's look that he'd chosen correctly, after all.

'What's this about?' said Nick.

Capello's face tightened with an inner fury, barely suppressed. Parallel jets of steam burst figuratively from each ear, themselves threatening to erupt with boiling mind-lava at any second. (Again, figuratively.)

'I've been hunting you down, Nick Steen,' Capello hissed. 'Tracking you. Chasing you. Pursuing you. So many times, I thought it was a lost cause. So many times, I thought of giving up. Of letting this madness consume the whole damned world. Of surrendering to the hell of this never-ending nightmare. But I thought, No, I will not surrender. I will carry on. And I picked myself up. I drove on, whatever the danger. Whatever the price. And now, an hour later, I finally have you. Here, in the sights of my gun.'

'Beretta 70, right? Magazine-fed, single-action semi-automatic.'

'That's right ...' Capello's eyes softened, slightly. Whatever he'd been expecting from Nick Steen, it hadn't been an ability to identify the make and model number of a conventional Italian firearm. But then Steen was a writer, so the authorities had said, and he presumed writers had to know these things. Good writers, at any rate.

'It was my driving instructor's.'

'Figures,' Nick said. 'They're all primed to go off someday, like cabbies. Nice piece. I favour the Smith & Wesson Model 29 revolver, six-shot, double-action. Massive barrel. It's currently at my mother's, though. Tell you what, put the piece down and maybe we can go over there and shoot some shit together. How about tomorrow? Then she can make us some lunch, and we can go bowling in the afternoon. I own a flame-thrower, too. Look.'

As Nick raised the incinerator's trigger-pump, Capello jabbed the Beretta's barrel hard against the writer's cheek.

'No games, Nick Steen,' he said, relieved he'd seen off the other man's subterfuge at the pass. 'No way are we about to start shooting off each other's pistols. Dammit, I hardly know you. Though I'd be on for bowling some time.'

'She has *Tafl* as well,' Nick continued, trying again to win back his assailant's confidence. 'The Viking game. It was my father's, originally, but he's in Valhalla now.'

'I don't give a shit about your family,' Capello snapped, suddenly.

Nick turned his head, staring directly into the other man's eyes. His writer's instincts sensed a dormant weakness there. A nagging rawness. A rising hurtity.

'What's this really about?' Nick said again.

Capello considered his prisoner for a moment, then spoke.

'There's been a breakout. At the asylum. The crazed serial killer Nelson Strain has escaped.'

'Don't be stupid. Nelson Strain is a fictional . . .' Nick froze, mid-sentence. Because nothing was ridiculous anymore, was it? Hell, his imagination had escaped, after all. Nick's fiction was coming to life around him. Why wouldn't Nelson Strain have escaped?

'Apparently you wrote a book about him.'

'I did indeed,' Nick said, nodding. '*Bone Death (A Sextology)*. There were going to be six, in total. Hence "sextology", with all the attendant erotic connotations of that word. But in the end, I only wrote the first one.'

'Why?'

Nick paused, recalling the horrors of those nightmares he'd bravely harnessed, transforming their threatened madness into killer fiction. 'Because it was too dark. Too disturbing. Too damned dangerous. Plus, it didn't break even.'

'But you know where he is?'

130

'Know where who is?'

'Nelson Strain, dammit! The insane lunatic who's broken out of the asylum.'

Nick sensed he had to play the proverbial cards close to his chest (also proverbial). It wouldn't help anyone in Stalkford if he started telling people the truth: that his mind had escaped and was now running rampant through their lives, killing and haunting indiscriminately. They'd probably call him insane. Burn him at the stake, then piss on his bones. It's what he would have done, after all.

'Like I say, Nelson Strain is a fictional character,' Nick explained, electing to stick with what had, until very recently, constituted conventional reality. Even if, deep within himself, Nick's mind was still reeling. For if what Capello was saying was true (not that Nick knew Capello's name yet), then Nelson Strain, one of the darkest, most terrifying monsters of Nick's imagination, was now making up his own story.

Meaning Nick's subconscious imagination was starting to write reality by itself. Nick hadn't yet penned a sequel, but Strain's story was evidently continuing to play out, way past the final sentences of Nick's original bestseller.

Hell truly had broken loose.

'You're confusing me with someone else,' Nick said. 'See you around, amigo.'

Nick pushed away the Beretta's barrel dismissively, stepped round Capello and yanked open the Renault's door. Then turned round again.

'Actually, I'm still blocked in. Can you move your damned car, please?'

'You're not getting in that car,' Capello said, aiming the gun at Nick once more. 'You're getting in my car. With me. Because you know something about Nelson Strain that you're not telling me.'

Nick breathed out another exasperated sigh. Could he risk it, he wondered? Could he chance telling Capello the truth (again, not that he'd yet learned what Capello's name was)? Perhaps if he could find Roz, get her to back up his story, he might just be able to get this gun-wielding pyjama-clad aggressor off his back.

'Look, buddy, here's the thing. You're right. Nelson Strain has escaped. He is a figment of my imagination, but that figment of my imagination has come to life. Like all the other figments of my imagination. We're under attack. From figments. See, I purchased a cursed typewriter from the reincarnation of a dead novelist, whose life's work I'd once shredded in front of his aging, watery eyes, and as a result of the guy's occult-fuelled fury, I was drawn unwittingly into a destructive psycho-sexual relationship with the machine, which eventually sucked me into it via nipple chains and sparklers, through to an alternate realm of lost words called the Prolix, ruled by a terrifying and all-powerful demon known as Type-Face, Dark Lord of Misrulery.

'My editor, Roz Bloom, also entered the Prolix with me, and together, following a bout of extreme physical torture and numerous terrifying encounters with hellish demigods and bizarre dream-demons, we eventually managed to escape via a portal housed behind my new fridge that connected both parallel worlds. Yet before we could break back through into our reality, Type-Face reached out, squeezing my brain, which was in a mug, sloshing about with my eyes, thereby releasing the contents of my conscious and subconscious mind into conventional reality, and thence to inner and outer Stalkford. Thus, the world as we know it is now drenched in the dark, supernatural horrors of my escaping imagination. Capiche?'

'You're insane.'

Nick knew he shouldn't have bothered. How could anyone believe all that? Except for the bit about Roz coming to his rescue because she couldn't bear life without him, it was totally implausible.

'I'm placing you under arrest,' said Capello.

'You're what?'

'I'm sectioning you. I'm sectioning you and taking you up the asylum right now. Perhaps the authorities will have some idea of who you are.'

It was as solid a plan as any, Capello figured. Because with Nick Steen incarcerated and unable to escape, he'd then be able to interrogate the supposed writer under the pretence of some emergency 'talk' therapy. Then he'd press the bastard by force for information. Find out exactly where Nelson Strain was hiding.

'I'm not coming anywhere with you. So back off, pal.'

Capello lowered the Beretta's barrel and shot the Renault's tyre. It erupted in a burst of escaping air, collapsing the vehicle awkwardly to one side.

'Roz is gonna kill you.'

'No, I am going to kill you,' Capello continued, 'if you don't do exactly as I say. You're insane, Nick Steen. Nothing but one of those damned crazies, and if you don't accompany me right now to the asylum, I'll blow your bloody balls off.'

Nick took a moment to assess the situation. The guy was clearly mad as a toilet brush. Nick didn't doubt for a moment that this lunatic would use that weapon on his balls. Maybe Capello himself had escaped from the asylum. Whatever the case, Nick would need to play things carefully from this point on. The guy was a livewire (hence his full name, Cliff 'Livewire' Capello – not that Nick knew that yet).

'Let me find Roz,' Nick said. 'She'll back up my story. Then you'll have to believe me. She's not far away. She's gone to an all-night pedicurist, to get her toenails done. It's off the Bramley Road.'

'Fine,' Capello said. 'That's on the way to the asylum.'

'It is indeed. Though there's a quicker route through Bobbington, if you were hard pressed to get there in a hurry.'

'Don't tempt me,' said Capello, thinking he ought to shoot his prisoner right here, right now. But if this Roz Bloom was prepared to back up the man's absurd story, that meant that she, too, might also be part of whatever scheme this Nick Steen had hatched to aid and abet Strain's escape. And if not, it was vital he get these crazies off the streets, anyway. Plus, if Capello could get two lunatics for the price of one, he'd earn double bounty money from the asylum when handing them over. Capello breathed a contented sigh. Two crazies no longer roaming the free world. And maybe, just maybe, this Nick Steen knew far more about Nelson Strain than he was letting on.

'Let's go,' he said.

'Can we replace my tyre first?' Nick said. 'Or we're likely to go round in circles.'

'I told you, we're going in my Peugeot.'

'Look, I'm technically the main guy here. As you can see from the flaming petting zoo to our right, I'm currently considered a hero.'

'Look yourself. My story began long before yours. If there's any heroics to be done around here, I'm the man who will do them.'

It was a stand-off, Nick realised. The two of them looked bound to spar and butt heads the entire night, probably, until this peculiar episode involving the machinations of evil Dr Strain was fully and finally resolved. Until then, Nick guessed he and Capello would be wrestling for prominence, with never the twain meeting eye to eye until they discovered some form of mutual co-dependence and/or newfound respect born of extreme and traumatic circumstance.

'Fine, we'll go in your car,' Nick eventually capitulated. 'As long as I can drive.'

'Fine,' capitulated Capello in turn. 'As long as I can keep my gun trained on you throughout, so that everyone who sees us knows who's really in charge of this bizarre and barely believable series of events in which we find ourselves embroiled.'

'Fine,' said Nick, capitulating yet again, while vowing not to capitulate a third time. He held out his hand. 'I'm Nick Steen, by the way.'

'I know.' Capello held out his free hand and shook Nick's. 'Cliff "Livewire" Capello.'

'I know.'

A look of confusion, almost of fear, crossed Capello's face. 'How do you know?'

Nick paused, thinking, then rapidly changed the subject. He'd suddenly realised exactly who Capello was.

Or wasn't . . .

'Let's drive,' he said.

★

Roz woke groggily from sleep. It felt like a hospital room. As she slowly opened her eyes, she glimpsed a small table, upon which sat a carafe of tepid water, a bag of grapes and the latest copy of *True Crime Atrocities*. She breathed a relaxed sigh. Her head felt groggy still, her thoughts muddled. But at least they'd remembered her murder magazine. As she slowly came to, she realised she was lying in bed, her right cheek resting on a soft cotton pillow. Was that it, then? Was her operation over already? Was her creeping avascular necrosis cured at last? She struggled to remember what had occurred the night before (it was actually only an hour ago, max). She remembered pleading with Nick not to flame-throw that family of mutated phasmids at the local hardware store, then a taxi drive and that bracing midnight stroll across the moor in freezing, adverse conditions, then a green light glowing in the distance like a mysterious supernatural beacon, then . . . then nothing.

Nothing at all.

She twisted her neck upwards from the pillow and stared up at the ceiling. It was tiled in white, though a vaguely greenish tinge coloured the far edges from some reflected light emerging from deep inside the hospital.

If this, indeed, was a hospital. Roz was beginning to have some doubts. There were no other patients, for a start, and no call-button for the nurse to come and empty her drip.

Hang on. Why the hell was she on a drip? And still dressed in yesterday's clothes?

Scarcely able to gather her racing thoughts, Roz tried slowing her brain by following the trail of electrical wiring that snaked from one side of the room to the other, running along the entire edge of the ceiling, down towards an old-fashioned loudspeaker perched on one wall in the far corner of the room. As she lay there, staring up at the raised mechanical box, it crackled suddenly into life, emitting a loud burst of audio static. Then the line went clear, save for a mild humming, and a smooth, youthful male voice came across the airwaves, piped directly into her room from some unknown area beyond.

'Good evening, Miss Bloom. Thank you for a truly wonderful operation.'

'Dr Strain?' Roz asked, her voice still croaky and dry from the anaesthetic.

'The toe in question,' the voice continued, ignoring her, 'is truly a remarkable toe. A beautiful toe. The most exquisite toe I have ever had the privilege of operating upon.'

'Why, thank you,' Roz said, flattered, despite her mounting confusion.

'I note that your other toes, Miss Bloom, are equally beautiful.'

'You're too kind.'

'Stop,' snapped the voice, its tone sharpening. 'Let me finish.'

Roz closed her mouth. Doctor knows best, she guessed.

'Beautiful as they are, I discovered that your other toes were also suffering from early signs of advanced avascular necrosis.'

No! thought Roz. They couldn't be. Could they? She forced herself up on to her elbows and stared down at her feet, which were poking free of the blankets at the foot of her bed. The left one was thickly bandaged, and a significant amount of blood had seeped through. That was okay. She'd expected that. But the others? Could those toes really be at risk, too? Did this mean she might have to forgo wearing her precious slingbacks entirely?

'The operation, though ...' Roz said, struggling to find her voice. 'It was successful?'

'Indeed it was,' the voice on the loudspeaker replied. 'Your necrosis was caused by a restriction of blood vessels to the foot as a result of your wearing a brand of extremely tight high-heeled shoes.'

'I know,' Roz said, sheepishly. Dammit, she should have listened to Nick, after all. Still, the hell was over now. Her other toes had been spared, thank God, and the disease was at long last vanquished.

She took a deep breath, prepared to accept the reality that the anaesthetic would soon be wearing off and she might soon start feeling some pain, then bravely flexed her damaged toe.

And felt nothing.

Unnerved, Roz examined her feet again. It must be the anaesthetic. Maybe it was far stronger than she'd suspected.

But something about her left foot bothered her. Roz forced herself to peruse more closely the crusted blood, which normally would have merited a mere nauseating glimpse. There was something about it, Roz sensed. Something about her toe and that small dent in the bandaging just above it. Something entirely unexpected.

It wasn't there.

'My toe!' she screamed. 'Where is my toe?'

'Unfortunately, Miss Bloom, it was necessary to stem and ultimately cauterise the relentless necrotic flow.'

Panicked, Roz thrust herself forwards across the bed and began winding away the bandage.

'Please don't exert yourself, Miss Bloom ...'

Increasingly anxious, she tore in desperation at the gauzed strips, dreading seeing for real the horrific image she'd already imagined inside her mind.

Then it was there. Or wasn't there, to be more precise. For between her big toe and her neighbouring pinkies, sat a red, mangled stump, with a whole lot of air above it.

'You monster!' she yelled. 'You said you'd cure it.'

'It is cured, Miss Bloom,' said Strain's voice, calmly. 'The toe in question is quite well, as I assured you it would be. For it is no longer dying. In fact, you might say it's positively thriving.'

Slowly, Roz became aware of a bubbling sound coming from an area to her left. She hadn't yet had a chance to take in the finer details of this part of the room, but soon her peripheral vision, drawn by the sound, became gradually aware of something else, close beside her left ear.

She glanced round and saw a glass tank beside her, attached by various wires to a bank of mechanical circuitry on the adjacent wall. The liquid within it glowed a strange, phosphorescent green, and in its centre, wriggling within the gently swaying fluid, floated the gnarled, blackened bone of Roz's missing toe.

It was ALIVE.

CHAPTER FIVE

'Looks like she cancelled her appointment last Friday,' said the pedicurist's manicurist, who was covering for the receptionist while she updated the cosmetologist on their dermatologist's optometrist, who suspected her nutritionist of cheating on an orthodontist with his hygienist.

'"Increasing agony in the second toe", it says here.'

'Figures,' said Nick. 'I told Roz a hundred times to ditch those shoes. She's been hobbling about like a crash victim.'

'There's another note below it,' the pedicurist's manicurist continued. 'No, hold on, that's for someone else.'

'We're wasting time,' Capello snapped, interrupting. 'Strain must be miles away by now!'

'Maybe he's in the shower,' said Nick, trying to calm his trigger-happy kidnapper. 'Or doing a number two. That might take hours in a strange toilet. Remember, he's used to doing it in a bucket. With the hoses on him.'

'Miss!' said Capello, turning away from Nick to address the pedicurist's receptionist, who was now returning to relieve the manicurist. 'This Bloom woman. Was she referred anywhere else?'

'To a chiropodist, you mean?'

'Or a podiatrist.'

'Well, she'd seen our podologist,' continued the receptionist. 'And the reflexologist . . .'

'But?' interrupted Nick.

'They could do nothing for her,' she added. 'She was in agony, though bravely tried to conceal it. For the sake of her shoes, I guess. I recommended she arrange a hospital appointment.'

'Hospital?' repeated Nick, ominously.

'She required immediate relief. It was a mildly serious condition, you know. Roz Bloom had developed avascular necrosis.'

'Necrosis ...' Capello whispered to himself, yet also aloud.

'Avascular necrosis,' Nick corrected.

'That's what I said,' replied the receptionist, misinterpreting Nick's response to Capello, thinking, wrongly, that it had been aimed at her instead. 'Avascular necrosis. Of course, we didn't diagnose it ourselves, but we knew all the signs.'

Nick raised an alerted eyebrow. 'Let me see that,' he said, reaching over the desk to grab the appointments calendar. Scanning his eyes over the list of dates, he located Roz's cancellation, then carefully read the note scrawled below it.

'Who's this referring to?' he asked, pointing to a second cancellation.

'Madame Peppier.'

'Who's Madame Peppier?'

'Well now, that's funny,' the receptionist muttered to herself, suddenly struck by a private thought. 'Two in one day ...'

She seems embarrassed, Nick realised. As if a certain metaphorical penny was at long last threatening to drop, metaphorically, so to speak.

'I guess we do see a lot of it in here ...'

'A lot of what?'

'Why, avascular necrosis ... You see, Madame Peppier had it as well.'

'Necrosis?' interrupted Capello, his eyebrow now also raised, alertedly.

'Avascular necrosis,' Nick corrected.

'That's what I said,' the receptionist confirmed. 'Avascular necrosis.'

Nick leaned across the desk intimidatingly. Although the receptionist wasn't technically a police suspect, nor he a policeman, desperate situations occasionally called for wholly inappropriate measures.

Avoiding his gaze, the receptionist ran her eyes over the page again, counting up the numbers on her fingers. She soon ran out of hands.

'There must have been eighty that week, I think. I really should have been paying attention.'

'You think?' Nick said.

'What's going on here?' said Capello, losing patience. 'Strain's an expert in necrosis, right?'

'Wrong,' said Nick. 'He's an expert in avascular necrosis.'

'Avascular necrosis, dammit!'

'Right.'

Capello waited, then rephrased the question. 'What's going on here? Strain's an expert in avascular necrosis, right?'

'Right. And here we have eighty women cancelling their pedicures before getting hospitalised for that precise condition. Right?'

'Wrong,' said the receptionist. 'None of them were hospitalised.'

Nick and Capello looked at her, dumbfounded.

'You see, they all attended a private clinic. Apparently, a newly formed medical company is offering cheap treatment, with a complimentary pair of shoes for all who sign up.'

'Nine-inch slingback heels?' proffered Nick, beginning to twig.

'Why, yes . . . How did you guess?'

'Call it writer's instinct,' he drawled.

'I do wish I had some of that avascular necrosis sometimes,' the receptionist said, starting to laugh. 'Then I could get a free pair of those shoes! But I guess I'll just have to go out tomorrow and buy myself some. If there are any pairs left, which I expect there aren't!' She laughed more loudly. Gleefully. Joyously. Insanely.

Nick and Capello exchanged a knowing glance.

'Don't do that, miss,' warned Nick. 'If you value your life.' He turned to address his pyjama-clad kidnapper. 'Let's go, Capello.'

'Hold your horses, mister. I give the orders,' Capello said, aiming the Beretta at him again. There was a look in the gunman's eye now, Nick observed. And though Capello might think Nick was the mad one, from where Nick was standing, that look of fury in the Italian's eyes was borderline deranged.

'Fine ... Well?' Nick said, carefully.

'Let's go,' Capello barked.

They went.

★

The Peugeot hit another deep puddle on the flooded lane and aquaplaned again, before Nick switched gears and swerved hard to the right, accelerating forwards at high speed in the direction of the moors.

'The asylum's the other way,' said Capello. 'Turn us round, dammit, or I'll plug you in the brain right here. I'll stop us first, obviously, so we don't crash.'

Nick shook his head. 'Roz is this way, Capello,' he said, stepping harder on the accelerator. 'And we have to find her, because not only can she alone vouch for my sanity, she's also the key to us apprehending Nelson Strain.'

'I see,' said Capello, pleased his hunch about arresting Nick's editor as well was paying off. 'How the hell you figure that?'

Nick glanced over at his kidnapping companion, smiling thinly. 'Because she's his prisoner.'

'Bullshit. You really expect me to believe such a chance, unexpected development? Such an insanely fortuitous change in our circumstances?'

'Not fortuitous for Roz,' Nick said, grimly. 'And we may already be too late.'

'Too late for what?'

Nick was glad Capello kept asking him questions. Not only did it help ease the tension between them, but it also allowed Nick to think through unfolding events clearly, logically and concisely, so that a taut and thrilling account of them might later be of some assistance to the police.

He gave the windscreen another burst of wiper fluid. Damn, the tubes were almost empty. Soon they'd have to contend not only with lashing rain, but also the chance that spraying mud from the road below might not be adequately removed, thereby potentially compromising general visibility and thus hindering further progress.

'You said you knew I'd written a book about Strain,' said Nick.

'That's right. The authorities told me.'

'Well, like I explained, that book was a fictional story. Now, whether or not you believe my books are coming to life, just hear me out. *Bone Death (A Sextology)* told the chilling story of Nelson Strain, a former child medical-research prodigy specialising in . . .'

'Necrosis?' said Capello, interrupting.

'Jeez Louise, Capello.'

'Fine, avascular necrosis!' he snapped. 'There. Satisfied?'

'I guess,' Nick smiled, enjoying their sparring, despite the underlying gravity of the situation. 'As much as I can be, at any rate, given the unspeakable horrors fast unfolding around us. But to get back to the fiendish plot of my best-selling novel, the young Strain was renowned for conducting cutting-edge research into methods of treating and potentially reversing the effects of avascular necrosis – that creeping condition whereby human bones, cut off from their blood supply by compressed or damaged veins, frequently as a result of previous injury or constricted clothing, eventually die inside the body, going all grey and black. Strain was determined to halt that process. Reverse the condition, if he could. Ideally before his eighth birthday, so that he could have the day off and go to the zoo. Unfortunately, he became obsessed. Immersing himself totally in his work in an attempt to block out the voice in his head.'

'Voice?' said Capello, confused. 'What voice?'

'Mrs Strain. Nelson's mother,' explained Nick. 'An overbearing, controlling and jealous old hagwitch, who constantly criticised, humiliated and psychologically tortured her son in order to control him. As he advanced into his teenage years, she convinced Nelson that there could never be any other woman in his life but her. That he'd never find the love of a woman outside her own foul, insane caress.'

'What a cow.'

'And she looked it.'

'I know,' said Capello, remembering the crime-scene photographs. 'Artificial hooves, plus udders.'

'So warped did Strain become,' Nick continued, 'that he eventually sought escape via the only world he knew outside her. Into that macabre and inner psych-realm of dead and dying bone.'

'Jesus . . .'

'Each patient admitted to Strain was routinely deprived of their ossifying bone matter. Strain would collect these fragments, piece by piece, hoarding them over the years, concealing them from sight in his private laboratory at the end of his mother's garden. And the more he collected, the more he desired, until eventually he began kidnapping his patients, physically restraining them in order to compress the bones further, until sufficient areas of their compressed skeletons had fully succumbed to the disease. Then, as his mother's criticisms continued throughout his late teens, Strain's mind naturally began to follow the calling of his groin, and, slowly but surely, he began to assemble the woman of his dreams from the accumulated matter. Piecing together the various sections, bone by bone, he created a hideous, malformed skeletal bride, whom he aptly named his Bride of Bone.'

'I know all this,' said Capello. 'Dammit, I saw the thing myself.'

Nick glanced briefly at Capello again, then continued, as if he hadn't heard him. 'So enraptured did Strain become with his new bride, that eventually he developed enough inner strength to finally confront his tormenting mother. He stood up to her, not with his bride present, as she had a tendency to collapse whenever he sat her up. But one wild night, exactly like this one, he stormed up to his mother's house and into her room (having propped his bride-to-be in the broom cupboard downstairs). And there, he murdered the old bag. The next thing he knew, police sirens were arriving at his dead mother's house, followed by the cars attached to them, plus their drivers. All bursting in on that perverse and grotesque 'wedding' ceremony he hadn't officially invited anyone to.'

'I said, I know all this,' barked Capello, strangely emotional. 'Hell, I was there!'

Nick glanced at Capello again, still saying nothing, then turned the car down another muddy lane, passing a sign marked 'Stalkford Moor Ahead'.

'I think you are insane,' Capello snapped suddenly, aiming the gun at Nick yet again.

'Then why haven't you shot me?'

Capello paused for a moment. 'Like I said, you'd have to stop the car first.'

Nick slammed on the brakes. The Peugeot skidded to a violent halt and he cut the engine. The rain hammered hard upon the roof above as Nick turned to stare Capello fully in the eye. When Capello finally turned as well, it was both eyes.

'So shoot me,' Nick said, unblinkingly.

Capello sat in silence, thinking. Then briefly moved the gun closer to Nick's forehead, before lowering it. He shook his head, sadly. 'I can't,' he said.

'Why not?' Nick replied, keen to know the details so he could potentially taunt Capello later and gain the upper hand.

'Because there is no Nelson Strain, Nick. No record of him at the asylum, I mean. They have no idea who he is, even though I've been treating him there myself for the last five years. All of a sudden, it's as if Nelson Strain never existed. And I need to know why, Nick. You're the only person in all of Stalkford who has any knowledge of him. That's the reason why I haven't shot you yet, or turned the car around to go back to the asylum. And because ...'

'Yes, Capello?'

'Because I saw something tonight that even I can't explain. And unless I can find a way to explain it, I may just have to accept that I'm as insane as you are ...'

'What was it, Capello? What was it you saw?'

'I saw him, Nick ... Nelson Strain himself ... I cornered him as he fled from the asylum ... I saw his hand ...'

'His hand, Capello?'

'His hand ...'

'What about his hand?' said Nick, getting impatient.

Capello looked up, fear of his own mounting insanity gleaming like crazed jewels from those frightened, widening eyes.

'It was bone. Nelson Strain's hand was nothing but a mangled skeleton. A crooked palm of gnarled and blackened bone ...'

★

Roz woke groggily from sleep again. She shook her head, struggling to recall those terrifying moments before she'd blacked out. She recalled her fear, an overwhelming terror at whatever it was that had caused her to faint. Then remembered ... Her toe! Her amputated, floating, undead toe ... Sickened within, unable to glance round again at that appalling, glowing tank of horror beside her head, Roz

146

turned away from it, hoping that this was all just some awful, horrific nightmare.

Except it wasn't, she realised. Anything but a nightmare. For this horror was real. Her toe had gone, and so, most likely, had that pair of incredible red slingbacks she adored so much.

Roz tried in vain to flex her missing digit, forgetting for a moment that she no longer could. God, how could she ever survive without her middle toe? It was one thing to take the thing off, quite another to leave it floating in a tank of green liquid next to her head. Why on earth had Dr Strain done that to her?

Something else was troubling her, too. Dr Nelson Strain . . . That name was familiar. Hadn't Nick written a book about someone called Strain? Yes, now that she thought of it, Nelson Strain was one of Nick's early characters, wasn't he? A crazed serial killer obsessed with the effects of avascular necrosis on compressed human bones! It was all coming back to her now. Nick had ditched the sequel on her advice, after a flood of complaints from a shocked and morally outraged bone doctor whom Nick had publicly castigated for failing to alleviate his writer's cramp. God, could it be true, then? Was this the latest of Nick's chillers to have come to terrifying life around them? Had she stumbled, unknowingly, into an as-yet-unwritten horror novel of Nick's own subconscious making? One in which she alone was its helpless and unsuspecting victim?

Yes, is the answer.

Roz forced herself upwards from the bed and stared down at her freshly bandaged feet. Beside the appalling bloodstained gap from which her amputated toe had once sprouted, lay a long and even line of more appalling bloodstained gaps.

'Good evening, Miss Bloom,' said a familiar voice through the overhead speakers.

'My toes!' screamed Roz. 'You've taken my other toes!'

'Please relax. Unfortunately, a cursory examination while you were convalescing revealed that your avascular necrosis had spread quite significantly in the last ten minutes, and I'm afraid it was necessary for me to remove all of your remaining toes.'

With mounting horror, Roz screamed, turning uncontrollably in her fright to look at the tank of green, bubbling liquid beside her head.

Within were Roz's amputated toe bones, floating and wriggling around like strangely animated coral. She screamed again.

'I regret to say,' the voice of Dr Strain continued, 'that this disease has taken such a strong hold of your body, that it will be necessary to remove additional bones from your afflicted skeleton in order to prevent its further spread. I recommend we begin immediately by removing all of your limbs.'

The door of the room burst open. Roz forced her terrified head back, away from the tank, hardly able to process the fresh horror advancing towards her from the doorway. There, shambling over the floor tiles, limbs clicking unnaturally as they rubbed together in a grotesque parody of natural motion, rose something tall and thin within a stained and sodden lab coat. Dr Nelson Strain himself, Roz realised, hardly able to believe her petrified eyes.

That hideously deformed, living skeleton . . .

CHAPTER SIX

Bone, thought Nick. So Nelson Strain now consisted entirely of bone. Then it was playing out just as he'd feared. Exactly like the story he'd planned for that first sequel, which Roz, in her infinite wisdom, had kiboshed before he could even put pen to paper. Now he was living out that unwritten sequel of his for real.

The facility lay a mile ahead of them, its illuminating green glow blending with the heavy rain to form an eerie, otherworldly bank of sprawling fog. Nick saw it and yanked on the car's handbrake, killing the engine, but kept the wiper blades going.

'There,' he said, pointing at the distant building. 'That's the place.'

'Dammit, you'll drain the battery if you keep these wipers going,' yelled Capello. 'Do you want to kill us?'

'Ease off, Capello. It's just while we discuss the abandoned facility ahead of us. Then when we've done that, I'll switch them off before we head out. In any case, there are worse ways of draining a car's battery without you realising. Leaving the main headlights on, for example. Ditto the radio, cassette or CD-player. Even leaving the car door open while you're outside is a killer, in all likelihood triggering the internal cabin lights without you realising. So less of the damned attitude.'

'Any other methods you wanna mention, Mister Battery-Drain King, or shall we maybe stop wasting our precious bloody time?'

'No, I think those are the main ones,' said Nick, keeping calm, aware that Capello was still holding a gun.

'Why this place?' Capello asked.

'Let's start with what this place is. Then that will flow naturally into your first question.'

'Sure. What this place is?'

'That's grammatically incorrect. What is this place?'

'You know what I mean, dammit!'

Nick buttoned his lip. This guy truly was a 'livewire'. Realising he needed to placate him, Nick switched off the wiper blades, then continued. 'No one knows. It was once a top-secret research facility for Stalkford's chemical and germ warfare association. They were briefly affiliated with the military, but in the main it was run by amateurs and enthusiasts. Until the place was closed down and taken over by NullTec.'

'Who's NullTec?'

'Who are NullTec? Either that, or what is NullTec?'

'You want me to bloody well frag your ass?' Capello shrieked. 'Who are NullTec?'

'No one truly knows,' said Nick, fairly confident now that Capello wasn't going to shoot him, no matter how much he ribbed him. 'Let's just call them a shadowy pharmaceutical tech company specialising in psycho-kinetic research and morally dubious brain experiments.'

'Oh, those guys.'

'But they, too, eventually moved on. Leaving the place abandoned, along with its deadly array of forgotten, half-perfected experimental medical and scientific apparatus. Who knows what kind of lethal munitions are lying about in there, just waiting for some passing crazed psychopath to use and abuse.'

'Like Nelson Strain, for instance?'

'You got it, Capello. You see, I dreamed all this up in my head. I never wrote a sequel in the end, but I kept a few outlines percolating in my brain. That's what we're seeing now. The contents of my unleashed psyche, awakening around us, playing themselves out for real. You know, I always imagined that if Strain ever escaped from that asylum, he'd be hiding out in a place like this, hatching an evil plan to avenge himself on those who'd imprisoned him in the madhouse. I have a hunch he's in there, right now. Waiting for us. Though I never got around to writing that first sequel, I always pictured a place like this, in a suitably wild and atmospheric location, far from society's prying eyes, where Strain might conduct his deranged research in secret. My subconscious is writing this, Capello. Perhaps even my unconscious. Ideas I had brewing deep within, yet never expressed or formulated in time. Now my own creativity is finally loose, threatening to destroy Stalkford, and possibly further. Maybe even outer Stalkford.'

'Thanks for the warning about leaving the car door open, by the way,' Capello said, his manner towards Nick softening.

'You know it makes sense, amigo. I guess we're both learning something out here.' He stared deeply at Capello. 'Learning from each other.'

They gripped hands manfully.

'What say we get down to business?' added Nick. Capello caught a dangerous glint in Nick's eye. Smelled the sharp, primal scent of imminent danger. As Nick nodded meaningfully, guiding him forwards with his mind, acquiescing him, Capello balked at the sheer notion. Deep down, he was terrified of what Nick would do to him. What unholy position this madman might put him in. What physical and psychological hell he'd force him through before this wretched night was over. And yet, deep down, he had a burgeoning respect for this man he hardly knew. And he felt a deep swelling within, a racing of the blood, and knew there was no longer any way of avoiding it.

'Okay, let's do it your way, Nick. Leave the wipers on.'

Nick switched them back on.

'Just tell me one thing.'

Was this it, Nick wondered? The moment Capello finally twigged? Was his new Italian buddy about to ask the very question Nick had been dreading?

'Speak your truth, Capello,' Nick said, reassuringly. 'Tell your tale. Share your story, even though personalised accounts of humdrum life-events aren't technically stories. Shoot.' He reached out immediately with his hand to stay Capello's own. 'Not with the gun. I mean, say what you were going to say.'

'I hardly dare speak it, Nick. The idea's crazy. A nightmare . . .'

'Try me, buddy. I wrote the book on nightmares. Till the book woke up . . .'

'Nice.'

'Thanks. Now go on.'

'Well, if Strain is a fictional character,' Capello began, forming the words slowly, like a primary-school child figuring out British math (mathematics). 'And this abandoned medical facility is a fictional abandoned medical facility . . .'

'Which it is.'

'Then . . . am I fictional, too?'

Did Capello want the truth? Or should Nick lie? Hell, he hadn't realised the escaping of his own mind would in turn create unexpected moral dilemmas like this. Though it was Capello's problem, and an existential one at that, it was even harder for Nick, who had to shoulder the additional burden of guilt. Like being a parent of Mankind. A reluctant messiah. Yet a messiah, all the same.

'I can't answer that, Capello.'

'Can't, or won't?'

'Shan't.'

Capello nodded, then in a burst of sudden rage, yanked open the door. 'Fine. Well, let's go then, Mr Mystery. If you truly think Roz is inside.'

'I know she is.'

They got out of the car. As the two men walked off in the direction of the facility, Nick clicked his fingers.

'Capello!'

He pointed at the vehicle. Capello turned and realised he'd left the passenger door wide open.

'Dammit, Nick, I'm sorry.' He walked back and closed it.

'I owe you a battery.'

'It's your car, so you owe yourself one.'

'Of course.'

'And the lights,' Nick said.

Capello reached in and switched those off, too. 'Technically, Nick, those were your responsibility, as designated driver of the car.'

'Except I'm not its registered owner, Capello, so any shortfall in battery capacity would ultimately affect your licence.'

'Dammit, Nick, I'm a gonna blast your bloody balls off if you keep it up like this!'

Nick knew he was being cruel, but he had to keep Capello sane. Insults were all that stood between the fiery Italian and a one-way passport to insanity.

They made off at last across the moor, Nick shouldering himself bravely against the rain, Capello cowering from it in his pyjamas.

'At least you're able to anticipate some of these bizarre twists and turns of events in advance, Nick,' said the Italian, trying to stay positive, despite the deep, existential fear nagging at him from within. 'It certainly speeds things up for us, knowing you have a plausible hunch within you that can guide us towards the most salient events in our ordeal without a whole lot of wandering around, searching for clues.'

'Exactly,' said Nick. 'It's like the 25,000-word novellas I used to write. Or short novels, which is the term I prefer. No room or time in those tomes for any extraneous info or vague, supporting subplots. They have to keep the story moving at all costs, as do we in this bizarre world of my unfolding tales we now find ourselves caught up in. And to continue the analogy, my innate ability to circumnavigate conventional "plot" elements we are now metaphorically facing, via the quick and sure-fire method of relating expositional elements through the logical and well-foreshadowed device of plausible prior knowledge, is certainly a bonus to us here, if not a positive boon, and we shouldn't lose sight of that amid all the attendant horror. Watch your step.'

Nick indicated a vast stretch of muddy, bubbling swamp to their left. 'That's the Stalkford Mire. Innumerable travellers and unwary wander-men have met their end in its dark, murky, mud-bespewen depths.'

'Innumerable?'

'It means uncountable. So many that it's not even worth counting. A catch-all phrase designed to convey an unknowable multitude.'

'Thanks, Nick. Thank God you're a writer, or I'd really be lost.'

Yeah ... thought Nick, guilt squeezing him tight. Like you're not lost, already, buddy. Lost in a book you never knew existed ...

A terrifying bestial howl broke Nick's self-castigatory ruminations. Nick and Capello stared up at the surrounding hills overlooking their position. Silhouetted against the grey clouds rolling overhead, was the stark, unmistakable outline of a giant, predatory wolf.

'What the hell is that, Nick?' said Capello.

'It's the werewolf from my book *The Howling Fur*. I'll deal with it tomorrow. Come on, let's get inside that facility.'

'Here, Nick,' Capello said suddenly, handing Nick his Beretta, along with the holster. 'You'd better take my gun. In case I really do lose my mind, and decide I want no more part of this hell, if you know what I mean.'

Nick strapped them on. 'It's the sane option, Capello. Because, though you may not realise it, I need you. And Roz needs you. And I can't risk you blowing your brains out because you're essentially weak, thereby jeopardising this entire venture. Though you do realise that by handing me this gun, you're now surrendering authority to me, your former prisoner, and in so doing, and to continue that analogy we spoke of before, making me the central hero of our ongoing tale. With you merely a subordinate, supporting character.'

'I guess so, Nick. But it's important that we find Strain, and if that means deferring to you in all things heroic . . . Well, you're the writer, I guess.'

'That's right. I'm the writer. And *I'll* end this.'

'We should get going. This seems like unnecessary padding, to continue the analogy. And there's been a fair bit of that during this whole car journey, if I'm honest.'

Nick smiled, ruefully. 'You've still got edge, Capello.'

'Thanks, Nick.'

They worked their way up to the main building, taking care to leap over the thick, muddy stream flowing from the rain-lashed mire, and eventually found themselves pushing through a line of broken fencing in the direction of what they soon discovered was a long-abandoned and thickly soiled security booth. Capello glanced inside it as they passed.

'See, that is why I go in the road,' he said. 'At least it washes away then, or a dog will eat it.'

'Quick,' Nick hissed suddenly. 'Get inside.'

They dived inside.

'It stinks so bad in here,' said Capello, glancing around at some of the wall graffiti. 'And I swear this message isn't ink.'

'Look,' said Nick, pointing.

Ahead of them, emerging from the doorway of the central building, clambered a tall, thin figure. It wore a stained medical lab coat, clicking unnaturally as it walked on uneven, bony legs.

'That's it!' hissed Capello. 'That's the thing I saw. That's Nelson Strain! Tell me you see it too, Nick. Tell me I'm not mad.'

'I see it,' Nick replied. 'And if I'm seeing what I think I'm seeing, then Nelson Strain has finally found a way, not only to reverse the effects of necrosis . . .'

'Avascular necrosis . . .'

'You got there at last, Capello. But also to go beyond the beyond and discover a way of revitalising dead bone matter itself . . . To bring to obscene, unnatural life those hideous skeletal fragments he so dearly craves. And yet something seems to have gone wrong, Capello. It looks to me like he tested the serum on himself somehow, reducing his own human body to the immortal remains of a living, breathing skeleton. What the hell was happening in that damn lunatic cell of his? You know, I have a hunch he wants to rebuild that bride of his dreams, the one he was previously denied. He wants his Bride of Bone back. And now that he's made himself a skeleton, too, he must think he's finally in with a chance.'

'I agree,' agreed Capello.

They watched as what had once been Nelson Strain got down on all fours and bounded off at speed into the night, like a skeletal wolf. They watched it run at full pelt over the moor, in search of yet more sacrificial victims.

'Okay, let's go,' said Nick.

'I've gone already,' replied Capello.

'I meant let's go in there, get Roz and get out again.'

'I understand. But what then, Nick? Once we've both gone in there, got Roz, and got out again. What happens to me? Where do I go?'

But Nick had gone.

CHAPTER SEVEN

Roz woke groggily from sleep yet again. How long had she been under? More crucially, how long were her limbs now? Was there anything left of her to flex? Dare she even check on the state of her potentially phantomised extremities?

She heard a familiar crackle as the loudspeaker system came back to life somewhere above her. No doubt she'd soon hear the familiar voice of Dr Nelson Strain, piping through from whatever bizarre piece of medical apparatus allowed his disconnected vocal cords to continue operating.

For how else could a skull and bones speak? How else could a dead skeleton scuttle and creep towards her like a living human being? The very idea was preposterous, and yet Roz had watched helplessly, insensibly, as that boned thing had advanced in her direction, then picked her up in its clicking joints like a rag doll. She recalled with mind-numbing horror how it had restrained her. Clutched her. Grasped her few remaining besieged and necrifying appendages in its grey, skeletal hands.

And yet had her limbs truly been necrifying? After all, Roz only had Strain's word on that. And could she really trust a skeleton? How ill had she really been? Sure, her second toe had been suffering from advanced bone-stricture. There was no denying that. Her fault for wearing those damned slingbacks. But had the necrosis really spread that far and that quickly throughout her compressed and ailing system? Was she, Roz Bloom, truly as ill as Strain had been claiming?

Was that thing in the lab coat really, honestly alive? She paused for a moment, exhausted by her own endless and now borderline irritating questioning. Then continued.

Had everything that had happened to her, each fresh horror unfolding before her tired and terrified eyes, simply been because of those damned over-tight shoes?

Then, finally, she remembered.

Nick.

Nick Steen.

Nick bloody Steen.

He'd done this to her. Nelson Strain was Nick's creation, after all. Nick's very own monster. Another one of Nick's unholy offspring. Yeah, Nick had caused all this. Caused Roz to stumble unwarily, unknowingly, into the skeleton's lair. And now Nick had left her. Abandoned her. Failed to stem the flow of his own warped, sadistic mind-rivers.

How she hated him.

Yeah, she hated Nick Steen, alright.

The bastard.

The overhead speakers caught their intended wavelength and came to life above her head. Roz prepared herself for the worst. Steeled herself against the sickening, saccharine tone of Strain's warped and perverted vocal cords.

Then heard music.

Sweet, gentle music.

Violins.

Cellos.

Sleigh bells.

That tinkly thing that's like a kid's keyboard crossed with a xylophone.

A glockenspiel.

What was it, Roz wondered? Was she dead? Was this that famed angelic host she'd heard so much about? Was she lying outside St

Peter's Gate even now, waiting for a duty angel to wheel her in to watch the Divine Chorus? Was she now clutching her cut-price ticket to the everlasting eternal?

Or was it just music?

It was just music. Yet something about this music's romantic tone, its heart-string tuggability, drew Roz's mind back from the horrors she'd witnessed. Back from the hurt she felt within. Something about its gentle melodic refrainery breathed of summer meadows and days gone yonderly by. Soft, fully-sanctioned caresses from an approved lover's arms. Fine boxed wines and meat-cheese platters under a waning sun. Heaven in Stalkford, Roz thought. Yeah, that was it. It sounded like Heaven in Stalkford.

Tentatively, Roz manoeuvred her head downwards and prepared herself for the worst. Which limb would she look at, or not look at, first? She elected for her left arm, figuring that if there was nothing there, she could at least vomit directly into the bin by her head.

She counted herself down slowly from ten, continued past zero, proceeding downwards to minus seventeen, then gave up and counted down from ten again. Finally, getting confused by which numerical system was best to adopt, she opened her eyes and looked.

Her arm was there.

She flexed it. Yes, this arm was definitely hers and moved like a dream. She rose from the bed and checked her other limbs. They, too, were all intact. Then she hadn't been operated on this time. Even though she'd blanked out, she hadn't been de-limbed.

Why not?

Then she sensed something else. The room itself. This prison around her ... It was subtly different. That bin beside her bed ... Now lined with a small plastic bag and freshly emptied. Those speakers in the far corners of the room. These were now joined by a third, mid-range speaker, presumably to utilise both surround and centre channels in order to create some form of primitive home-theatre system. The glass tank beside her head filled with her floating toes was now gone, replaced by a bouquet of fresh, blooming roses with the words 'My darling lover' penned in delicate calligraphy upon a tiny cardboard note.

And beside them, a silver tray, with Belgian chocolates arranged in the shape of a human heart, with 'To Roz' added over the top in squirty cream.

She'd been relocated.

This room was somewhere else entirely. But where exactly had she been moved to? And who, or what, had moved her?

What in hell's name was going on?

She heard a familiar sound. Then watched in terror as this door, like the last door in the previous room, the room she'd been in prior to this room, flew open.

And the thing that had fallen deeply in love with her staggered in.

I.e. the skeleton again.

★

'Smells like an operating theatre of some kind,' said Nick, as he and Capello forced open yet another door and emerged, their suspicions partly confirmed, into the ruined remains of an abandoned medical laboratory. Sure enough, there was an operating table in the centre of the room, but that didn't explain the numerous rows of glass display cases arranged along each wall, nor the blackened, preserved semi-organic husks contained within each one.

Nick tried the light switch in vain. There was no electricity working in the entire building, it seemed, and the two heroes, one infinitely more heroic than the other (Nick, that is, i.e. he is the more heroic) had been forced to navigate their way through each corridor, guided only by the dim green glow that seemed to be emanating from somewhere deep inside the building.

How it managed to spread itself so far outwards, if indeed the light was spreading, which it was, was beyond the comprehension of either man.

'I just don't know how it's doing it,' said Nick.

'Me neither,' concurred Capello. 'It's as if the glow is somehow coming from the wall itself, like that "glow in the dark" material they make spooky toys from.'

Nick knew what he meant. Once, he'd released an entire trilogy of books employing specially manufactured 'glow in the dark' paper. Sales had rocketed, but so had the number of lawsuits when Nick's readers had subsequently developed partial blindness from the illegal chemicals Clackett had used at a slight reduction.

Nick prayed inwardly that this paint wasn't worse. That his rampaging mind hadn't turned yet another problem of his past into a violent supernatural horror of the present, perhaps giving those who looked upon this green light a third eye, or X-ray vision, allowing them to glimpse the horrors of their insides, and the vast miniature cosmos therein, floating just below the pelvis. The chances were that it had. Or would do, now that Nick had just thought of it. That seemed to be the crazy, terrifying way in which this world of his now worked, and Nick alone stood in the path of its horrors. With Roz and Capello as potential human shields.

'What the hell were they experimenting on here?' Nick asked aloud, examining one of the glass cabinets on the wall beside him. Illuminated by the green glow emerging from the forced doorway, Nick made out what looked like a preserved simian's bottom adrift in the luminescent preserving liquid. This fiery red floating protuberance was connected by an intricate system of underwater wiring to a primitive battery circuit, itself connected through one side of the tank to a wide bank of dials and electrical levers, presumably connected up to the powerless mains.

'Looks like a baboon's arse,' said Capello. 'A gang of them attacked my Peugeot once, at a safari park. I grabbed one through the sunroof and tore it a new one. But the old one looked just like that.'

They snaked past the remaining tanks, counting over 200 more baboons' arses and a bank of assorted animal udders meshed semi-organically with the primed ammunition belt of a modified M60 machine gun.

'Wait, Nick,' said Capello, holding up a familiar-looking cardboard box he'd retrieved from a small pile on the floor. 'I know this box. It's a shoe container. See? Look here.' He handed the box to Nick. 'There are hundreds, here on the floor.' Capello kicked one aside.

The hollow sound caught Nick's ear and he, too, tapped the box in his hand. 'Empty,' he said. Then flinched at the diagram printed on the box's edge, outlining the specific shoe it had formerly contained. 'It's Roz's,' Nick said, realisation slowly dawning. 'That's her nine-inch scarlet slingback. The one that's been crushing her pods. Her size nine, that's in reality a size seven. I'd know it anywhere.'

Capello picked up another of the boxes and examined the address printed on its underside.

'But these are old shoes, Nick. They belonged to Nelson Strain's mother.'

Nick froze, staring hard at Capello through the dark, green-tinted shadows.

'She collected them. It was her hobby. Like all ladies. These were among the millions of boxes we had delivered from a police ware-house on the outskirts of town, directly into Nelson Strain's cell.'

'And, of course, shoes, like people, were smaller in the days of yore . . .'

'Two sizes too small. Oh God, Nick, it's too horrible to contemplate.'

'Yet contemplate it we must, Capello. Strain must have sent these shoes out to his potential victims, knowing the sizes were potentially

confusing, and yet knowing that ladies are too proud to admit unnecessary pain if the shoe is right. That's the horrid, appalling beauty of
his scheme – he made it their fault, ultimately, thus ensuring their
continued silence. He offered these freebies initially, knowingly stran-
gling and squeezing the feet of his victims. Then, when they realised
they desperately needed urgent toe surgery, he offered them a course
of private treatment through which they would also receive yet more
complimentary shoes. Agonising retro-shoes, that would continue to
destroy the integrity of their dying bones. Ultimately, he brought
them here, to this newly formed base of operations. To create his new
Bride of Bone. But something doesn't add up. He can't have needed
all these shoes, all these victims, for one single Bride of Bone?'

'I imagine if we keep looking and searching, we'll find there's
more to this wretched scheme than meets the eye.'

'Maybe. In fact, probably. Let's continue.'

They carried on, and upon reaching the far side of the room, Nick
thought he heard the sound of distant voices. 'Listen, Capello,' he
said.

'I can't listen while you talk, you fool,' snapped Capello. 'In order
to listen, I need you to be quiet, too.'

'Now *I* can't hear, Capello.'

'So shut up, then.'

'No, you shut up.'

More tussling, Nick reflected wryly. But that was good for Capello.
He needed the natural nip and tussle of nascent buddy-dom; the
manly badinage of jostling, jockeying heroes in a joint fight against
the dark wildfires wrought by the forces of supernatural tyranny and
oppression, in order to stay sane.

Hell, if he had to, Nick would taunt the living daylights out of
him.

'Sounds like voices,' said Nick. 'Just beyond this wall. And yet . . .
there's no door.'

He reached out and pressed his hands hard against the brick.

'Wait,' said Capello, crouching down to listen near the floor. Following the course of the sound emanating from somewhere beyond, Capello crawled along the ground until he paused by a raised metal bar, set just above the surface of the floor.

'A boot scraper!' he declared.

'Then there must be a door here,' said Nick, moving up beside Capello. Together, they felt around the wall, attempting to trace the contours of its shuttered opening, occasionally stopping when they accidentally touched fingertips in the darkness.

Then, at long last, Nick found it.

'Here,' he said. 'At long last, I've found it.' He reached down with his hand and, sure enough, discovered a lock that had been painted over and concealed by someone many years before. Capello leaned forwards, pressing his ear up against the hidden plate.

'It's louder here, Nick,' he said. 'And they are voices, just like you said.'

'It must be the women Strain's kidnapped,' said Nick, whipping out Capello's Beretta, which was now effectively his. 'Roz must be inside with them. Let's burst in, Capello. Before Strain returns here with yet more lambs for the slaughter.'

He levelled the gun at the concealed lock, waited for Capello to protect his face from any potential ricochet with the folds of his dressing gown, and opened fire.

The lock exploded in a blaze of smoking metal. Nick raised one knee and kicked the door in violently, screaming loudly and rolling backwards on to the floor as his foot met the full force of an obstruction. Reeling from the blow, the door, which opened the other way, sprang back with him as he fell.

Capello stared down at Nick, who was out for the count, and braced himself for the potential suicide mission. He no longer had a gun in his hand, but he was the last man standing. With a yell of primal rage, Capello hurled himself through the opening and into the room beyond.

Alerted from semi-consciousness by Capello's bravery, Nick shook off his torpor and dived in after him. Together, side by side, the two men stared into the darkness.

Then saw them.

Illuminated by the green, fluorescent glow of the fluid in which they slumbered ...

... a legion of skeletal warriors.

Row upon row of them, Nick observed. Twitching like electrified mice, slowly waking from their sleep of death.

'*Boners* ...' he whispered. For deep down, Nick knew exactly what they were. His intuition, his subconscious leanings, his unconscious creative energy, had created these beings from the darkest regions of his exposed id.

These were his children, he thought, self-disgustedly.

'An army of Boners ... This is it, Capello. This is the sequel I feared would be unleashed. I imagined a plot development like this at around book four or five, but evidently Strain's grown impatient. Brought things forward to book two.'

'Good God, Nick,' said Capello. 'You're one sick bastard.'

'Tell me that back in the car,' said Nick. 'Right now, we've got to run.'

They turned back to the door behind them and found it blocked by a familiar-looking figure in a bedraggled lab coat.

A vast, black-boned skeleton.

'Doctor Strain,' said Nick, addressing the thing directly. 'What the hell happened to you?'

'I'm Doctor Strain,' said a voice behind them. Smooth, almost gentle sounding. Together, they turned back round and saw a young, nervous, adolescent-looking male emerging from behind one of the glowing tanks. A pair of long, black rubberised gloves encased both mitts, right up to his elbows.

'The question is, what's going to happen to *you*?'

The distinctly human Nelson Strain reached out and pulled a nearby lever. At once, the tanks began to drain themselves, emitting a violent roar of rushing pipes as the green fluid glowing within them began to bubble and disperse through released plug apertures embedded in every floor.

As the strange fluid drained away, each skeleton inside began to grind and rattle their bones, clutching at the smooth glass surface of the fragile glass with dripping, exposed finger joints.

As Nick and Capello backed off from this waking army of death, they each felt a rigid, bony hand seize their respective shoulders.

Nick sighed in defeat.

They were prisoners.

CHAPTER EIGHT

'What's that smell?' said Nick, gagging. His keen nostrils were becoming momentarily overpowered by a sharp, musky scent slowly filling the room. A complex blend of corrosion and decay, he noted, one gradually revealing subtler shades of corruption as the dank aroma unfurled around them. Nick caught several notes of intestinal rot infused with layers of degenerated surface corrosion, balancing finer hints of regurgitated worm and moist cemetery shroud. Strongest, though, was the heavy, almost faecal stink of crusted, decalcified bone.

'Delectable, isn't it?' said Strain, inhaling deeply as he stepped towards the two intruders. 'The unmistakable aroma of bone putrefaction, magnified tenfold by the rejuvenating qualities of my soon-to-be patented reviving fluid.'

He clicked his fingers and the tall lab-coat-wearing skeleton behind them relaxed its grip on the men's shoulders, stepping back into the shadows to block the passage behind. Meanwhile, Strain held up a glass phial containing a small amount of the green, glowing liquid. It seemed to shimmer inside the bottle, as if attuned to some unseen psychic energy – perhaps even a higher cosmic power, Nick posited.

'Radiation fluid,' Nick whispered, the unspeakable fear of untold generations realised at last in the contents of this conventional, nondescript sample bottle. 'The juice of destruction.'

'Not quite, Mr Steen. Although it is a man-made agent, and hugely destructive. As you will soon discover.'

Strain held out something else in his other hand. Prone and still upon the black rubberised surface of his gloved palm, lay the small, skeletal remains of a diseased human toe.

'You can see, it's quite dead,' Strain said, nudging the toe bone with his thumb. 'Necrified beyond repair. Yet behold . . .'

Carefully, yet evidently enjoying every second, Strain slowly tipped the phial in his other hand sideways, until a small, single drop of the liquid gathered at its spout, growing heavier as it hung suspended briefly in mid-air over the grey, rotten toe husk below, then dropped.

It hit the toe directly in the central phalanx. There was no hissing, Nick noted. No sudden burst of steam. No loud crackle or electrical sparking. Yet within seconds, before their astounded eyes and shocked comprehensions, the toe in Strain's palm began to move.

'Kill it!' yelled Capello, half-mad with terror. 'Stamp on it. Crush the bastard. Spray that sonofabitch with Raid. Anything!'

'We can't, Capello,' Nick said, eyes trained at all times on the crawling toe bone as it wriggled confidently over Strain's palm towards the ends of the doctor's fingers. 'I don't have a tin of it with me. Though ironically, I could easily have picked one up from B&Q.'

'Yes, but would it work on a toe?'

'Probably not. But you're the one suggesting using a tin of Raid, not me.'

'Look, it wants to say hello,' said Strain, holding the zombified digit closer to Nick's face.

'Hello, toe,' Nick replied, trying in vain to make friends with the miniature monstrosity. As it leaned out over the abyss beneath Strain's palm, millimetres from plunging into the dark region of Nick's particulars, Steen forced himself to look up, defiantly.

'What's it made of?'

'Like I said, human bone.'

'I meant the liquid.'

'Oh, I see. Well now, Mr Steen ...' Strain glanced briefly at his second prisoner. 'And Mr Capello ...'

There was a look of recognition there, Nick noted. Capello, too, was glaring at Strain with a look of barely concealed contempt. Nick knew there was a backstory between these two men – that Capello had been there when Strain was first arrested, that he'd subsequently spent five years trying to cure Strain of his lunacy before giving up and imploring the authorities to see sense and kill this dangerous lunatic rather than releasing him back into an unsuspecting society. But although he knew all this, there was something else going on here that Nick suspected he didn't know.

Maybe it had only been put there by his unconscious mind, seeded via his liberated subconscious imaginings, but he couldn't help feeling that there was something personal going on with these two. Not quite an understanding 'twixt opposites, one that might be expected to arise naturally between patient and therapist, say, but more an implied yet firm commitment to mutual destruction. A rift of some nature, Nick ventured to guess. Perhaps a blood feud. Maybe a terrible crossed path of two-way vengeance.

'To answer your question, this tincture I hold in my humble hand is my own creation. A surprisingly smooth yet simple combination of basic elements, all of which were in abundant supply at the very asylum you and those so-called "authorities" elected to imprison me in. A heady concoction of high-energy drinks from the asylum's vending machines – Lilt, Tizer, Quatro and Diet Irn Bru – mixed together with a generous solution of diseased rat urine, which, as you know, possesses a life-force strong enough to withstand nuclear apocalypse.'

'So you're building an army,' Nick spat, unable to conceal his anger. 'An unholy force of skeletal evil.'

'A legion of Boners, who will rise upwards, forcing Mankind to do its bidding. Thrusting it deep into a titanic struggle for its very survival. Yes, soon my Boners will stand proud, hardened against the withering, wilted flock of flaccid prannies you call Humans. Against you, my Boners will rise, their spirits stiffened within, and at my command, they will plunge themselves into all who oppose them.'

Nick grinned wryly at Strain's choice of words. The kid's development must have been severely arrested. No one called humans 'prannies' these days.

Strain laughed maniacally, the green glow from the phial in his hand lighting his face demonically in the semi-darkness. It was a crazed visage of ultimate insanity.

'I should have strapped you in the electric chair myself!' snapped Capello when the young doctor had finally stopped laughing, approximately three minutes later.

'Save it, Capello,' said Nick. 'We're the prisoners now, remember?'

'Your companion is right, Clifford Capello,' said Strain. 'Except you won't be prisoners for much longer. For you will both soon be dead. And I will take great pleasure in ensuring that *you*' – Strain jabbed his gloved finger at Capello – 'die slowest, longest and lastest.'

The young trainee doctor picked up the big toe, which had been rearing upwards on his palm like a miniature cobra python, and tossed it into a jam jar on a nearby table. The jar was filled to the brim with green reviving fluid. The two men watched as the digit commenced to float and wriggle around like a fat tadpole.

'Nice theory, Strain,' said Nick, transferring his eyes back to the doctor. 'But I think you're after something else entirely.'

'Oh, really?' Strain replied, his voice feigning boredom, yet nevertheless betraying a hint of concern.

'Something these Boners are merely a substitute for. Something you've never had, Strain. Something you could never have, despite years of yearning . . .'

'Silence!'

'The love of la femme,' Nick stated, boldly. 'That's what you want, deep down. And it's something you'll never have. Because your mother wouldn't allow that, would she, Strain? Your mother was the only woman your mother allowed into your life. She wouldn't even allow you to marry a dead bride, would she?'

'I said, be silent!'

'Now you're trying to lure some real feminine interest by marketing your mother's vintage unsold shoes, popular again with today's jaded, heel-starved female, and deliberately marketing them two sizes too small in an effort to crumble and destroy the toe bones of innocent ladies. What's next, Strain? Their foot bones? Their ankle bones? Maybe even their thigh bones?'

'Which are connected to their hip bones,' explained Capello.

'Their backbones?'

'Which are connected to their shoulder bones.' Capello was enjoying this now. Finally, a chance to get one over on his sworn enemy. 'Maybe even their spine bone?' he yelled.

'Which is connected to the dem bone,' explained Nick.

'The dem bone?' Capello looked confused again.

'Technically dem *bones*,' corrected Nick. 'They're what allow humans to dance.'

'Seize them!' Strain yelled at the lab-coated skeleton, who stepped forwards again from the shadows to grab the two men. There was a moment of stillness as it reached for Capello, as if it were sizing up the prisoner's potential for explosive violence. But before the Italian could resist, he and Nick felt the guard's cold, bony grip tighten once more on their shoulders.

'We are seized,' Nick quipped, slightly too late.

'Throw them in a cell. Soon, they too, will be donating their dead and dying skeletal fragments to my army of rising Boners.'

'How are you gonna do that, Strain?' Nick said. 'My bones are healthy. I'm lithe, trim. Physically supple.'

171

'Your bones may be strong at the moment,' Strain warned, ignoring him. 'But not once you've begun wearing ... these.'

He snapped his fingers, and a pair of armoured skeletal assistants clicked forth from the shadows. They were, Nick realised, having created them himself for one of his proposed sequels, members of the terrifying Skeletorian Guard, the elite military wing of Strain's Boner army. Clasped in their calcified hands were two pairs of tight, elasticated Speedos.

'I can't wear those!' cried Capello.

'I believe that's the idea,' said Nick, grimly.

'You can choose the colour, of course,' said Strain. 'They come in Lincoln Green or Canary Yellow. But both squeeze just as tightly, and rapidly reduce the blood-flow to your more crucial extremities ...'

With that, the lab-coated skeleton behind gave Nick and Capello a hard shove, forcing them forwards. Strain stood by to let them pass, laughing maniacally again.

'What have you done with Roz?' Nick yelled.

'You'll find out, soon enough,' Strain bellowed in response. 'In one hour's time, gentlemen, you will both become my guests of honour. At another wedding ceremony. My second, in fact. This time, to Roz Bloom, deceased. My brand-new BRIDE OF BONE!'

'Fiend!' yelled Nick, hopelessly.

'Yes!' cried Capello. 'That's the perfect phrase to use in this context. You fiend! You absolute fiend!'

'You absolute bloody fiend, you!' Nick bellowed, before he and Capello were finally steered away by the lab-coated skeleton behind, past yet more tanks of drained Boners into a small pathway to their right, leading onward to what looked like yet another concealed door.

Upon reaching and opening it, for it was indeed another concealed door, as they'd suspected, the Skeletorian Guard took charge of both prisoners, confiscating Nick's Beretta (which had once been Capello's, but which Capello had effectively bequeathed Nick for being the better hero), and led them through into another dark corridor beyond.

Capello turned his head as both he and Nick were marched off into the darkness. The tall skeleton in the lab coat stood behind them, watching the two men leave from his position at the doorway. Evidently, his immediate duties lay elsewhere, but for a moment or two, the undead creature waited there, alone. And stared.

While Capello stared back.

Then the starer and the stared-at parted at last, both ceasing the aforementioned stare.

And were gone.

★

'Please! Please!' cried the Italian as the skeletal arms tugged the pair of small green Speedos further up his thighs, his flesh turning milky white as the elasticated lining clamped down on fragile blood vessels.

'Take the pain,' said Nick, as his own appointed armoured bone-bag tugged back the pant-lining of his yellow pair with a crooked undead finger and let it snap back hard against his exposed groin. 'You skeletal sonofabitch,' Nick hissed, once the shock had subsided and some semblance of circulation had returned. 'I give it half an hour before our penis bones start to shrivel, Capello. After that, we'll need to start fantasising something in order to pump extra blood to the region.'

'And what in hell am I gonna think about?' Capello raged. 'A skeleton with massive bazookas? Such a thing doesn't exist, Nick.'

He had a point. It was unlikely even someone as imaginative as Nick could train his mind well enough to drum up some plausible erotic fantasy amid the physical hardship of this dank, abandoned medical cell. Unless he went for full-blown kink.

The two undead guards checked the ropes binding their prisoners' hands to the rafter beam above, then scuttled back across to the cell door, locking it behind them as they left.

'We're finished, Nick,' Capello said. 'Strain has us strung up like a couple of sexy kippers, and in one hour we have to be guests at his wedding. And what the hell have they done with my pyjamas?'

'They're over there,' said Nick, thrusting himself in the general direction of their blocked khazi, trying to force some circulation. 'Though one of them nabbed your bow tie. I'll tell you something, Capello. I wish I'd opted for Lincoln Green, after all. These Canary Yellows are playing havoc with my tinted shades. Which aren't glare resistant.'

'Come on, we have to think of something, Nick.'

'I'm aware of that, Capello.'

'Well? Any ideas?'

'None,' Nick said, dejectedly. 'As far as I can see, we have approximately fifty-nine minutes left of supple bone flexibility below, then we slowly turn into dying necrotic skeletons from the groin upwards. Or downwards. Most likely both.'

'And Roz? What of her?'

'I'm trying not to think of her, Capello. Because if Roz is shortly to become Nelson Strain's Bride of Bone, then that means only one thing.'

'What, Nick? What is that one thing?'

Nick twisted himself round to face his fellow captive. 'She's already dead.'

Capello nodded, gravely. 'And potentially skeletal.'

'Fine, two things,' Nick conceded.

CHAPTER NINE

She was flying. Soaring through sun-kissed clouds not yet heavy with the weight of rain. She beat her limbs like phantom wings, feeling light as a bird, which was probably due to her missing digits.

This was death then, she mused. Not so bad, when you came down to it. Once you were through the veil, and the whole universe opened up, blowing your hair backwards, away from your eyes.

Except she still felt fear. Why was that, she wondered? With mortality put to rest at last, and infinity beckoning her towards an eternity of casual flying, why was she still scared?

The cosmos was beautiful, after all. The kind of beauty only glimpsed in a Jack Vettriano calendar. Sand, sky, wine, shoes, some dancing, more wine, big fedoras, plus an entire shelf of best-selling 'Feminism' novels to read on her stain-resistant fabric sun-lounger.

And/or a good murder magazine.

Heaven.

But then she remembered something else. Her toes. Or lack of them. No more shoes for her, she reflected, starting to sniffle. Or socks, tights, clogs – flip-flops, even. Life, as she knew it, was over. She must stay here now. Here, in this windy land of Death.

And yet . . .

And yet she could sense something wanting her.

Craving her.

A presence respecting Roz for who she was.

Something that loved her.

175

She could feel him – for it was a him, of that she was certain – close by yet perhaps eternities away, drawing her back, urging her back behind the veil she'd previously passed through.

She had to return.

She couldn't die here. Not yet.

Roz awoke from her dream to the smell of flowers. Gently, as if unable to fully believe she was back on earth, even though she hadn't remotely half-died and was simply hallucinating on morphine, she turned her head once more to the table beside her pillow. There, upon it, stood a fresh bouquet of roses, arranged neatly in a newly rinsed (she hoped) sample bottle.

Then she remembered. That thing . . . That tall skeleton in the lab coat . . . Dr Nelson Strain . . . Or *was* it?

Because it hadn't taken her arms and legs from her after all, as Strain had threatened to. Hadn't kept her a prisoner in that operating room of hell, but had instead moved her to this alternative operating room of hell, leaving her chocolates, kind notes and flowers. Surely this meant the thing in the lab coat wasn't Nelson Strain, after all? Surely Nelson Strain wouldn't have gathered up her toes in a box of travelling sweets, sealed and concealed them inside her own handbag in the belief that one day they might be grafted back on to her stumps, now that her digits were alive and kicking once again, not that we've actually seen any of that happening . . .

No, it was all too horrible. Too horrible for words. As Roz reeled from a fresh flush of nagging terror, she could think only of escape.

For this was a madhouse, she realised. She had to get out. Whatever insane creatures had trapped her here, she must find a way to flee them. Get back to Stalkford.

She rose from the bed and attempted to walk over to the door, collapsing halfway, lacking the requisite balance formerly provided by her full set of toes. But, dammit, she was determined to get out. She had to treat this escape like she treated editing one of Nick's books. Yes, the journey would be tough. No doubt she'd face inevitable opposition, an endless barrage of abuse if she dared to locate a way out of the proverbial mess, then cackles of derisive laughter at any hint of suggestion that the way out might not lie that way, but this way instead, followed by a shower of assorted stationery and ink toner as Nick finally got to grips with some of the notes. But she had to try.

Grasping the proverbial nettle, along with her figurative mettle, Roz rose once again from the floor and prepared to fling herself violently at the door.

Which suddenly opened.

Roz sprawled backwards in terror as that dreadful skeleton in the lab coat strode towards her, a small cardboard box clutched in its bony hands.

'If that's ink toner, I've dodged it before!' she yelled, defiantly.

The thing shook its skull, emphatically, from side to side.

'Paper clips, then?'

The shaking continued.

'A bottle of apology perfume?'

The lab-coated skeleton stared at her for a long moment, then placed the box it was holding to one side, reached down with both bony arms and gently lifted Roz upwards.

'I'm sorry,' said Roz, softening. Sure now from the creature's relaxed demeanour that it wasn't Strain, after all. 'I was simply searching for my digits,' said Roz, bluffing. 'I think they've crawled out of my handbag.'

She stared upwards into the thing's dark, sunken eye sockets, sensing something hidden there. A feeling, perhaps. A yearning . . .

A *sadness* . . .

As if brushing the notion aside, the tall lab-coated skeleton snapped into sudden action, carrying Roz over to the bed. It set her down gently on the soft, freshly laundered mattress, then scuttled back to the small box it had dropped. It picked it up and brought it over to Roz.

She backed off, terrified that the thing was about to unleash some fresh bone-revived horror she wasn't yet aware had been extracted from her. Perhaps her teeth had been removed without her knowing and been swapped for falsers. Maybe they were about to start chatting to her from inside the box. Berating her. Lecturing her. Ridiculing her.

But when the skeleton finally removed the box's lid, all it contained was a brand-new pair of retro-styled high-heeled ladies' slingbacks.

In Seville Orange.

'What beauties,' Roz said, almost dazed. Then noticed the size on the box. Suddenly, a flash of fury ignited within. 'They're two sizes too big, you fool ...'

The skeleton raised its greying mandible, inclined its zygomatic bone slightly to one side, so that a ray of light touched briefly against its supraorbital notch, and carefully patted Roz's knee. Then it took her ankle delicately in its metacarpals, and gently slipped the shoes over her stumps.

'They're perfect,' Roz whispered, dreamily. 'The perfect fit.' She looked up at the skull of her mysterious, unknown suitor. It couldn't be Nelson Strain. It just couldn't be ...

She stared deeply into its sockets. They were so dark. So dreamy. So alluring ...

Maybe it wouldn't be quite so bad becoming a living undead skeleton, after all.

Then they did it.

★

'Good God, Nick, it's cupped my swingers. They've both turned hard as marbles.'

'Hang tight, Capello. Actually, I'll rephrase that. Hang loose. You have to think of something saucy. You've got to get fresh blood to the area.'

'It's no good, Nick. With my briefs twisting like this, I can't think of anything remotely saucy. Help me, for God's sake!'

But Nick couldn't. Since his physical love affair with a cursed typewriter, he was no longer confident airing his own particular pillow preferences in public. He was mixed up, he guessed. Unable to know what exactly rocked his boat anymore. Woman or machine evidently both did it for him, but the former was absent, and the latter wasn't exactly common territory for the fellow hetero in peril. But he had to try something.

'What about a typewriter with no cover on it, Capello? All inked-up and ripe for hammering?'

'What the hell are you talking about?' gasped Capello.

'Okay, scratch that. Do you like knockers?'

'Of course.'

'I mean brass knockers. You know, like the ones on big doors?'

'No, Nick, those don't turn me on.'

'Okay, let's forget it. Do you actually need your balls? I mean, could you ultimately do without them?'

'God forbid,' said Capello, despairing. 'I need offspring, dammit. To continue the task I have undertaken. To kill Nelson Strain.'

'Well, that's a long way off, Capello. First you need to meet some-one, court them, propose, then marry, procreate, conceive, bear and raise a child together – all inside this room within the next half an hour. And with the best will in the world, getting these pants off is a prerequisite to any of that happening. So unless you can start getting hot under the collar for a mechanical writing implement, I don't think I can help you.'

Capello breathed out a defeated sigh and hung his head low over his chest.

'That's it, Capello. Maybe the sight of your own Speedos will turn you on.'

Capello ignored him, sinking slowly into what increasingly looked like self-absorbed reflection.

'Dammit, Capello,' said Nick. 'All this death and destruction, and all for a skeletal bride. Strain tried it once, but got interrupted. That's partly your fault, by the way. But I sometimes wish he hadn't been apprehended at all. At least until after his wedding. That way he might have died happy in the asylum, knowing he'd achieved his life's aim and escaped his mother's psychological clutches. Even though hundreds of victims died to provide those bones for his skeletal betrothed.'

'Including my *brother*,' said Capello, tears falling from his eyes on to his bare chest.

'What do you mean, brother?' Nick asked, barely comprehending. Though he knew it was something about a brother.

Capello looked up at Nick, his face wet with flowing tears, which were now starting to flow even more fully, though not heavily enough to constitute a fully blown bawl. A tastefully vulnerable volume of tears that still smacked heavily of innate masculinity.

'My brother ...' he repeated, pointedly. 'Dwayne Capello. My older twin. He was a therapist, too. He was engaged to a beautiful lady called Brenda. Sadly for her, she developed an in-growing toenail that one day led to a bad case of creeping necrosis.'

'Creeping avascular necrosis.'

'Sorry, Nick. I must keep trying. Creeping avascular necrosis. One day, she was sent for an operation at the clinic of a renowned junior doctor.'

'Nelson Strain ...' whispered Nick.

'No, another guy. But he was spending the week at Thorpe Park with his parents, so they sent her on to his replacement.'

'Nelson Strain ...' whispered Nick.

'The very same. But she never returned. Dwayne waited and waited, but always heard nothing. Eventually, he set off to see where she'd got to, knocked on Strain's door . . . then he disappeared, too.'

'What, right there at the door, like David Copperfield?'

'No, no, he went in. Presumably then something happened to him inside the house, which stopped him coming out again alive, because he was never seen again. It wasn't a magic trick, or anything like that.'

'I see. So, almost as if he was murdered, then?'

'Exactly,' said Capello, fresh tears starting to flow.

'By Nelson Strain, presumably?'

'I'd put five pounds on it . . . When neither he nor Brenda returned, I knew something must be up. So I alerted the authorities, who began to watch Strain. Observe him, and his mother. Then finally, one day someone heard the old woman being murdered in her kitchen and phoned the authorities, because something just wasn't adding up. The following week the police went over there, and I went with them. I would have killed Strain there and then, but he alone knew where my brother and sister-in-law-to-be were buried, and he blankly refused to tell. So that's when I trained to become a therapist.'

Nick knew all this, of course, having made the entire story up himself, but decided to let Capello have his moment. Not only would it take his buddy's mind off the immediate horror, but it would also allow Nick to work up some potential erotic thoughts to save his below area while pretending to listen.

'Day and night, I worked my way up the therapy ladder so I could one day treat Nelson Strain myself. Find out from his warped mind, where the remains of my brother and sister-in-law-to-be were concealed. But it was useless. He stayed mad as a cucumber. Which is when I decided to kill him. But before I got a chance to do that, he escaped. And so here I am, with the bones of my particulars rapidly greying like the hairs on my own head, no offspring, and no hope of vengeance. It is over. I just wish I knew what had really happened to my brother . . .'

'Probably melted down into glue, or used as fertiliser,' said Nick, realising Capello had finally stopped talking. 'Unless bits of him were used as part of Strain's original Bride of Bone.'

'No, I think that was mainly Brenda.'

'What I'd like to know – and you've been talking for ages, Capello, so please don't interrupt me – is how Strain managed to create a living skeleton while he was inside the asylum? If that thing in the lab coat is what got Strain out, then how the hell did it get in? And who in God's name is it?'

Suddenly the door burst open, admitting a legion of strutting Skeletorian guards. As they piled en masse into the small room, a pair of overhead loudspeakers crackled into life and Strain's soft and well-spoken voice sounded across the airwaves.

'Gentlemen, you will be delighted to know that your programme of tightly panted groinal-compression is to be temporarily halted. Until the grand ceremony itself is concluded.'

'Thank God,' Nick said, breathing an audible sigh of relief as his shrinking squeezers were at last cut free. Then Capello was also released from his twisted Lincoln Greens and collapsed to the ground beside Nick, hardly able to assist the bony warriors as they dressed him in his pyjamas once again.

'I'm afraid I've been forced to bring the entire ceremony forwards,' Strain continued, 'as the subject of the rite had briefly absconded from her holding cell. Yet I am pleased to say she has now been located, and the culprit who had removed her has also been caught and apprehended. Gentlemen, you will now accompany my guards to the acid room. As guests of honour. At the wedding of Dr Nelson Strain and his . . .

'. . . BRIDE OF BONE!'

CHAPTER TEN

The two men were herded along several corridors, forced down four flights of stairs, led along numerous additional corridors, then steered back up two more flights of stairs, before being pushed along another series of numerous corridors that veered almost imperceptibly to the left through a vast connecting lobby, where they were then coerced back down three more flights of stairs and forced finally through a dank underground tunnel, ending in a steel-lined enclosure situated deep inside one of the neighbouring facility buildings, into which Nick and Capello were then ignominiously thrust.

'And this is the acid room?' asked Nick.

'Wrong,' Strain replied. Fortunately, the system of overhead speakers carrying Strain's voice had been wired through each building and tunnel in the complex, meaning he was an ever-present presence and thus able to conduct conversations whenever the evolving plot woven by Nick's escaped imagination required it.

'The acid room is next door,' Strain continued. 'This is a holding area where the soon-to-be-acidifed can change out of their work clothes into jogging bottoms if they prefer, and grab a quick snack from the machine. Though it doesn't currently give change.'

Capello tucked his five-pound note back into his pyjama pocket.

'Also, it won't accept notes,' added Strain. 'But we can exchange for coins upstairs?'

'Maybe later,' said Capello, noting the machine was out of Lilt.

'Can I just confirm that we aren't the ones being acidified?' Nick asked.

'Not immediately. First you will both watch your friend, Miss Bloom, being acidified. Once you have beheld her bony corpse rising up again, having been ceremoniously dunked in a tank of my reviving fluid, to become my living BRIDE OF BONE, then you, too, will be acidifed, and your revived skeletons compelled to become bridesmaids.'

'No way! That is bang out of order!' Capello yelled.

Nick could tell his friend was losing it. He had to think fast. 'Wait up, Strain. Neither myself nor Capello have yet developed symptoms of avascular necrosis, despite our bout of intense groin-tightening. So why would our bones be in any need of reviving? Surely you can't revive living bones?'

There was a brief pause as Strain considered both questions.

Nick took the opportunity to reassure the flagging Capello. 'The advantage of living out a horror fable penned by my subconscious, Capello,' he whispered, 'is that many of the finer plot points usually refined and perfected by my conscious mind, often while I'm in the bath, haven't yet been integrated into the evolving plot-in-action in which we now find ourselves. Meaning we may yet outsmart Strain's self-evolving narrative, and perhaps locate some plot hole he hasn't yet thought of, giving us a potential last-minute chance of wrapping up this unfolding tale to our own advantage.'

Strain's voice piped through again. 'In answer to your questions, Mr Steen, the particular acid I have developed here in record time – yes, merely a few hours, that's right, I stand by that – contains a unique necrifying agent that effectively kills the bone before it can be acidified, thus allowing any subsequent deep immersion in my reviving fluid to create, unimpaired, an aforesaid living, seething mass of ossified bone.'

'Figures,' said Nick. 'Thin, plot-wise, but still works. My own unconscious is outsmarting me, Capello.'

'Enough!' yelled Strain. 'Put them both in the acid room!'

Immediately, warriors of the Skeletorian Guard grabbed the two prisoners and forced them through a neighbouring door, not even pausing to open it. As the men tried in vain to brush the fragments of shattered steel from their outer garments, Nick heard a faint church organ playing wedding hymns in the distance. He glanced over in the direction of the sound and identified a scarlet-robed bone-bag in a wizard's hat, playing two separate keyboards simultaneously.

Damn, they'd got Rick Wakeman as well, Nick mourned inwardly.

Yet there was little time for reflection. On either side of the vast hall-come-temple they now found themselves in stood row upon row of tall glass tanks, brim-full of green bubbling fluid. Each contained a floating skeleton, exactly like the other room of glass tanks they'd previously stumbled into. Only a bit bigger.

'See, he's flagging,' Nick whispered to Capello. 'His own narrative sense hasn't yet developed a more impressive-looking stage for this final confrontation. It's no good repeating a set of impressive-yet-familiar-looking glass tanks. That's sloppy writing. He needs to up the ante visually, and he hasn't. I think we may yet be in with a chance, Capello.'

'Then what's that?' Capello said fearfully, pointing towards a gigantic metallic green vat at the far end of the room, set upon an even taller raised stage. Evil-looking steam rose from its open lid, wafting a terrifying, hissing cloud of death towards their vicinity.

'Ah, that, presumably, is the giant vat of acid containing Strain's newly-developed necrifying agent, which is, admittedly, much bigger and more impressive-looking than I had imagined.'

'And that?' Capello pointed to just above the vat.

'True, that's a vast windowed ceiling above said stage, opening up to reveal a heavenly vista beyond, where, instead of rainclouds, there now floats a vast billowing mass of acidic vapour, just waiting to be unleashed upon an unsuspecting Stalkford. Which, to be honest, is indeed upping the ante.'

'And those?'

'You mean the terrifying visions of damned humanity partly visible within said vapour, crying out in vain to their unjust gods, pleading for a deliverance they will never see? Okay, I admit it. Strain has truly upped the ante. Meaning we could well be doomed, after all.'

'Meanwhile, Nick, look,' said Capello, forcing Nick's attention towards several figures now appearing from what was presumably a door located immediately behind the vast tank of steaming acid. In mounting horror, Nick realised the Dead-yet-Alive Rick Wakeman skeleton was already playing 'Here Comes the Bride', while employing a none-too-subtle Moog synth wave oscillator for additional atmosphere.

Among the group now appearing before them, Nick identified Strain talking with a rather confident-looking skeleton in a suit. This particular Boner was occasionally greeting other skeletons, evidently guest skeletons, while showing them where to sit.

'That must be the Best Skeleton,' Nick whispered, then caught sight of two more figures who'd been tied together, back to back.

Nick gasped. One of the bound figures wasn't a skeleton at all. It was a human being.

Roz.

'Look. There's that tall lab-coat-wearing skeleton we keep bumping into,' said Capello. 'Tied up to that woman who I presume is Roz.'

'Whom,' said Nick. 'Look, we have to get closer.' But before he could formulate a plan on how to achieve that, the unit of the

Skeletorian Guard still holding him and Capello thrust the prisoners forwards, marching both men up close to the unveiling ceremony, which was already commencing at pace above them.

'Well, that was easier than we thought,' said Capello.

'Don't write home yet, buddy. There's a reason we're being thrust up here to the front, and I don't think it's for a glass of celebratory champagne and a miniature burger.'

'No, it most likely means we're going to be dunked in that huge vat of acid ourselves, and forced to become bridesmaids for Roz in some sick parody of the male usher role.'

'I'm sorry, Capello,' said Nick. 'Ultimately, it's my sick mind doing this. I take partial responsibility.'

'Save it, Nick. Right now, we need to get out of here.'

Capello was right. Nick couldn't give up. Not here, not now. Even if it meant becoming a bridesmaid to his former lover and editor-in-arms, he had to go down fighting. Otherwise, the whole world as they knew it would soon be chock-full of necrothed Stalkfordians. Strain's skeletal Boners would rule the entire world.

'Nick!' yelled Roz, suddenly catching sight of him from her position on the raised platform. 'I knew you'd get here eventually! Did you have any trouble finding us?'

'We had a few teething problems, didn't we Capello?' said Nick, winking at Capello.

'Just a few!' laughed Capello. Then he stared, confusedly, at Roz. There was something about this woman, Capello thought to himself. Something strangely familiar . . .

'We can discuss it all later over a coffee and perhaps a Danish pastry,' said Nick, interrupting Capello's thoughts. 'Right now, we need to get you out of here.'

'And my fiancé, too,' said Roz, nodding behind her at the lab-coated Boner clamped to her back.

'Don't be crazy, Roz,' said Nick. 'That thing has to die.'

'Never, Nick!' yelled, Roz, suddenly crazed. 'He's my betrothed. He was planning to help me escape. He moved me into a different room and gathered up all my necrified toes for me, not that you or anyone else witnessed that happening, given that your sense of narrative typically focuses almost entirely on your own exploits in this fictional world you've created. We were all set to flee this place together when the Skeletorian Guard burst into our room while we were busy at it and hauled us up here.'

'She's gone insane,' said Nick to Capello. 'She's fallen in love with the very lab-coated skeleton who originally kidnapped her. It's Stockbone Syndrome. She's gone, Capello. Completely gone.'

There was no way Nick was going to rescue any skeleton, living or dead. Even if they managed to defeat Strain and get Roz and her chosen Boner safely out of here, a pet skeleton was going to be hell to look after. Admittedly, there'd be no food requirements or toilet training needed, but what if Roz and it decided to produce mini-skeletons one day? A creche-full of rattle-armed rattlers shaking each other's bones all day long?

It would be a bloody nightmare.

'I don't know if you realise this, Roz, but you're not here to marry that skeleton on your back. You're going to be permanently shacking up with Nelson Strain.'

He nodded his head over at the doctor, who was desperately trying to locate the ring his besuited Best Skeleton had lost through a hole in his lower rib cage.

'And,' continued Nick, 'that Boner you've fallen in love with is in fact the very one who kidnapped you and handed you over to the insane doctor in the first place. He's the one who enabled Strain to necrify your toes. So he's guilty as hell, Roz.'

'But he's seen the errors of his ways, Nick,' Roz said back. 'He loves me. And if that means I have to become another living skeleton to love him back in a way that doesn't cause unnecessary chafing, then I'm completely prepared to do that.'

'You think Strain will let that happen, Roz? You think he'll let you and that skeleton waltz off into the moonlight? Clicking and clacking with each other all hours of the night in any tomb or vault you elect to rise from? Wise up, Roz. You're Strain's new Bride of Bone. And he won't let anyone or anything else win your metacarpal.'

'But Strain never gave me these,' Roz said, raising one foot to reveal her brand-new pair of Seville Orange-coloured slingbacks. Nick noticed Roz's severed toes had been temporarily replaced with someone else's glued-on skeletal fragments, enabling her new shoes to remain fully on.

'That's right,' Roz declared, defiantly. 'I'm wearing some of *his* toe bones. Until we can find a way to reattach mine.'

Capello leaned across and whispered to Nick. 'I recognise that shoe, Nick. The one Roz is wearing.'

'The one shoe or both shoes? They're technically a pair.'

'Both shoes. They belonged to Strain's mother. They were among those we supplied to Strain in order to decorate his cell with her belongings.'

'I know all this, Capello. This truly is wasted wordage for our big finale. To continue that analogy we had going with each other some time back.'

'Wait, Nick. Shoes weren't the only items we sent over to Strain. There were also her old clothes, those massive corsets she loved so much, her electric chair, as I explained . . .'

'And?' prompted Nick.

'And . . . her chess set. Except it was no ordinary chess set, Nick. The individual pieces were a design we'd never seen before, and they filled over twenty boxes. Nick, I think those boxes contained . . .'

'Bones?' said Nick.

'Bones,' confirmed Capello. 'Meaning what was transported into Strain's cell was a disassembled skeleton, just waiting to be reassembled.'

It all began to click for Nick. 'Strain must have put those bones back together in his cell ...' he whispered, his brain slowly working through the hellish details of the crazed doctor's mad, malevolent scheme. 'Then added his patented reviving fluid ...'

'And the skeleton came to life right there, inside the very asylum cell he was imprisoned in,' concluded Capello.

'Then the skeleton went on an immediate rampage,' Nick added, contravening Capello's hasty conclusion, 'murdering all the asylum staff and allowing his new master to escape.'

'Except that now,' Capello countered, contravening Nick's conclusion that had contravened his previous conclusion, 'he's turned against that new master, having himself fallen in love with Roz, whom he craves as his own Bride of Bone, and whom, I have slowly realised over the course of this scene, never having glimpsed her physically prior to this moment, resembles in uncanny detail my sister-in-law-to-be ...'

'So finally, it almost adds up,' Nick said, racing against time to work out precisely what it almost added up to.

'Oh, Nick ...' said Capello. 'You don't think ... those bones ... those bones in the chess set ... Could they be?'

'Your brother's bones, Capello ...' said Nick. 'The bones of Dwayne Capello. Great, now it does all add up.'

'Can it be true, Nick? Can that lab-coated skeleton be none other than my long-lost brother, Dwayne "the Mane" Capello?'

At the sound of his name, the lab-coated skeleton strapped to Roz's back turned wildly around to face them. Miraculously – nay, supernaturally – glistening tears dropped from both eye sockets as the pathetic creature cranked opened its mandibles in a doomed effort to cry. Then discovered it couldn't, and made do with some unpleasant rattling.

'On a technical note, Capello, I would imagine Strain murdered your brother via his preferred process of necrifying the bones first, in light of Strain's previous explanatory statement that he'd only recently invented a necrifying agent that works within acid itself, which therefore wouldn't have been available to him at the time of your brother's murder. Meaning, I'm afraid, that Dwayne was probably forced to wear those pants, too.'

'These ones?' said Capello, horrified. The Speedos had been tied around his neck for later use, as had Nick's.

'Not that pair, specifically. Although who knows? In any case, this means Strain hasn't yet fully ironed out all potential plot holes concerning his preferred ending to this terrifying tale-in-action.'

'Plus, while we're at it,' Capello added. 'Doesn't acid actually destroy bones? I thought it was just kidney stones that survived. Like in famous murders.'

'Roz would be your expert there,' said Nick. 'But I wouldn't hold out for an explanation any time soon.'

'Enough!' yelled Strain, who'd now located the ring in his Best Skeleton's lower sacrum, having rolled in there unseen via the pelvic ilium. 'The specific acid I've created contains both a necrifying agent and a bone protection salve, which allows the necrified bone to remain intact at all times, even as the acid supply disintegrates the remaining matter.'

'He's on the ropes,' said Nick.

'Now back to my wedding, if you don't mind,' Strain continued, haughtily, holding up the ring in question. 'This will probably require tightening once you've been acidified,' he declared proudly to Roz, 'but it's genuine tungsten alloy, and I'm proud to say, once belonged to my mother.'

Strain turned to the unit of Skeletorian Guard currently guarding Roz and what had formerly been Dwayne Capello. 'Put them in the vat.'

'Why put Dwayne in the vat?' Nick asked. 'You said the acid would have no effect on his bones, so essentially that's an empty gesture not quite befitting a supernatural mastermind.'

'Fine. Leave Dwayne out and put Roz in by herself,' Strain snapped.

Nick winked at Capello. 'That's one for us, Capello. We've used Strain's own logic against him. Now he's fallen victim to his own plugged plot hole. With Dwayne left outside the vat to help us, we may yet stand a chance. So get ready. When I say "Now", explode into action.'

'But how, Nick?' said Capello, despairing. 'Our hands are tied, and the Skeletorian Guard still have hold of us.'

Nick glanced down at the ground and spotted a small shard of glass lying a few feet away.

'Damn,' said Nick. 'My conscious imagination has left a shard of glass close by, but Strain, who's effectively steering my unconscious mind, has ensured we can't reach it by keeping us slightly distant in this final scene, which he's dreamed up himself.'

'Look, Nick!'

Nick did so. Up on the raised platform, the royal unit of the Skeletorian Guard now severed the ropes binding Roz to what had once been Dwayne Capello, lifting her up to the top of the vat via a small stepladder, which Strain's Best Skeleton and his bony ushers had presumably erected the night before. Together, he and several other skeletons began dangling Roz over its steaming rim.

She began to shriek with terror. 'Stop this!' Roz screamed. 'I don't want to fall into this vat of acid and become a skeleton, after all. Not even for you, Dwayne,' she cried, yelling back over her shoulder to address her lover below. 'It was so perfect, the idea of running away with you and bearing your skeletons, but now that I'm staring my own acidification in the face, the very idea of being stripped down to my bare bones is making me feel physically sick.'

The thing that had once been Dwayne Capello looked up at Roz gravely, brushed away a tear it could no longer feel or produce, but which perhaps it still recalled from its former life, and gently nodded.

'Throw her in!' shrieked Strain.

'Didn't you hear me?' Roz pleaded. 'I said I don't want to be acidified!'

Nick stared up helplessly at the hellish scene. Dammit, he had to make her angry. Had to blow her damned fuse. 'You don't stand a chance, Roz!' he yelled up at her. 'Like when you try and edit one of my books. You're effectively useless as a human being!'

'Is that so, Mister Nick Steen?' roared Roz, exploding at last. 'It's your fault I'm in this pickle! It's your overblown writing that's caused this entire catastrophic state of affairs in the first place! It's your fault I'm slowly losing my own personality and acting and talking like one of your damned cardboard cut-outs!' She lashed out suddenly, hurling a couple of nearby skeletons into the vat.

'Way to go, Roz,' shouted Nick, pleased he'd got some of her own personality back for her. 'Trouble is,' he said, turning again to Capello, 'she might be able to hold them off for a little while, but there are too many of them, I fear.'

'Can't you insult her physically as well, Nick? Call her a shitting dipstick or something?'

'I could, Capello, and certainly have done frequently in the past, but it's too late now. See?'

Far above them, all signs of physical struggle had suddenly ceased. Nick looked away, unable to face the reality that Roz, once again, had been skeletonally overwhelmed.

'Dammit, it's hopeless, Nick,' Capello said. 'Our hands are literally tied. Unless . . . Unless . . . Yes, look again!'

Nick looked again. A strange transformation was now taking place on the raised stage. Before their disbelieving eyes, the skeleton that had once been Dwayne 'the Mane' Capello, now raised his de-shackled arm-bones high over his shoulder blades ... and tore off his own skull.

'Bloody hell, that's horrific,' said Nick, as the Dwayne 'the Mane' Capello skeleton poised his frame and hurled his dead head across the room towards the Boner General (esteemed leader of the Skeletorian Guard), who was currently preparing to dip Roz into the acid pot. It struck the monster full in the cranium, propelling his scattering bony frame backwards, directly into the bubbling vat.

All hell then broke loose. The guards clutching Roz immediately let go of her, turning as one to attack the now headless form of the Dwayne 'the Mane' Capello's skeleton. As Roz scrambled frantically down the ladder to save her own life, the famed unit of the Skeletorian Guard clutching Nick and Capello's arms also released their grip, advancing as one upon the headless liberator.

'Now's our chance,' yelled Nick, lying down on the floor. He rolled over to the glass shard that his own imagination had placed there, freed his bonds, then Capello's, and leaped forwards, snatching the Beretta (that had once been Capello's, but which he'd given Nick for being the better hero) from one of the departing skeletons' shank bones before opening fire at Nelson Strain.

For Nick knew, deep down, that bullets weren't going to do much damage to ossified bone, even the revived kind, but they could – and would, dammit – penetrate the forehead of a crazed lunatic, hope-fully splattering his insane brain cells over the smoothly curved surface of that gigantic vat of acid.

The shot missed.

'Damn,' he said. 'I forgot to adjust for headwind.'

'Tell me about it,' yelled Capello, then held out his hand. 'Hand it to me, Nick! I can nail the bastard!'

'No, Capello, it's my gun now.'

'Dammit, Nick, he killed my brother! Let me plug the sonofabitch.'

Capello had a point, Nick guessed. It was only right to let Capello wreak personal vengeance, and yet he'd won this gun from Capello fair and square.

It was his Beretta now.

'Please, Nick,' Capello pleaded. A tear dropped from his eye. 'Look,' he said, his voice betraying a deep, emotional pain that made it croak as he spoke. 'I know I'm not real ... I realise that now ... I know I'm simply a creation of your subconscious mind. I know my life has been a sham, Nick. A total fiction. But please, please let me do this one thing, to prove to myself that I once *was*. Let me die, Nick. Let me die ... as a man.'

Nick choked back a tear, not wanting to show Capello how much more this thing was hurting him. It was his mind causing all this, after all. It was Nick's responsibility, ultimately. Nick's tale. Nick's tragedy. And Nick must now shoulder that weight himself. Alone.

But maybe he should spare Capello the worst.

'Sure,' he said, at last. Then bravely, stoically, selflessly, handed the Beretta back to Capello, the second-most heroic man in the room. Third if you counted Capello's skeletal brother, Dwayne, who was also more heroic.

'Thanks, Nick. I know this must hurt you, too ...'

'I'll get there,' Nick said, his voice a brave whisper. Then smiled. 'God speed, paesano.'

Capello nodded, exchanging a final deep look with Nick. 'Now get the hell out of here!' Capello yelled suddenly, immediately after the deep look. 'Me and Dwayne will hold these bastards off while you two escape.'

'Dwayne *and I*.'

'Sorry. Thanks, Nick. Though it is hard for a man to die alongside his brother.'

There were harder ways, though, Nick reflected. If you and your brother were spiralling to the ground in a flaming hot-air balloon, say, or choking on pretzels after daring each other to scoff as many in one minute as possible, or in a pointless blood feud where you ended up shooting each other dead at a family barbecue in front of the children.

Yeah, there were harder ways than just dying beside each other. But sure, let Capello have his moment. He was about to expire, after all.

As Nick nodded at his friend one final time, the Rick Wakeman skeleton ennobling the moment further with a suitably melancholic overture, Capello turned, white hot with years of vengeful rage, and aimed Nick's Beretta at Strain's balls.

With a scream of defiance that was unnervingly high-pitched, he blasted six full rounds of bullets into Strain's protesting body ('You murdering bastard!' it shouted), from the groin upwards, each shot propelling Strain's blasted body further up the side of the vast acid vat, splaying his innards over and across the metallic tank as his severed body rose continually, sliding upwards with the force of each slug, until, as the sixth bullet finally blew the doctor's brains into a red cloud of spraying bonce matter, the mad junior pathologist was thrust upwards one final time.

No longer supported from behind, Strain's body flew backwards over the rim, landing directly in the hissing pool of steaming acid. As his body sank beneath the furious, bubbling waves, already melting away as the grim concoction immediately went to work, Capello turned back to Nick, handing him the Beretta.

'This won't work on those skeletons,' he said. 'So take it, Nick, and remember me.'

'I won't forget you, Capello,' said Nick.

'Or Dwayne.'

'Or Dwayne.'

'Or Dwayne's murdered bride-to-be, Brenda.'

'I did write all this, Capello. No, I won't forget them.'

'Go, now! Go, go, go!' Capello screamed suddenly, realising they were both wasting time, and hurled himself headlong back into the fray.

But Nick didn't go. Not yet. Instead, he turned to watch the thing play out. Beyond him, Dwayne's headless frame was struggling to fend off the horde of Boners, enraged by the lone rebel among them who'd dared to wrench off his own cranium and fling it at their exalted leader.

Then Capello dived hard into the melee, wrenching bone from bone, de-skulling and de-femurising as he went, in a crazed effort to rescue his besieged brother. Nick watched in horror, realising there was little he could do. That it was only a matter of time before Dwayne and Cliff were both overwhelmed. Suddenly, he felt some-one seize him by the wrist.

It was Roz.

'Please, Nick!' she yelled. 'Do something to save him. Do some-thing to save Dwayne!'

But Nick knew there was nothing he could do. Both her favourite skeleton and his brother were doomed.

'Look, Roz, you never were Dwayne's betrothed,' Nick said, real-ising that stark emotional cruelty was the only way to shake her out of her madness. 'He thinks you look like his old flame, Brenda. He was merely using you as a substitute. He was on the rebound, Roz. It's his own dead Bride of Bone he loves. Not you!'

'The *bastard*!' Roz yelled, shoving her middle finger up at her former paramour. Not that Dwayne could see it without his skull.

'This way, Nick. Run!' she cried, sprinting off into the shadows.

As she disappeared through the far door that led back into the changing facilities, Nick looked back one last time to see if there was

197

anything at all he could do for Capello (who was currently, like his brother Dwayne, in the process of being deboned). He saw something grey and round roll across the floor towards his feet, having dropped downwards from one of the stepladder rungs.

Dwayne Capello's skull.

Nick picked it up, staring into its dark and empty eye sockets. All too briefly, and perhaps it was only a mere trick of the light, or Nick's escaped imagination playing one final card, Nick thought he glimpsed a twinkle of distant starlight.

A spark of understanding . . .

Then he turned and hurled the skull back in the direction of the skeletal fray, where an alert and death-defying Capello caught it in his remaining hand, turned, nodded meaningfully at Nick, and set it back upon the top of his brother's headless spine.

Fully revived, the Capello brothers gave one final joint battle-cry (though Dwayne's was essentially still a rattle) and commenced fighting together like warriors, to the death.

There was nothing more Nick could do. Bar helping them.

So he ran.

★

Outside, he found Roz drowning in the Stalkford Mire and heroically dragged her out.

'That's two lives you owe me,' Nick said, then turned to open fire on the huge werewolf leaping at Roz's throat from one of the surrounding hills. It sprawled backwards across the heath, slowly turning into the local lycanthropy expert from *The Howling Fur*.

'Three,' he said to Roz. 'Good job I loaded this with silver bullets from that box of silver bullets that was sitting on that table labelled "Silver Bullets" inside the "Silver Bullet" room I just entered. Whoever had been in that lab last had been developing ways of employing silver bullets to combat the spread of lycanthropic disease.'

Roz was busy examining her feet. She'd have some trouble walking back across the moor in those new shoes, Nick realised. Even with a batch of Dwayne's glued-on toes to assist.

'*My* toes are in here, Nick,' she said, rattling a small tin of what looked like boiled travelling mints her ex-skeleton had gathered up for her, although no one except Roz had witnessed that happen. 'I want his off my feet right now.'

'No time for hysterics, Roz,' Nick said. 'We have to get out of here first. Capello can only hold off those Boners for so long. Let me run to his car over there, carrying you in my arms, seeing as you can't walk normally, as usual.'

Despite heavy protestations, Nick picked up Roz and carried her heroically over the stretch of sodden moorland, before dumping her in the back of Capello's Peugeot. Then he got in himself and keyed the engine.

The battery was dead.

'Capello, you fool,' Nick shouted, switching off the hazards his friend had left on.

'Look out, Nick!' Roz yelled in terror, pointing at something she'd just seen through the windscreen. Nick stared out through the same windscreen (by this time, the rain had pretty much stopped, so it was clearer than before, despite being out of wiper fluid) and saw, pouring through the abandoned facility's gates, Nelson Strain's unleashed horde of seething, rattling Boners.

'Then it's over for us too, Roz,' said Nick, stifling a sense of mounting horror. 'We're dead ducks. As is Stalkford. Humanity is doomed. My mind ... My damned mind has won ...'

They looked out one final time together at the approaching army of skeletal Boners, preparing to meet their end as one. An end Nick's own mind had created in a moment of madness when he'd first decided to purchase that cursed typewriter. They watched, helplessly, as one by one, the living, breathing army of raging Boners advanced inexorably towards them . . .

. . . then stumbled, flailing, and sank below the sodden, unseen surface of Stalkford Mire.

Where they will remain, Nick vowed, breathing a deep sigh of relief. Until they rise up again next month, when the swamp gets drained by the authorities in order to unearth the suspected remains of Strain's numerous missing victims.

But that was a different sequel, Nick mused. He keyed the car's engine, which now worked, Nick having located a spare battery in the boot, put there by his sub-conscious.

'Come on, Roz. Let's go kill something else.'

'Sure, Nick,' Roz said, yawning and nestling her cheek against her precious box of severed digits. 'Just don't let any hellish demon fly off with my toes in its beak before I can find a way to graft them back on!'

'Relax,' Nick said, reaching for the flame-thrower in the back seat. 'I can solder them back together with this.'

But Roz was already asleep.

★

The vat of acid was calm now. As if nothing had ever disturbed its once frothing, steaming mass. Protruding across the tank's rim, from a position on the top rung of the neighbouring stepladder, lay a small, upturned vessel. A glass phial, now empty, from which a measure of liquified content had recently been spilled.

Below, in the stillness of the becalmed acid, a greening pool of tiny bubbles finally broke the surface. A cloud of greying fragments followed, floating like scattered pieces of a dissolving bath bomb. One by one, these shapeless, gently-bobbing shreds of parted bone matter began to wriggle, propelling themselves steadily through the softly lapping fluid in a life–or–death struggle to locate each other. At length, the bubbles began to thicken, as larger parts of bone began to break the surface, each piece slowly gathering, forming itself with the others into the vague semblance of a doctor's face.

Which began to smile ...*

* i.e. Nelson Strain was coming back to life. As a skeleton, probably (and ironically, given the tale you've just read, where we thought he was a skeleton to start with, but in fact wasn't, but *would* be now), although there's no immediate sequel planned.

THE DARK FRACTIONS

CHAPTER ONE

Nick Steen was hiding from himself.

Through the window overlooking the cabin's outer porch, he caught the faint hint of a russet-leather blouson amid the swaying cornstalks. Then the cloud overhead passed by, taking with it the patch of shade tanning this remote and sun-drenched wheat field of rural Cornfall, where Nick was now a prisoner.

Just a shadow.

Nick poured himself another whisky, then hurled it at the wall.

No way was he getting drunk on *his* watch.

You will, Nicky Boy. You will. Just wait.

'Make me,' Nick said, aloud.

Oh, I will, Nicky Boy. I will. Just continue to wait.

He ignored his internal voice, if that's what it still was, poured himself a double and hurled that at the wall as well.

You'll drink eventually, Nick. Every damned drop.

'Including those I've just thrown?' drawled Nick sarcastically.

Sure. You'll stagger over to that wall, soil yourself halfway, then lick the timber dry.

Dammit, the voice seemed to know his innermost thoughts. Nick drew the revolver from his holster, ejected the barrel and counted his remaining bullets.

Four left. He'd missed his head two times already. No way could he risk another shot. He'd have to wait until he was finally face to face with himself.

And he didn't mean looking in a mirror.

He'd first suspected what was happening two months back, when a waiter at Stalkford's Spice Palace had refused to serve Nick extra portions, warning him it was perilous to consume multiple servings of prawn masala four days running, even though Nick had only reordered the same dish in immediate succession on two consecutive evenings.

Then there'd been that market trader who'd chided Nick publicly for querying the herd provenance of a taupe cowhide blouson at his local leather wagon. Nick hadn't had a clue what the man was talking about, his near-permanent vestment of choice being a black tweed jacket with matching roll-neck sweater to reflect both his advancing age and all-towering intellect. Then the man had told him about the *other* Nick.

The Bad Nick.

The *Dark* Nick.

That's when he'd finally understood.

Nick Steen was haunting *himself.*

Top marks, Nick, old buddy. And I know exactly where you are. Hiding inside that cabin, right?

'Come on in and find out!' yelled Nick, snapping the revolver barrel shut.

Oh, I will, Nicky Boy. I will. And when I do, maybe we'll both *have ourselves a little drink. Maybe we'll sit and drink and chat together about your* book ...

'Never!' Nick bellowed, releasing a sudden burst of pent-up rage.

Hell, he'd caused all this, hadn't he? This bleeding of his own crazed mind into the very substance of the known universe? Stalkford was warping on Nick Steen's watch. Against his will (and without his express permission), Nick's extensive bibliography of best-selling horror tomes were now coming to life around him, ever since the day he'd inadvertently opened a portal to a cosmic demonic realm, having sexed himself raw on the teasing sprongs of a cursed but sentient typewriter.

Now all the devious, sadistic imps of Nick's subconscious mind were escaping, currently marauding through inner and outer Stalkford via his bursting neurons. Every book Nick had ever penned was suddenly real, emerging from the dark, swirling ocean of his subconscious imaginings. Incarnating themselves into physical form, turning the entire county into a living, breathing Nick Steen chiller.

And now the most terrifying book of them all had woken up.

From the blackest corner of Nick's mind, the murkiest depths of his doom-ridden soul, had risen the Dark Fraction, a petrifying figure from Nick's unreleased psychological chiller, *The Dark Fraction*. A fictional writer's demonic fictional alter-ego, hellbent on avenging itself against its creator's perceived misdemeanours, now transformed from the pages of Nick's unsold novel into a living manifestation of his very own destructive, subconscious authorial urges.

Now, wherever Nick travelled, his Dark Fraction was close by. Tailing him. *Taunting* him. Telegraphing insulting messages to various hotel lobbies. Warning Nick it was closing in, while at the same time notifying staff members about the author's embarrassing personal habits. Vile traits of private behaviour only Nick himself could have been aware of. Like picking his blisters after a long day and warming both hands in his underpants at night.

A demon from Nick Steen's own particular brand of id.

Nick poured himself another glass. Damn, if only Clackett had agreed to publish his earlier masterpiece, perhaps none of this would be happening ...

He edged the drink closer to his lips. Maybe just *one* ...

That's it, Nicky Boy. Drink up, buddy, and let's talk about the book.

'Leave me alone!' yelled Nick, hurling that one at the wall as well. Then immediately poured another.

He grit his teeth, forcing down the fresh pang of anguish rising in his soul. Sure, he could drink. That was easy. He could neck it back, howling into the void about abandoning Roz in Stalkford, leaving her to face the unleashed horrors alone while assuring her he was off fighting demons, when all along he was simply going behind her back to find a new publisher, but deep down, Nick didn't feel *remotely* bad about that.

For Roz above all others had been the one who'd wanted every single printed copy of *The Dark Fraction* pulped before it even hit the shelves. It was *her* fault that Nick had left her to face near-certain death in order to seek alternative representation for his spurned masterpiece. And if Nick felt remotely bad about anything at all, it was that this search had been cut prematurely short. Not just by those he'd approached, who'd all rejected the novel as well, but by the very monster whose literary life Nick was ironically attempting to save from destruction.

Even if *it*, evidently, wished to destroy *him*.

Nick looked through the window again, narrowing his eyes against the sun's relentless glare as he scanned the distant field of windblown grains. As far as he could make out, there was nothing at all moving out there in the cornstalks.

But I'm close, Nick. Watching you. Stalking you.

'Good one,' said Nick. He had to admit, that pun on 'cornstalk' was funny. Hell, maybe this entire thing was just a joke. Maybe it wasn't his demonic alter-ego talking to him in his head, after all. Maybe it wasn't a malevolent spirit embodying his worst moral failings, attempting to stir up Nick's feelings of repressed guilt (which were luckily non-existent). Feeding off Nick's unfathomable, innermost secrets (nothing actionable, as far as he knew), having initiated squatter's rights in the dark core of his cerebellum. Maybe this *was* just Nick Steen's own internal voice at its wittiest, pithiest best.

I see you, Nicky Boy. I see you at the window. I'm coming in real soon.

Nick shuddered. Who was he kidding? The thing was real, alright.

That's right, Nicky Boy. Your sins finally found you out.

Nick sensed a strange internal darkness swelling deep within, which he suspected wasn't entirely down to the prawn masala, and forced himself to look through the window again. He gazed out at the field beyond the cabin, shielding his eyes from the sun's relentless, blinding rays in an effort to penetrate the stalks of swaying corn.

Was he feeling a vague sense of guilt, after all? Surely not. Nick hadn't felt a shred of remorse his entire life. Unless it was that matter of ousting his wife and child from their family home via a team of bailiffs. But he'd paid the company eventually, hadn't he?

Yet it was out there, dammit. Whatever it was, *wherever* it was, it was *out there*.

And getting closer all the time, buddy. So close. So damned *close ... That's really, really close, in case you were wondering.*

Nick heard a rustling sound and spun his head too late to see anything more than a blurred shape dart from the front edge of the surrounding field, leaving behind it a distinct and unnatural tunnel of *flattened corn ...*

Then a spring of footsteps pattered across the pine boards outside, ending abruptly at the front door of Nick's cabin.

Cautiously, Nick stepped back from the window. He mustn't make a sound. Although, given his Dark Fraction knew full well he was in here, sound probably wasn't a massive issue. Assuming a defensive position several feet behind the front door, Nick raised his revolver, aiming it just left of and slightly above the door's handle. Then waited ...

And waited ...

Until ...

Finally ...

There was a knock.

Then another knock.

And another knock.

Three knocks in total.

Each knock slowly spaced from the preceding knock (except for the initial knock, which itself had no antecedent knock).

The sum of all these three knocks created an eerie effect.

Making the tension completely unbearable.

He had to wait, dammit. Had to *see* it. His own Dark Fraction ...

The tension and suspense, meanwhile, increased exponentially.

Nick waited a while longer. Waited to face his deepest, Darkest Part.

That's a better title, by the way ...

'Balls, it is!' Nick yelled, opening fire.

The revolver blazed four times, splintering the wooden door and drilling three ragged holes through the timber (the first shot missed, taking out the hall light instead, but that's not important here).

As smoky carbonite billowed ceiling-ward, something heavy outside collapsed to the ground.

'Got you, *buddy*,' Nick barked, yanking open the door.

It was the postman.

Nick prised an envelope from the man's already-stiffening palm. Though self-addressed in his own handwriting, as requested by all publishers he'd approached, this particular missive *wasn't* a rejection letter.

It was *worse*.

CHAPTER TWO

'Open up, Roz!' Nick yelled, clasping the letter in one hand while hammering on Roz's front door with the other. 'It's me. Nick!'

'Is it?' a terrified Roz yelled from behind her security chain. 'It wasn't Nick Steen at Clackett Publishing last night. Though they said he looked *exactly* like you.'

'*Exactly*, Roz?'

'Well, apart from the russet-leather blouson, military bandana and horseshoe moustache. And the tiger claw scar running down one cheek, knuckles tattooed with the words "hate" and "hate", and a six-a-day Bourbon habit you don't have. Not to mention muscles they never knew you possessed, Nick. And according to Beryl in the accounts department, a not-altogether-displeasingly-manly body scent.'

'That was my Dark Fraction, Roz. From my novel *The Dark Fraction*, remember?'

'Wait, Nick, I hadn't finished. Plus a smoothly gravelled vocal timbre, tightly squeezed leather trousers and a throbbing custom Honda.'

'Did he mention hitching a ride to Hell with him at any point?'

'Apparently he did, Nick. Once he's finished hunting you down and destroying every last fibre of your being, they said.'

'That's what I want to talk to you about.'

Nick pressed his palm more firmly against Roz's door, but the security chain held.

'Not so fast, Nick,' she said, motioning him back from the doorstep. 'That was *last* night. What about the night before? The Nick Steen who dropped by Clackett's that evening looked just like you, too, apparently. Only they say *that* Nick was wearing nothing but underpants and a pair of decorative wrestling boots.'

'Scarlet zigzags on banana yellow?'

'That's right, Nick. How did you know?'

Nick grimaced inwardly. It was the demonic entity from his proposed sequel; a 1940s matinee wrestler version of the writer's subconsciously wrought darker self's darker self. So they were *all* coming to life now, were they?

'It's my demonic fictional alter-ego's demonic fictional alter-ego, Roz. Let me in and I'll explain.'

'How do I know you're not one of *them*?'

Nick thought for a moment. 'Ask me something only the real Nick Steen would know.'

'Okay,' said Roz, casting her mind back. 'Where were we dining when I first agreed to publish you?'

'Haven't a clue.'

'Oh,' replied Roz, a trace of sadness in her voice. 'Then tell me, what was the welcoming gift I gave you?'

'I don't remember it, Roz. Ask me something else.'

'It *is* you, Nick,' Roz sighed, opening the door.

Nick strode straight past her into the lounge and claimed the main armchair by the fire. Then he handed her his crumpled letter. 'Read it, Roz.'

She took it from his hand and read.

THE DARK FRACTIONS

Nick Steen,
Various Hiding Places,
Stalkford

Nicky Boy,

It's me. Or should I say 'you'? Wrong. It's 'us', buddy. The dark parts of your psyche. The Dark Fractions (although The Dark Parts *is a stronger series title).*

There's a rumour going around that the book you wrote, the one introducing the entire concept of 'us', isn't going to be published, after all. Rumour is, you're set to pulp 'us'. Well, 'us' don't like that, Nicky Boy. 'Us' think otherwise. 'Us' totally disagree. So 'us''re coming to get you, buddy.

Guess you'd best publish 'us', after all. Or 'us''ll have no choice but to avenge 'us'.

With hate from 'us' all,
Your Dark Parts
(aka The Dark Fractions) (again, we'd scrap that name)

Various Infernal Realms,
Ninth Circle of Hell,
Assorted Hells

'They're coming to life, Roz,' said Nick. 'All of them. Every demonic fictional alter-ego in the proposed series. The one in the banana-coloured boots is from my first sequel.'

'You mean *The Darker Fraction*?'

'No, Roz. As I explained to you back then, a better title would be *The Dark Fractions*.'

'I still think *The Darker Fraction* is superior, Nick.'

'Except I sent you a *series* proposal, Roz. Meaning that if you name the first sequel *The Darker Fraction*, you're then faced with calling book three *The Even Darker Fraction*. Whereas if you name the series itself *The Dark Fractions*, you can then distinguish all additional titles thus: *The Dark Fractions Book Two: The Dark Quarter*, *The Dark Fractions Book Three: The Dark Eighth*, et cetera.'

'But then what about that first book, Nick? Would it still be named only *The Dark Fraction*, or does it make better sense to call it *The Dark Fractions Book One: The Dark Fraction, aka The Dark Fifty Per Cent* from the get-go?'

'Like I explained, Roz, you can alter its official title on a reprint to bring it into line with the rest of the series, while creating at the same time a rare first edition of vastly inflated value for the second-hand collectors' market. Incidentally, that *Fifty Per Cent* sub-subtitle you keep suggesting is unworkable. That would mean calling the second book *The Dark Fractions Book Two: The Even Darker Fractions, aka The Dark Twenty-five Per Cent* and *The Dark Fractions Book Three: The Increasingly Darker Fractions, aka The Dark Twelve and a Half Per Cent*, surely?'

'I always liked *The Dark Third*.'

'I did too, Roz, but Tony Clackett didn't understand the word "throppelganger", remember?'

'Well, it's all immaterial now, Nick. Because your series proposal was roundly rejected by everyone at Clackett, and the initial book pulled from sale at the last minute due to "terminal narrative confusion". Quite simply, the book has to go. And frankly, I think our refusal to distribute the initial printing actually protects *your* reputation.'

'They're trying to *kill* me, Roz.'

'Oh come on, Nick, they can't *all* be after you. After all, shouldn't one of them be haunting the fictional novelist featured in your original book? And shouldn't the rest instead be haunting their own corresponding Dark Fraction or Fractions?'

'Except that they wouldn't be haunting their own corresponding Dark Fractions, would they, Roz? Their own corresponding Dark Fractions would be haunting *them*.'

'No, Nick. Technically, they'd be doing *both*. Haunting one Dark Fraction while also being haunted by their own corresponding Dark

Fraction. Like I said before, we rejected your series proposal for a reason. Numerous reasons, in fact.'

'But if you'd bothered to read that proposal correctly, Roz, you'd realise that the *Dark Fractions* series features a troubled pulp-horror author named Gareth Meringue,* who was to all intents and purposes a thinly veiled semi-autobiographical portrait of myself.'

'Another reason I disliked the book, if you *must* know.'

'I see, Roz,' intoned Nick, stunned at her candid aggression. Roz *never* spoke to him like this. Only once, after he'd used her toilet for the first time. But something was different now, he sensed. Something had *changed*.

'Well, Roz,' he continued. 'They've murdered the incarnated form of Gareth Meringue already, dicing him into a thousand shreds and adding the remains to a large cauldron of prawn masala I narrowly avoided additional helpings of. I imagine they've moved on to me now, as I'm essentially the chief orchestrator of this entire narrative concept. And as chief orchestrator of this entire narrative concept, I'm demanding that you distribute my original book as planned, right now, and save my life.'

'Publish and be undamned, you mean? Sorry, Nick. That's out of the question. Plus, the rumour is that you've actually been gallivanting around Stalkford, trying to source a new publisher to get the series commissioned *elsewhere*.'

'Touché, Roz,' Nick replied, tartly. '*Touché*. But so what if I have? Hell, if you guys are so concerned about recouping your investment, I'll get my *new* guys to buy you out.'

'Sure. In which case, that's absolutely fine, Nick. Who's the publisher?'

Screw Roz and her damned bluff-calling.

'Well, I've yet to get confirmation on the figures, Roz. Or a meeting. But as soon as they answer my letter . . .'

'Please, Nick. No one's interested in it, as you well know.'

---

* Heh heh heh. Keep up, traveller.

'Then you're going to sign off all existing copies of *The Dark Fraction* for immediate pulping against my express wishes, are you, Roz? Leading to a deep and irredeemable rift in our creative partnership, plus my death? Is that correct?'

'I'm afraid so, Nick. My priority is to protect Clackett's interests and *your* writing reputation. To do that, all existing copies of *The Dark Fraction* must be destroyed. Now, I have every faith you can see off the threat of these real-life Dark Fractions without assistance from me. After all, you've destroyed every other horrific manifestation of your inner id invading our reality thus far. Plus, it looks as if they'll all die anyway once the books get pulped. Therefore, why don't you go off and do what you do best, and leave me to do what *I* do best? Which is making sure the books you *do* put out are in tip-top reading condition.'

Nick rose from his chair. 'I have a feeling it's your editing reputation you're concerned about *most*, Roz.'

She looked away, embarrassed.

Nick smiled at her coldly. 'I guess I'll be facing my *real* Dark Fractions alone, then. Seeing as you've got your panties in a right royal scrunch this morning.'

'I guess so, Nick,' Roz replied, staring out of her lounge window at her distant privet hedge.

Nick nodded slowly to himself and headed over to the door. Then turned back again. 'Where are my books at the moment? The ones scheduled to be pulped.'

'Somewhere you'll never find them, Nick. Believe me, it's for the best. And like I said, as soon as they're pulped, those Dark Fractions of yours will disappear. Every single one of them will be dead.'

'And what about *me*, Roz?' said Nick, staring at her intently. 'Will I be dead, too?'

'In all likelihood, yes, Nick. I would imagine so.'

★

Nick slammed hard on the accelerator of his Honda Civic and sped out of both Roz's road and her life, immediately braking hard to negotiate a cul-de-sac, before roaring back round again, passing Roz's house a second time and speeding off in the direction he actually needed to go in. As his car hurtled towards the approaching junction at the end of the road, Nick heard a vague snicker of laughter through his open window and glimpsed, in his rear-view mirror, a puff of what looked like rising cigarette smoke circling over Roz's privet hedge.

Probably my tyres, thought Nick. I tore that cul-de-sac a new one.

Yeah, lightning-fast, Nicky Boy. Practically burned a hole through the Neighbourhood Watch sign.

His internal voice again. Or *was* it?

For your information, buddy, I took that curve at ten or over.

Bullshit, amigo. Four m. p. h., tops.

Ten, compadre. Probably eight.

Seven. Possibly six.

Look, I don't have room for two internal voices. It completely confuses things.

Just like Roz said . . .

'Get the hell out of my head!' Nick yelled, aloud.

Sure thing, buddy. You keep talking loudly to yourself. It's only madness, *after all. Just some damned voices in your head.*

'Begone!'

You're not crazy . . .

'I said, get the hell out of my head!'

Not crazy at all . . .

'Up yours!' yelled Nick, pausing at the junction for an approaching cyclist to pass by. The guy flipped him the bird, so Nick subsequently roared past at a full twenty or more, before reaching the main road and shifting gears, maxing out the full thirty down the main high street while narrowly avoiding the bus lane, which wasn't properly indicated from the side street he'd just left.

'No way am I going mad,' Nick yelled through his window at passers-by. 'Not on *my* watch, dammit!'

Jeez, what was happening to him? Was his *Dark Fractions* series proposal really *so* confusing? Roz certainly thought so. But what was it about *this* particular series that had rattled his erstwhile editor so badly? Was it because *The Dark Fraction* itself was Nick's most personal work to date? Did the book and his proposed series perhaps reveal too much about his own internal demons and questionable bathroom habits? Maybe Roz found that uncomfortable – exposing the raw flesh-wounds of Nick Steen's emotional innards.

But it was no excuse for condemning his unsold series to an industrial pulping mill, albeit a series that required a degree of book-keeping and mathematical prowess beyond the natural arithmetic ability of most readers. Nick, too, if he was honest. Which he wasn't.

Hell, the *Dark Fractions* books were his *masterpieces*, though, easily matching the quality of all his other masterpieces. Sure, if Roz destroyed them in one fell swoop, it might get *these* Dark Fractions off his back, but at what cost to humanity? The loss of such timeless works of literary art would be nothing short of a tragedy inflicted on the entirety of Mankind.

It looked as if Nick was going to have to fight this battle with himselves alone. A group of demons hellbent on catching up with Nick Steen and editing *him* out of existence. Dammit, for once in his life, he needed guidance. Direction. Someone to chew the cud with and work a way out of this whole damned mess. He was all out of angles, dammit.

He needed Bruford.

Nick swerved right after indicating in good time and accelerated back up to thirty, slowing gradually while passing some double-parked cars, then gently increased his speed back up to thirty again as he approached the side road leading towards Stalkford's oldest aquarium.

Bruford would know what to do.

As the glass-panelled water-zoo came into view, Nick braked hard, kicking the pedal repeatedly as the Civic continued to roll forwards despite him, aquaplaning down a road flooded by what was left of the aquarium's tanks. He looked up at the building in horror. Jets of water streamed at all angles from its smashed and shattered panes . . .

Nick switched off the engine as the car finally ground to a halt, bobbing gently in the flowing current. As he stepped out, rays of sunlight dappled the brightly coloured scales of dying fish on the pavement either side of him. Ahead, the aquarium was a broken wreck. Each pane of glass in the building, every single tank, had been smashed to pieces. Nick noticed more of the ejected marine life struggling amid cascading torrents of water flowing rapidly down the street towards waiting drains and gutters. He watched the stricken and stranded as they gasped their way to a waterless grave.

'Jesus . . .' Nick said in quiet panic, hoping to God that Bruford was still alive.

Who'd *done* this? Who'd gone around every glass tank in Stalkford Aquarium and pounded every pane loose with a four-foot sledgehammer? *Including* the outer glass panelling, presumably to rub metaphorical salt in their initial wound? (Metaphorically speaking, obviously, as real salt would have been dissolved by the escaping water, thus having no effect whatsoever – in point of fact, the antiseptic qualities of the salt may even have aided some of the ailing fish.)

Dammit, was Bruford already *dead*?

A dark suspicion began to form in Nick's mind. About whom *exactly* might have committed this abhorrent fish-based atrocity. And as he made his way through the aquarium's outer gate, removing a flapping turbot from one of the fence spikes, Nick was forced to

219

acknowledge that, if this really *was* the work of his Dark Fractions, ultimately, Nick had caused this *himself.* As chief orchestrator of this entire narrative concept, *Nick* had massacred Stalkford's fish.

Nick had killed Bruford.

Then an unfamiliar voice spoke to him.

'Sluice me, Nick. For God's sake, sluice me.'

CHAPTER THREE

It seemed to come from deep inside Nick's mind (like his two internal voices) and at first he was convinced he'd been psychologically possessed by the departed spirit of Liam Neeson, who presumably had just this moment expired and re-entered Nick's mind in an effort to maintain some form of professional presence on this mortal plane (in all likelihood to secure additional voiceover work, being easily the most profitable avenue of employment for a professional actor in terms of hourly performance rate plus usage residuals). It certainly sounded like him. Yet why the freshly undead Irish actor would wish to be 'sluiced' upon an inaugural psychic melding was unclear.

'What do you mean by "sluiced"?' asked Nick aloud, desperate to get this over with so he could find out what the hell had happened to Bruford.

'*I need sluicing, Nick,*' said the voice that, again, was just like Liam Neeson's.

'Listen, Liam,' Nick replied, forcefully. 'I'm not about to enter any brain-based partnership contract without professional advice from a specialist solicitor and reliable witness signature. Besides which, I already have two internal voices roosting inside my head. My own internal voice, plus another internal voice that sounds like me but isn't me, although technically he's an aspect of me, as he's an alternate version of me – so, as you can see, things are already getting quite confusing. I appreciate the offer, but I'm afraid the internal voice thing is getting too complex, like Roz did point out, and therefore I'm going to have to decline your interest in my headspace and get on with investigating what's happened to Bruford.'

'*Wait, Nick. It's me. I am Bruford.*'

Nick shook himself, trying to make sense of what he'd just heard. Bruford didn't sound like *that*. Bruford's voice was more like Roger Daltrey's. Not Liam Neeson's.

'*It's a result of this recent calamity, Nick. The scene of aquatic devastation you see around you. I'm so close to death that I've been forced to shed my vocal skin in order to convey an increased sense of urgency via altered vocal inflections. It's a survival instinct.*'

'So now you sound like Liam Neeson in my head, as opposed to Roger Daltrey?'

'*That's correct, Nick.*'

Roger Daltrey sounded better, Nicky Boy.

'*Forgive me intruding, Nick, but is that intrusive and insulting comment from the other internal voice you mentioned?*'

'That's correct, Bruford. My Dark Fraction.'

'*Then permit me to fade him out, Nick.*'

'You can do that?'

'*It's one of the few psychic skills I still possess.*'

No, wait. You can't do th—

'*There. That's better. Now sluice me.*'

'Where are you?'

'*Round the back of the aquarium, Nick, expiring in the scrapyard they don't like anyone knowing about. There's a broom sticking conveniently out of one of the dustbins, with which you can commence my sluicing.*'

Wasting no time, Nick pressed himself past the iron gates and sloshed his way around the side of the smashed building. Why had they attacked his childhood friend? What could the Dark Fractions possibly hope to gain from destroying Nick's loyal sea-mammal pal, Bruford the psychic dugong?

'*Nick, I have about one minute of life left. No more will I feel the cool wash of oxygenated water in a cramped, irregularly sanitised tank. No more will I bob repeatedly in a murky slick of my own greased effluence as members of the public stare in at me, laughing at my comically swollen proboscis. Please sluice me.*'

'I'm coming, Bruford!' yelled Nick as he burst into the scrapyard at the rear of the aquarium.

'*The broom, Nick. Quick.*'

'Which broom, Bruford? There are two brooms.'

'*The densely packed corn-husk-fibre model with additional tufts of finest horsehair. That broom.*'

Nick grabbed Bruford's preferred broom and cast his eyes over the pathetic scene before him. Clearly, this yard was concealed from the public eye for good reason. A neglected dead zone of spent marine life, past-its-prime seafood and unsold aquatic-themed plastic goods.

Nick pored through the scattered detritus, hurling aside layers of rusted tank piping and sun-faded pond furniture, but there was as yet no sign of his old friend.

'*Can you see me yet, Nick?*'

'No, Bruford, I can't see a bloody thing.'

'*Focus on that large round object, eight feet to your right.*'

'The beached whale?'

'*That's no whale, Nick. It's a dugong.*'

'Then it's a *fat* dugong.'

'*I'd like to see a* thin *dugong. Anyway, that's me, Nick. I've been bloating in the sun for six hours now, and am likely to emit a cloud of extreme toxic gas if I burst. Please hurry.*'

Nick made his way over to the vast mound of swollen blubber he'd prefer to have avoided. Now he was up close to it, he could see that it was indeed his best friend, Bruford, the telepathic dugong he'd known since childhood. Yet, despite a loyal camaraderie lasting decades, Nick had always resolutely avoided writing about Bruford in his fiction. A psychic dugong was a being so strange, so wild, so goddamned *out there*, that the primitive mind of Man was in no position to accept what society might deem an obscene aquatic aberration, albeit one ultimately signalling a glorious future for both species; a world beyond current human ken, where Man and Dugong could splash forwards, hand in flipper, towards a brighter and moister future.

Grasping the broom in one hand, Nick lost no time in sluicing water up over his dying friend's dry and blistered exterior.

'*Aah, that's better, Nick. And behind my neck, please.*'

Nick sluiced more water behind the dugong's neck.

'*Now my flippers.*'

Nick sluiced Bruford's flippers.

'*And now my love cudgel.*'

'I'm not doing your love cudgel.'

'*Nick, I'm the last of my kind. If I am to survive this flood and seek out a lady dugong, I will need my love cudgel in full working order. Or there will be no more psychic dugongs for the rest of eternity.*'

Nick sighed and sluiced the dugong's love cudgel.

'*Oh, sweet mama . . .*'

Averting his eyes, Nick took in more of the devastation around him, calculating from the number of nearby expiring fish still flapping about in their death throes that his Dark Fractions had hit the place around ten or fifteen minutes ago. So they'd guessed correctly that Nick would be out here, consulting with his psychic dugong. And, he realised grimly, if he hadn't been held up by Roz's damned cul-de-sac, he might well have found himself directly in the firing line.

Hell, they were getting *closer.*

'*They came for you, Nick.*'

'I know.'

'*They destroyed the whole place. Then tortured me.*'

Nick shook his head in disgust. 'Those bastards. To think they'd have tortured *me*, too.'

'Tell me, Nick. Now that I've been sluiced, and my life temporarily extended, how may I be of service?'

Nick took a deep breath. Where could he even begin? How crazy did all this sound? Would even a psychic dugong comprehend the madness of these last few weeks?

'Relax, Nick. I think I've got the gist from a brief psychic melding conducted without your prior knowledge. I see that Roz has abandoned you after refusing to distribute The Dark Fraction, *and has left you to do battle alone with various physical manifestations of the aforesaid Dark Fractions.'*

'Please. Call her Judas.'

'That's a shame, Nick. I heard you two described as being like Dempsey and Makepeace versus some monsters. A perfect media pitch that in some alternate reality might have led to a highly successful and profitable genre-based television series. What's preventing you two seeing eye to eye on this particular case, given your previously feisty yet sexually tense, water-cooler-friendly, potential ratings-hit badinage?'

Jeez, thought Nick. Did he really have to spell it out *again*?

'Not really, I can briefly read your mind again. So, Roz thinks the series proposal is too confusing. Roz therefore intends to pulp all existing copies of book one, title to be finalised, and yet the incarnate versions of your Dark Fractions, which are now slowly coming to life as a result of your imagination leaking out into reality, are under the mistaken assumption that you're the one who wants your books pulped, and are thus hellbent on destroying you, instead of her.'

'Correct.'

'Presumably because they'll die if their fictional selves are pulped?'

'Exactly.'

'Then pulp your books, Nick, like Roz says. Problem solved.'

'That doesn't solve anything, Bruford.'

'*Because you're torn between seeing your life's work needlessly destroyed and your own existence needlessly destroyed?*' The dugong stared intently at Nick, its oiled moustache twitching.

'Precisely,' said Nick.

'*Then, Nick, I believe you should sacrifice your work for the greater good. It will not only save your life, but Roz's, too. I suggest you head back to her place right now and protect her. Because if they've already got to me, she'll no doubt be the next in line.*'

Bruford had nailed it, dammit. *Roz* was the one who wanted his Dark Fractions dead. Not Nick. *She* was the one pulping Nick's books. So why the hell weren't his Dark Fractions after *Roz*? Unless they had no idea yet that *she* was the one threatening their existence . . .

'*Nick, I hope you're not thinking what I know you're thinking.*'

'Tough,' said Nick, putting the broom down. 'Thanks, Bruford. You've given me the answer, after all. I'll hand Roz over to them.'

'*You can't be serious, Nick? You'd happily sacrifice the life of your editor in order to preserve the existence of a flawed, problematically structured horror series?*'

'Maybe not happily . . . Actually, yes, happily. Because if my Dark Fractions aren't able to destroy my sense of self by guilt-tripping me, owing to me never feeling guilt because I've always been right about everything I've ever done, then they'll no doubt give up on the preliminaries and try to destroy me immediately on sight, and by any means necessary. Yet if I hand Roz over to them as a bargaining chip, then my books will be saved and I can start negotiating some sort of reality time-share agreement with them. Legally supervised, of course.'

'*I don't believe I'm hearing this. You truly do have a Dark Fraction, Nick. If you don't come to your senses soon, and allow Roz to destroy your books, these Dark Fractions of yours will corrupt and destroy all life in their wake. Except me. I'll be dead in a bit, anyway.*'

Nick yanked a hose-reel from the wall and switched on the outside tap, setting the revolving spray nozzle so that it would continue to douse Bruford at ten-second intervals.

'For old times' sake,' he said. Then headed back over to the alley running alongside the destroyed aquarium.

'*Come back, Nick. If you leave me now, I may not be able to help you again. Please, Nick. Just one more sluice of my love cudgel.*'

But Nick had already gone.

CHAPTER FOUR

Nick drew his revolver and hammered on Roz's front door.

Was it really so bad, handing Roz over to them? Ultimately, wasn't his work more important than Roz's survival? Then again, certain things his editor had thrown up about his novel's internal logic were proving uncannily accurate as the thing slowly came to life around him. Like how the internal voice of the Dark Fraction currently haunting Nick was proving fairly inconsistent, appearing to pick and choose when and where it interfered with Nick's existence. Sometimes it was right there inside his head, seemingly aware of all he was thinking and experiencing, and then at other times it seemed completely oblivious to his whereabouts. Or, like earlier when he was communing telepathically with Bruford, the psychic dugong, it seemed to rise up out of nowhere for a brief insulting interjection, then was silenced almost immediately.

Nick winced internally. Hadn't Roz pointed out all this? That employing internal voices as a literary device simply didn't gel well on the printed page beyond one or two internal voices, which themselves needed to be distinguishable from each other either via the use of alternative fonts, italics, italics in speech marks or carefully delineated character traits? Maybe she'd been on to something, after all. But that didn't justify destroying Nick's books.

With no response at the door, he kicked it open.

The house had been ransacked.

'Roz?' he yelled out. But there was no reply. 'Roz? It's me. Nick Steen. Best-selling horror author and dark architect of worldly destruction. Are you in?'

But Roz was nowhere to be found. Nick stepped over her upturned Madagascar Dragon Tree and made his way through to the lounge. Clearly there'd been some sort of violent struggle. Broken furniture and shattered ornaments lay strewn about the floor.

Dammit, they'd got to Roz already. That meant Nick had just lost his leverage. Now there'd be no way of using her as a bargaining chip, or convincing his Dark Fractions that Roz was the one who was intent on destroying them, and not him. Instead, they'd simply assume he and Roz were in this thing together. Unless Roz could explain things her end and get Nick off the hook by sacrificing herself instead – but he sincerely doubted that would happen, especially having flipped her the bird before he left.

He reached down and picked up a cracked photograph frame lying beneath Roz's mantelpiece. It showed her and Nick at ShriekCon '85, where *Distendus Rectus* had won 'Best Novel' in the 'Hellportal' category.

Now she was gone.

As Nick placed the frame back above the fireplace, he caught sight of some crumpled paper tucked deep inside the chimney base, as if Roz had been interrupted halfway through lighting a fire. A *fire*? On a hot summer's day?

Nick reached in and grabbed it.

He unfolded the crumpled sheet, grinning slowly to himself. It was a receipt from a local industrial firm, confirming delivery of 10,000 copies of Nick Steen's *The Dark Fraction* to Warehouse C on an industrial estate opposite the old paper mill by Stalkford's south river.

Clearly Roz had been determined to hide the evidence from him. Now Nick had a chance again. If he drove over there now and immediately ordered the staff to unload his books at gunpoint, he might yet be able to convince the Dark Fractions he was on *their* side.

He paused suddenly, hardly able to believe what he'd just said (in his mind). On *their* side? *Seriously?* Was he *really* rooting for his Dark Fractions? Maybe Bruford was right about him. Maybe there *was* a dark part of Nick Steen that he'd never realised existed. One that would rather live in a world of evil Dark Fractions, than a world *without* evil Dark Fractions.

What the *hell* was he becoming?

The phone rang. Nick made his way through piles of over-turned furniture and found it down the back of Roz's shattered television. Luckily, it had landed with its receiver intact so that the line was still properly connected. He picked it up and held it close to his ear.

'Who's this?' he said.

'Hey, Nicky Boy. It's *you*. Or should I say me? Or how about "us"?'

An eruption of laughter from several voices cackled down the line.

'You've already done that joke,' said Nick.

'Now we're gonna do *you*, buddy,' continued the voice, which was exactly like Nick's own, but more gravelly from butting back endless cigarettes. 'We know *exactly* where you are.'

'Except you didn't know where I was in the cabin at the start of this – for want of a better term – "story", because in the end you actually turned out to be a postman. And why are you no longer speaking inside my own mind?'

'The effect of that dugong's psychic blocking is still pretty strong, Nick, hence us communicating with you via phone. But it is indeed both inconsistent and a logical flaw, like Roz told you.'

'Whatever. Let's do a deal,' said Nick. 'I want my books to exist just as much as you do. Surely we can work out some sort of Nick Steen time-share deal?'

The voice on the end of the phone began to laugh. Cruelly. Scornfully. *Tauntingly.* 'Not interested, buddy. By the time I've finished with you, Nicky Boy, I *alone* will be the real Nick Steen.'

Nick's Dark Fraction laughed again, but was suddenly interrupted by a slightly quieter yet near-identical voice, as if coming from a figure standing immediately behind it. 'Wrong, buddy. *I'll* be the real Nick Steen.'

'No way,' said the original Dark Fraction, seeming to move away from the mouthpiece. '*I'll* be the real Nick Steen.'

'No, *I'll* be the real Nick Steen.' It was an additional quieter voice, perhaps another of Nick's Dark Fractions, standing either directly behind or perpendicular to the former Dark Fraction, which was itself standing directly behind the initial Dark Fraction.

Roz was right about one thing, at any rate, Nick thought to himself. This multiple Dark Fraction thing is more confusing than it needs to be.

'We're endless, buddy. Like holding a mirror of Nick Steens up to a mirror of Nick Steens. And we're *all* coming to get you.'

As a cacophony of raucous laughter burst down the line, Nick slammed down the phone and raced out into the hall. Roz's jacket with the big shoulder-pads was still on the hook, along with her favourite pair of high-heeled slingbacks. The ones he'd bought her after he'd grafted her toes back on.*

If Nick knew one thing about Roz, it was that she'd never leave the house without putting on her favourite publishing gear. They must have dragged her out of here kicking and screaming. He had to get over to the warehouse on Stalkford's south river, and fast. If he could beat his Dark Fractions there, he could take the books themselves hostage *and* work out some sort of survival deal for himself and Roz.

---

* See *Bride of Bone.* Which presumably you've already read, as it appears directly before this tale. If not, and you're reading this story first, then you're potentially deranged and should seek medical attention.

Really, Nick? Roz, too?

Well, he could rescue her, at any rate, then potentially use her as leverage again, depending on how the situation unfolded.

Nick ducked outside, running back along Roz's garden path towards his waiting Honda Civic. As he wrenched open the driver's door, a thunderous roar filled the air. Nick glanced up, catching sight of a gleaming metal motorcycle tearing along the street behind the furthest hedgerow.

Then a heady flash of metallic black and silver burst into view at the far end of Roz's road, and Nick stood face to face with *himself*.

'Me,' he whispered, aloud. 'My Dark Fraction.'

'Your Dark Part sounds better, Nicky Boy.'

It was precisely as Roz had described, the horseshoe moustache being particularly impressive. But Nick sensed something more in this un-helmeted biker double, perched atop his 1968 Honda CL350, which now blocked off Nick's only available exit from Roz's road. Something cold and dangerous. Nick watched as his Dark Fraction flicked a metal Zippo down the front zip of its russet-leather jacket and lit what Nick suspected was not the first bottle of Bourbon that morning.

'You drink it ... *alight*?'

The Dark Fraction grinned, gulping the entire bottle down, flames and all. Then belched fire. '*Neat*,' it added, a plume of black smoke rising from its mouth. 'Though a little water wouldn't go amiss.'

There was no option. Nick would have to drive *through* it.

As his double glanced away momentarily, lighting a cigarette with its own breath, Nick seized his chance and ducked inside his vehicle.

His Dark Fraction looked up, grinning, then revved the bike's engine. There was a tumultuous racket of throbbing noise that Nick felt sure would draw complaints from Roz's neighbours.

Nick didn't think he'd stand much of a chance against his doppelganger, given the flaming toxic fumes still wafting upwards from between the demon's teeth. Instead, he'd have to slam his Civic into a hard reverse and hope his double would follow him down the road behind. He was banking on his Dark Fraction not realising the end of this alley was a vicious cul-de-sac, in which case he'd already be performing a high-speed backwards turn around the circular dead-end before his evil double even knew what it had run into.

He buckled up, then keyed the Civic's ignition. The distant biker revved his engines even louder.

Then suddenly, things got a lot worse.

As Nick sat there, helpless, a mass of armed and bearded biker-Nicks roared into Roz's road on identical machines, drawing up beside their near-identical-looking leader. A gang of biker doubles, Nick observed. An undead mob of literal Hell's Angels on an unholy path of supernatural vengeance.

Nick depressed the clutch lever and slammed the Civic's gear into reverse. He whipped his head rearward, leaning back over his shoulder to spot any lingering pedestrians immediately behind him, then pressed down with his foot on the accelerator.

The Civic sped backwards at over five miles an hour. Immediately, the biker gang roared after him, their leader yanking back on his bike's handles to perform an electrifying wheelie.

'Keep it coming, buddy,' drawled Nick, as he continued to kick hard against the accelerator pedal, pushing the car to an extreme speed of seven miles per hour.

Before he knew what was happening, the cul-de-sac was upon them. Praying he'd got his calculations just right, Nick wrenched his steering wheel left, twisting the vehicle round in a deathly backwards curve, narrowly missing two dustbins and the rear fender of a stationary Citroën.

Nick yelled a swear word as he continued to wrench the wheel leftward, weaving it slightly to and fro as the Civic navigated his dangerous reverse-turn, the heady chaos of this unconventional manoeuvre threatening to derail both the vehicle and also Nick's sanity, with such a brazen affront to the established laws of physics.

Damn, if he got out of this alive, it would be a miracle. A god-damned miracle.

Fighting to keep his concentration fixed on the road behind, Nick risked a quick forwards glance at the bikers ahead of him, who were now approaching the self-same dangerous cul-de-sac entirely unawares and at petrifying half-speed.

Nick watched as several careened into the enclosed semicircle of parked vehicles, wobbling dangerously and chipping the occasional small piece of paintwork.

'Screw you, *meatheads!*' Nick yelled as he transferred his gaze back over his shoulder. He was still wrestling with the wheel, which fought like a wildcat against his hardening will, daring Nick to give up, to surrender to the laws of science and lose control; wreck this hard-fought state of ultimate concentration and hurl him and his Civic against the edge of the pavement or – God forbid – someone's newly painted fence in some uncontrollable blazing fireball of exploding death and metal.

But no. Nick held fast. Nick held the line. Until finally . . . by some *miracle* . . . he saw that he'd twisted the full one-eighty back into Roz's road.

Then suddenly, out of the very eye of that crazy storm of clatter-ing, collapsing motorcycles, burst one that appeared to know what the hell it was doing.

The leader of the pack.

Nick's Dark Fraction.

As the blazing Honda bike sped directly at him, behind yet

technically still ahead of Nick's car, Nick realised, with mounting horror, that he'd finally run out of road.

No way could he perform a three-point-turn in time now. Not with his Dark Fraction bearing down on him at such insane speed.

He knew it, and his dark double knew it.

Bye bye, Nicky Boy. Nice knowing you.

Nick closed his eyes and did the unthinkable.

CHAPTER FIVE

The unthinkable being a hard reverse swerve turn – or *J-Turn** – back against the left-hand kerb (or right-hand, if the car is accelerating from a forwards position), which should *never* be attempted as kerb bouncing is an instant fail in any driving test, followed by a risky gear-change and immediate forwards acceleration back into the main road without checking for pedestrians or oncoming vehicles. If Nick happened to clip a passer-by, it would mean an instant fine, licence points and a possible jail sentence, depending on the severity of damage to the wounded party, but Nick no longer had a choice.

Instead, he must fly straight into a metaphorical dead man's curve of ultimate nightmare, a fiery hard-turn to hell that had haunted his nightmares ever since the day he'd accidentally revved his cousin's toy car into an open fire and been ordered by his uncle to crawl into the flames and retrieve it (luckily, the alcohol seeping from his uncle's pores caught fire first.)

There was no escaping destiny any longer. This manoeuvre, crazy as it was, *had* to be attempted. Bracing himself, Nick took one last look at his Dark Fraction, who was in the process of lighting another bottled Bourbon while upping another gear, then swung the wheel left.

Nick's head swayed sideways, lurching back and forwards slightly as the Civic bumped the kerb. Lightning-fast, Nick applied the brake

* Look it up if you're lost. GM

236

pedal, slammed the car's gear into first and kicked the accelerator, yanking the wheel right again as the car moved forwards into the road and moved off in the direction of the main junction at the end of Roz's road.

'Nick Steen, you damned *lunatic!*' he yelled, scarcely able to comprehend what he'd just done. 'You could have mounted the pavement!'

But no. Nick Steen knew what the hell he was doing. Nick Steen was out clean – and more importantly, still ahead of his Dark Fraction.

He glanced up at the rear-view mirror, but there was no longer any sign of the bike behind.

He looked back at the road. The route ahead was empty, save for an old pensioner woman crossing the approaching junction with a trolley of cheap shopping.

Where the hell had his Honda-riding Dark Fraction got to?

Suddenly an almighty boom burst in his ears as the motorcycle came into view directly above Nick's car, bouncing hard on the Civic's bonnet before accelerating forwards into the road ahead of him.

Dammit, it had jumped right over him. While Nick was at a diagonal angle bouncing off the kerb, his Dark Fraction had damn well jumped right over him!

That's right, Nicky Boy. Wheelied my way up on your own damned fender.

Nick tried his best to ignore the sudden psychological intrusion of his Dark Fraction, no doubt a subtle subterfuge intended to break his concentration, and watched instead as his russet-leathered double skidded twice around the old lady ahead, who was still crossing with a trolley of shopping, because she was so damned slow due to her age. The biker braked hard, swinging its machine round to a sudden halt, facing Nick across the road.

Nick slammed on his own brakes even harder, swerving to a gentle halt in front of the crossing pensioner. The biddy continued at a snail's pace across the tarmac, oblivious to the sound of Nick's Civic and his double's Honda as they revved engines angrily at each other across the smoking blacktop.

'Move it, you old bag,' yelled Nick. Normally he avoided swearing at the elderly (where possible), but he was still pumped with adrenaline from his own daredevil antics; a necessary state he'd had to get himself into in order to get the hell out of that hell-hole behind him, tout suite.

He stared across at his Dark Fraction opposite, whom he saw was now in the process of swallowing another bottle of flaming Bourbon, while extending its remaining middle finger in Nick's direction.

Dammit, he had to keep calm. Just wait for the old croc to cross and we'll be on our way again. But what if that demon opposite decides to throw that bottle *at* me? What if it's just feinting over there, and is in fact about to hurl a Molotov cocktail up my ass?

Hey, nice idea, buddy.

The Dark Fraction pulled back its bottle arm and prepared to fling the flaming liquid at Nick's Civic.

Then Nick was on it, slamming his car into gear. The vehicle leaped forwards, swiping the old lady side-on and sending her flying into a nearby hedgerow. Before his double knew what was happening, Nick was away again, tearing along the side road towards the second junction.

Damn, if that old biddy hadn't just saved his life.

Nick slowed, pausing for a break in the traffic, then carefully moved out into the main high street, looking both ways and avoiding entering the bus lane, which was tricky to do from this exit.

Suddenly, his Dark Fraction was at the passenger window, having accelerated forwards at an illegal speed to catch up with him.

'Pathetic!' Nick yelled. 'Joke's on you, pal, because Stalkford Council have secret cameras hidden all along this stretch, and they'll have more than likely clocked your speed all the way back to the previous junction.'

But Nick's warning fell on deaf ears. His Dark Fraction merely turned towards him, laughing raucously while swigging from another flaming bottle. Then it belched fire at him again.

Nick swerved the car right as a huge plume of black smoke burst against the car. He felt the heat sear his sideburns as he turned his face away from the fiery maelstrom. When he next looked back, the dashboard was smoking, and his Dark Fraction was sitting right beside him in the passenger seat.

'I've killed her, Nick,' it said to him, smiling. 'I've killed Roz.'

'You've *killed* Roz?' Nick roared, hardly able to believe his ears. Even if the sentence itself was actually quite simple.

'Read my lips, Nicky Boy. *I've . . . killed . . . Roz.*'

For a brief moment, Nick's peripheral vision clocked that his Dark Fraction had failed to attach a seatbelt. Then he slammed on the brakes.

Nick felt himself flung slightly forwards. The seatbelt locked and Nick retained position as the car braked to a final halt. When he looked up at the windscreen, his Dark Fraction had vanished.

Incredible, Nick thought to himself. His head should have at least cracked the glass, even if the car wasn't going at sufficient speed to send the bastard flying out over the bonnet and into the road, to be crushed again and again by his reversing wheels.

At the familiar roar of the bike's engine, Nick looked up. His Dark Fraction was back out in front, astride its machine and lighting another bottle.

'Roz is *dead*, Nicky Boy,' it yelled. 'And now you're gonna die, too.'

Terrified, Nick reared backwards against his seat as his double swung another flaming bottle high up over its head, preparing to fling it directly inside Nick's car.

He didn't have time to react. This was it. The moment of death.

He watched as the flaming glass arced forwards to meet him ...
then paused mid-air, failing to leave the Dark Fraction's hand.

A look of fear crossed the double's face.

Then Nick heard the sirens. Saw the familiar blue flashing in his
rear-view mirror and realised his doppelganger most likely had insufficient insurance and probably no paid-up tax on this particular
mortal plane.

As Nick's foe swung the bike around and roared off into the
distance, Nick collapsed backwards, against his seat.

The thing had killed Roz.

It was decided, then. The books had to go, whatever the loss to
humanity. No way was Nick going to accept Roz's death as payment
for allowing his Dark Fractions series to survive.

He'd pulp the damned books himself.

He reached into the glove compartment and drew out some extra
rounds for his revolver, plus some Murray mints. Then turned the car
around and drove immediately south, in the direction of the old
paper mill.

As Nick passed over the long stretch of wasteland beyond the
edge of town, the ground below him played havoc with the Civic's
suspension.

But no way would that stop him. Nick was on his own path of
vengeance now, and exterior damage to his car's exhaust system was
the last thing troubling his mind (though he made a mental note to
bring his annual service forwards by a couple of months). He saw the
sign for 'South Road Industrial Estate' and increased his speed,
daring to push the meter past thirty miles per hour, aware all the
while that hitting anything above that limit might entail an imminent garage visit in addition to the main service.

But this was for Roz.

She'd warned him after all, hadn't she? Told him the books must
go. But had he listened to her? Had he hell.

He'd get them for that, too.

He swung his car into the industrial estate and drove ahead cautiously, searching for Warehouse C. It was getting late and the entire place looked deserted. No doubt most of these labourer sorts had bunked off early for the bank holiday weekend.

Meaning the entire estate would be empty. Just him and his damned Dark Fractions facing off. Maybe Roz hadn't told them where Nick's books were, after all. Maybe she'd held out. Maybe Nick still had the edge. All he had to do was sneak in and pulp the entire print run before anyone even knew he was here.

Then, maybe, he'd go write something else.

Dedicate it to Roz.

Maybe.

Nick swung the car into the front drive of Warehouse C, parked the vehicle and stepped out. He looked up at the building, which resembled no other on the estate. A tall, dark and imposing structure of blackened brick, with numerous boarded-up windows adorning each side.

Nick drew out his revolver and shot the lock apart. Then swung open the warehouse door and stepped inside. The place was pitch dark, even before the door swung back behind Nick, sealing him in.

He removed a small cardboard box from his jacket pocket, then cautiously lit one of two matches he had left.

And saw the room was full of Nick Steens.

CHAPTER SIX

'Keep back!' Nick yelled, unsure which one to aim his revolver at first.

A strange voice spoke. 'Hold your horses, boy. Let me just stack all these in one corner.'

The overhead lights snapped on and the warehouse entrance lit up suddenly, revealing row upon row of cut-out promotional display headboards featuring the real-life Nick, brandishing a brand-new copy of *The Dark Fraction*.

Of *course*, thought Nick, recalling that the printer's machine had broken down during production and accidentally octupled the number of cut-outs Clackett had ordered for his short-lived promotional tour. Nick's heart sank as he caught sight of the surrounding walls. There, piled against each other, stood all the unused elements of Clackett's comprehensive yet ultimately doomed display package.

Nick looked around, trying to locate whoever had spoken to him from the darkness. Finally, a grizzled, bearded pensioner in denim dungarees, red plaid shirt and lumberjack cap clattered slowly down a portable stairwell at the back of the room.

'Now what the cotton-pickin', hellzathumpin', trash-bang-whallop-whizzlin', howlereenin', yankee-doodle-dandee-guzzlin', cracka-thumpin' Hellbellery is going on here? You cain't jes' go blasting on in here, boy.'

Nick lowered the revolver as the decrepit-looking time-ticker continued to hobble precariously down the metal steps. Nick sighed, realising he'd no doubt be expected to help move the displays.

'Evening, old-timer.'

As the old buzzard's eyes finally fell into focus, his grizzled features flashed with sudden panic at the sight of Nick's face.

'What the whipple, if it ain't one o' them cardboard-shiftin', statue-breathin' ghost-boy promotional display fuckers come to life!' Panicking, the old man slipped on the iron rungs and plunged head-first down the stairwell, landing with a sickening thud at Nick's feet.

'Easy, grandpa,' said Nick. 'I'm the *real* Nick Steen.'

He knelt down by the old man, whose legs had bent backwards at the waist and were now protruding upwards, beneath his head.

'Gone an' snapped ma damn pelvis,' the old man growled. 'Dang it, if my lower half ain't flipped the full one-eighty.'

'Where's the rest of the staff?' asked Nick, growing increasingly concerned that this frail geriatric had been left in sole charge of his books.

'Ain't no one here but me, boy. Dang it all, give me some whisky, will ya? I can't move ma damn legs.'

Nick picked up one of the old croc's feet and used it to smooth his ancient brow. 'Where are you from?' asked Nick, trying to keep the coot conscious.

'Hackney,' spat the pensioner. 'Rode west to Stalkford back in eighty-five. With ma lovin' Martha by my side. Dammit, where is she, boy?' he yelled suddenly, starting to panic. 'Where's *Martha*?'

'I don't have a clue,' said Nick. 'Carry on.'

The old man began to weep. 'She was on her way here . . . With a trolley of shopping . . . I gotta hold on till she gets here, dammit. My dear Martha . . . I can't leave her all alone . . . not when she *hates* crossing them roads . . .'

Hold on a moment, thought Nick. It couldn't be. *Could it?*

'I told her . . . I said to her . . . lemme go with ya, Martha . . . let me cross them roads with ya, but dang it, if she don't *insist*. That's ma Martha, Lor' bless her soul. She be out there all on her own, crossing

243

them damn roads all on her lonesome. Danged miracle she ain't been *hit . . .*'

Nick weighed things up. He *could* tell this terminal case the truth, but he'd no doubt get delayed comforting the old rust-bucket while his Dark Fractions finally caught up with him. He *had* to prioritise destroying those books. Only then could he let this sunken wreck know he'd slammed Martha side-on into a muddy ditch and smeared her halfway down his car.

He shoved his revolver under the dust-husk's chin.

'Where are those books, pop?'

'Thataways,' said the senescent grizzler, pointing up at the stairwell he'd just plummeted down. 'Thirteenth floor. Right by that there pulping pit.'

'Pulping pit?'

'Near that darned conveyor belt, jes' waitin' for ol' Slim to set that there lever goin' and send 'em all to kingdom come.'

Nick bristled instinctively at the thought, and was sorely tempted to blow the man's head off. Then he realised this cracked and yellowed spine-shatteree was just doing his job.

Not only that, but he was probably also the only person here who knew how the pulping machine worked. Nick grabbed the fossil's shoulders and hoisted the dinosaur up, carrying him over towards the stairwell. He was light as a puppet and unusually quiet given that both crushed legs were swinging loose like jostling marbles in a sock.

At the top of the steps, Nick kicked aside more cardboard versions of himself to reveal an old-fashioned see-through elevator directly ahead, with a manual sliding scissor gate. The pensioner began to whimper as they approached, as if troubled by some nightmarish vision only he could see.

'They're coming, boy. I see 'em. Just like you, they is. Maybe a *little* taller.'

Nick slid open the metal gate, stepped into the lift's interior and hit the button for floor thirteen. 'Just show me where the pulping room is, old man,' he said, reassuringly. 'Then I'll put you out of your misery.'

A minute or so later, the lift bell chimed and Nick pulled open the door to reveal a long, dark corridor beyond.

'See that door at the end?' gasped the old man, now resembling a decrepit chimpanzee hanging from the neck of some kindly vet prepped to administer a final injection. 'Them books o' yours are all in there.'

Nick nodded, moving forwards cautiously into the corridor. Then glimpsed a sudden movement beside them.

'Jeez!' he yelled, whirling round with his revolver to face whatever was pacing them.

'No, son!' yelled the pensioner, slapping down hard on a nearby light switch close to Nick's head.

Blinding light dazzled Nick's eyes as the interior of the corridor suddenly lit up like a chandelier, revealing row upon row of additional Nick Steen doubles.

'Down, old-timer!' Nick yelled, opening fire.

'No again, son!' screamed the paralysed dangler as Nick's weapon blew the nearest mirror into a million flying fragments.

A *reflection*, Nick realised, lowering the revolver again. He stared, dumbfounded, at the blank space where his double had previously stood. A damned reflection.

'Now they can *all* get through,' howled the grey man-bag on his chest.

But Nick wasn't listening. Who the hell had lined up a row of full-length mirrors in a warehouse already lined with an endless procession of cardboard Nick Steen doubles? That was bound to confuse things, particularly as the one thing Nick needed to be able to identify without any margin of error was an army of Dark Fractions looking *exactly* like him.

Then he remembered. Clackett had been recouping some of their financial losses on his ill-starred book by allowing the Stalkford Mirror Company to house their current stock overspill in a shared rented space. Ever since that outbreak of the undead in Vampton, which Nick had yet to contain, people were returning mirrors to suppliers all across the region. Meaning Nick would now not only have endless cardboard Nick Steens to contend with, but also additional multiple reflections of himself.

He moved on, trying to concentrate on the door ahead, yet keenly aware he was still being followed by his own reflections on either side. They looked stranger now. As if they were walking slightly faster than him. Or were their heads turning slightly sooner than his whenever he angled his face side-on to keep an eye on them?

He tossed the old man aside to get a better look. As expected, his reflections did likewise. Then Nick turned around to examine the mirror directly opposite. He stared deeply at that familiar uncanny illusion created when two mirrors are placed opposite each other. An endless corridor of infinitely retreating mirrors, and at its centre, an ever-shrinking image of the reflected Nick Steen.

He raised one arm, and a thousand receding Nicks did likewise. Surely they were all him? And yet the reflection closest to him was smiling.

And Nick never smiled.

He watched its hands rise upwards. Reaching outwards, towards him. Then Nick finally clocked the banana-yellow wrestling boots.

As the Dark Fraction hiding in the mirror *stepped out*.

CHAPTER SEVEN

It was largely naked, save for a pair of extremely tight purple pants and a mess of ragged medical stitching over the heart area, where it had evidently survived multiple operations. Its garish wrestling boots sported two red zigzagged arrows pointing upwards. The thing was a version of Nick that could neither speak nor form its busted jaw into anything other than an inane, toothless grin. Only able to communicate via primal grunting, the creature slammed itself further through the mirror (which evidently doubled as some form of supernatural portal), its heavy torso glistening with beads of oily sweat.

My Darker Fraction, thought Nick. To use Roz's inferior phrase. Or throppelganger, to use a phrase they both liked but which Tony Clackett didn't.

The wrestling demon.

A shiver of fear ran down Nick's spine. For this particular creature was an adversary specialising in an ancient form of weighty muscular combat known as the *grapple*. In its human years, as sketched briefly in Nick's series outline, this grease-skinned hell of human tannery had never once been taught to punch, or kick, or even stomp. Instead, the dumb tank of thundering man-meat knew only the harsh, clammy slap of the wrestler's Sweat-Grip.

Nick tore off his jacket, prepared to face the heavy, clammy smack of its outstretched palm. He was about to rip off his black roll-neck sweater, too, in order to free up what extra friction he might eke out of his closely-thatched chest hair, when the thing in boots launched itself through the air towards him.

The barrel of human flesh slammed head-first into Nick's chest, knocking the revolver from his hand and throwing him backwards against the mirror behind, which cracked violently under Nick's weight.

Before he could tell what was happening, Nick found himself unable to breathe. As motes of dust fell from an overhead bulb, sprinkling downwards into his straining, bloodshot eyes, Nick sensed in horror that the thing had wrapped itself tightly around his chest, and was now squeezing him tight.

He felt a terrible crushing in his buttocks, fiercely aware that one of the creature's hands was now splayed there, forcing his left cheek in an attempt to wrench it upwards, over the hip. If Nick didn't do something fast, his left flank might tear off completely.

Bracing himself, Nick leaned in close to his opponent's face, ignoring the beads of sweat dripping from his double's brow, and inhaled the sharp, caseous scent of his Fraction's thickly rolled neck fat. He clamped the wrestler's ear unwillingly in his mouth and bit down hard.

As he tasted the nauseating metallic tang of blooded ear-meat on his lips, sensed the salted crunch of decimated lobe-gristle giving way between his teeth, the pressure upon him suddenly softened, and Nick realised he was free once more. As the Darker Fraction rose to its feet, Nick kicked out hard at its glistening man-breasts, sending the paunchy demon flying, back towards the mirror through which it had entered.

But the massive grappler was back on its feet in an instant, springing at Nick with unexpected speed thanks to its low centre of gravity, off-balancing him physically and mentally as both arms flung outwards from the thing's barrelling body, slapping at Nick's face with spanned, corpulent fingers.

248

Nick fought to evade the spread of those stinking, slippery stubs, gripping the mug's jaw in his own mitts and pushing inwards and upwards, crushing the wrestler's lips and face together to form what soon resembled a promotional live tour poster for some gurning local comedian. After a minute of mutual grunting, not to mention heavy sweating, the demon finally howled like a dart-struck bear and released its grip once again. Then, as Nick roared loudly in triumph, the thing struck him unawares with a short, sharp digit jab to both eyes.

Nick yelled loudly, collapsing to the deck. 'You clammy *sod* ...' Nick spat, just before the Darker Fraction once again gripped his cheeks in its reddened, pinguid fingers and pressed Nick's jaws tightly together. Nick prepared himself for the worst. No way could he get out from underneath the creature now. As he felt a final burst of air escape from his crushed lungs, and heard the slow yet inexorable cracking of his crushed, protesting ribs, Nick stared into his double's strangely familiar-looking eyes and prepared to meet his Maker (presuming that said Maker would still have him).

Then the thing grabbed his left buttock again.

As the huge hand squeezed and twisted Nick's flesh in a crazed attempt to tear off his whole arse, he sensed his death throes finally approaching. Lashing out uselessly one final time with his booted heel, singularly failing to upend the human keg, Nick prepared himself gravely for the imminent rending of his rump. Until, all at once, the pressure lifted (yet again). As Nick's vision slowly refocused, he saw a frail, familiar form clasping what little skin it had strength left to squeeze, swinging like an old neckerchief from around the demon's neck.

The half-dead octogenarian.

Dammit, the spent fag-end had saved Nick's life, like his wife had before him. Despite being completely paralysed. Yet the victory was pyrrhic. For with one heavy swipe of its hand, the Darker Fraction slapped the spent geriatric sideways, so that his broken body swung round its throat in fits and starts like the connector cord circling a spiral swing-ball, until the old fool was finally at rest upon the thing's chest, staring directly upwards into the eyes of his opponent.

'Hell, you ain't *Martha* . . .' the failed coffin-dodger wailed as the wrestler ripped him free, grabbing both mangled legs in its mitts and swinging him round and round at increasing speed, until, with a nauseating crack, the corpse-in-waiting's splintered spine gave way at last, and the top half of his torso ripped free, flying off at an angle and shattering another mirror.

Seizing his chance, Nick leaped aside and rolled himself over and over towards his dropped revolver. He grabbed it from the floor, whipped round and blasted several slugs into the chest of his Darker Fraction.

The enraged grappler howled, staggering backwards against the mirror. Then steadied himself. Bullets were useless, Nick realised. Only the destruction of his book, *The Dark Fraction*, would send this demon back to wherever it had spawned from.

Abandoning the fight, Nick turned his attention to the door at the far end of the corridor, where his books were stored, then realised he'd never get there. For in between him and the door there now appeared a long procession of demon Nick Steens, stepping as one from each mirror lining the route.

They were the numerous Dark Fractions from Nick's proposed series, each leaving the shadows of its own dark reality to invade Stalkford's own, in every configuration of Nick Steen one could possibly imagine.

There were dark magicians, ghostly cowboys, Egyptian pharaohs, deep-sea divers, trapeze artists, diseased flesh-eaten astronauts, tax accountants, even a Lizard Nick.

They turned their heads as one to face him.

Realising the path was now blocked, Nick turned the other way, hoping to flee back down the corridor to the lift.

Yet more Dark Fractions were stepping out from the mirrors *behind* him, too. Amid this terrifying army of Steen alter-egos stood a Medieval Jester Nick, a Hunchback Nick, a 1920s Crooner Nick (with ancient microphone), a 1950s Prison Jailer Nick, a Prohibition Gangster Nick, a Tap Dancer Nick and an Archive Children's Television Presenter Nick. All deranged. All hellbent on erasing the *real* Nick Steen from existence.

They, too, turned their heads as one to face him.

A version of Nick wearing a doctor's lab coat grinned at him, brandishing a lethal-looking scalpel.

'Want me to cut out your Dark Parts, buddy?'

'You look familiar,' replied Nick, quizzically. 'Haven't we met somewhere before?'

'I once starred in a supernatural-based medical drama.'*

'Of course,' said Nick, remembering. It was the Dark Fraction from his final book in the proposed series, in which the latest incarnation of the writer's demonic fictional alter-ego's demonic fictional alter-ego's demonic fictional alter-ego's demonic fictional alter-ego's demonic fictional alter-ego's demonic fictional alter-ego's demonic fictional alter-ego's demonic fictional alter-ego's demonic fictional alter-ego's demonic fictional alter-ego's demonic fictional alter-ego's demonic fictional alter-ego's demonic fictional alter-ego's demonic fictional alter-ego assumes the identity of a warped medical practitioner from an imagined supernatural television soap playing continually inside the head of the demonic fictional alter-ego it's been haunting.

Yeah, Nick thought. There *were* too many.

Realising both ways were blocked, Nick turned back to the glass pane opposite, still reflecting in on itself from the mirror directly behind him. Once more, he saw a never-ending procession of

* Heh heh heh.

receding Nicks stretching off into the darkness of that infinite, unreal tunnel.

These included Violent Skinhead Nick, Burned-Up Grand Prix Racing Driver Nick, Garden Pond-Drowned Nick and Vampiric Traffic Warden Nick, all moving directly towards the very mirror frame through which Nick was observing them.

Except these particular Nicks were no longer walking towards him.

They were *running*.

Nick whirled round. Ahead lay the opposing infinitely reflected tunnel.

Yet in this one there were no Nick Steens in sight. Not even himself.

How could that be? How could he suddenly fail to project a reflection of his own face? Had he, Nick Steen, ceased to exist? Had he suddenly become ... a vampire?*

Nick felt the brute force of a thousand hands hurling him violently forwards, hard against the mirror.

It exploded around him as his head struck the glass.

Then he fell through.

* No, he hadn't.

CHAPTER EIGHT

He woke in slow motion. Nick wasn't sure how he was doing it, but every movement he made was suddenly laboured, from the shifting of his various limbs to the travelling soundwaves formed by his tortured yell of 'Fucking arsehole!'

He was inside the mirror tunnel, he realised. Surrounded by glass fragments that seemed to be flying past him at incredible speed (yet slowly, remember). Ahead, and behind (which he discovered when he finally managed to turn round, a full minute later), was an infinite corridor of mirrored frames, leading off into the far distance, growing darker and murkier the further they receded.

A terrifying feeling of déjà vu struck Nick like a hammer blow. Immediately he was back on the intensive therapy ward, waking groggily, still half-drugged from sleep, glasses sequestered in his wife's bum-bag on a nearby counter beside his untouched grapes, eyes lacking crucial focus as they fixed themselves upon the monitor he'd had no idea had been placed there, staring in abject horror at his own emergency colonoscopy.

No one on the private medical team realised he'd woken from the anaesthetic, least of all Nick, who'd spent the next half an hour convinced he'd died on the toilet and woken up inside his own impacted bowel. Only when he'd lunged at the screen with ragged nails, weakened by endless nocturnal haemorrhoid raking, laughing hysterically at the top of his lungs, attempting in vain to scrape a fresh layer of aged beef from his intestinal wall, did the surgeons realise what had occurred, and duly gassed him back to oblivion.

He'd gotten a decent book out of the experience,* but this was no colonoscopy, Nick realised. He began to walk forwards, into the gloom. It took him five minutes to cross approximately ten square metres of tunnel,† but once he was there, he realised that he'd made no progress whatsoever. The same stretch of tunnel ran on and on endlessly, its furthest reaches only becoming visible the further Nick travelled.

After several hours, he knelt down on the ground, exhausted. Experience as a horror writer told him that he ought to have encountered *something* horrific by now. If he'd been constructing a supernatural portal of infinitely receding reflections, for one of his own books, say, Nick would have put in a dream demon by now. Certainly a haunted toilet or two.

But instead, the place was empty. Eerie. Otherworldly. *Creepy.* Plus other words meaning the same thing. The worst part of being here, Nick decided, was that he was now completely lost. He couldn't for the life of him recall which particular mirror frame he'd entered the tunnel by, and he hadn't been keeping track of the number of steps he'd taken. Partly a result of that relentless *slow motion* he was experiencing, which messed with his natural rhythms and also prevented him whistling his favourite marching tunes.

'Hell!' he screamed, breaking down suddenly and falling to his knees. 'If I'd known I'd inadvertently invoke an army of spirit doubles

---

* *Colonicum Irrigatum Spiritus Rectum.*

† For 'ease of reading', the publishers have edited out all future references to supernaturally induced slow motion, including crucial time and distance calculations conducted in my own private time. Those who wish to read the text *as author intended* may compensate for this oversight by slowing their natural reading speed to half or three-quarters their standard pace while imbibing full-strength antihistamine, but the effect will, I warn you now, be a poor imitation of the original vision. Pray continue. GM

hellbent on my own destruction, cause a permanent rift in my life-long friendship with a psychic dugong, lose the friendship plus life of a loyal yet imperfect editor, then get attacked by a demonic wrestler before falling into an infinite tunnel, I wouldn't have written that bloody book about the Dark Fraction in the first place.'

He wept. Big, Nick-sized tears flowing from both eyes, falling to the ground and then past it towards an eternity of featureless black below. Why hadn't he listened to Roz? Hell, every damned book would have been pulped by now.

But he hadn't, and now Roz was gone. Dead as that zombified Nazi U-boat captain they'd decapitated last month while it strode blindly out of the ocean towards Nick's waiting ice-cream van. Dead as the inhabitants of Silth village, destroyed by a colossal 'Terror Shriek', which may or may not have had something to do with Nick's own primal scream on his last family holiday, during which his daughter's persistent interest in idle recreation had completely wrecked his copy-edit responses.

Dead as his own soul.

Jeez. Nick slapped himself. Was he getting soft? Surely it was only natural to despair like this, when all his friends and family had either deserted him or died, and he found himself now in a lonely tunnel of self-reflective endarkenment?

Oh, Roz . . . Dearest, kindest, but not necessarily cleverest Roz . . .

She's right here, Nicky Boy.

Nick looked up. That internal voice again. There really was no rhyme or reason to its appearance. It just seemed to float in and out of Nick's existence whenever it was most needed for an ironic comment on events, or to seemingly shoehorn some supposed narrative development into proceedings for the warped and nightmarish real-life horror novel Nick now found himself the star of.

'What do you mean, "she's right here"?' Nick cried out.

But he didn't need to be told. Already he could hear the distant roar of the heavy motorcycle engine as it sped towards him from somewhere just beyond his visible range. Was it coming from the tunnel in front of him, or the tunnel behind?

In the darkness, a dim light flared, growing increasingly brighter as it drew near, until Nick saw at last that it was formed by the bike's headlamp approaching up ahead.

Correct. It was the tunnel in front of him.

Nick could barely believe his eyes as a huge cloud of fire burst upwards from the machine, followed by a dense plume of smoke that vanished past the tunnel ceiling into the eternal blackness beyond.

The bike was close now. Nick saw his Dark Fraction raise another flaming Bourbon bottle to its lips. Should he turn and run? What would be the point? There was no way out, either way. Just the same, relentless tunnel of receding mirror frames.

Then he saw the passenger. A pair of arms extending outwards from behind the Dark Fraction, clasping it tightly about the waist. And below, a pair of leathered legs, tucked in closely behind the rider's own.

A long rush of blond hair flew out from beneath the passenger's helmet. As the motorcycle skidded to a sudden halt in front of Nick, facing him side-on, he realised that this second rider was female, shapely and dressed from top to toe in tight black cow-wear.

She pulled off her helmet and shook her hair freely. Her appearance had changed, Nick noted. Her lips were fuller now, her eye make-up heavier, and that welcoming smile of hers was subtly different, now almost bordering on genuine. Yet it was still Roz.

'Those are some hot boots,' said Nick. 'I don't recall you ever "digging" leather, Roz.'

'Really, Nick?' she replied, sliding her legs tightly and somewhat provocatively over one side of the Dark Fraction's throbbing engine. 'I thought I mentioned it numerous times. Or is that just another thing from our past you *don't* remember?'

Nick smiled thinly. 'Touché, Roz. Maybe I do tend to forget things we've done together because ultimately, I'm not too interested in lady stuff. But I'm certain of one thing. If you really *had* worn biker boots like that at any point in our friendship, things might have worked out very differently, believe me. By the way, are you dead, or what?'

'She's very much *alive*,' said the Dark Fraction, inhaling more ignited spirit. 'Right, babe?' It laughed somewhat lecherously (not surprising, since it was a demon), as did Roz, which wasn't quite as becoming for a literary editor, Nick thought. Still, at least Nick could throw that back at her when she next ribbed him for conducting kinky nooky sessions with his own typewriter.

So, Roz had shacked up with his Dark Fraction, had she? Suddenly, it all made sense. That wisp of cigarette smoke behind Roz's privet hedge earlier that morning. Not Nick's own tyre smoke at all. Instead, a product of that very Zippo lighter Roz was now clutching in her hand.

It had probably visited her as soon as Nick had left her house. Maybe even before then. Evidently, they'd planned the whole thing. Left that invoice sheet in the fireplace next to Roz's fallen photograph in an attempt to lure Nick here.

He'd been duped.

'There's something you should know, Roz,' Nick said, keeping his voice calm and intentionally dismissive.

'Yes, Nick?' Roz replied, grinning and lighting a fresh bottle of Bourbon for her new lover. '*What* must I know?'

'Those leather trousers it's wearing, the eyepatch, the throbbing hot rod, that six-a-day-hot-Bourbon habit?'

'Seven,' said his Dark Half, gargling on flames. Nick ignored it.

'They're all me, babe. Deep down. Even those wrestling underpants on my Darker Fraction. They're just myriad physical and psychological signifiers, Roz. Heightened characteristics stemming from idealised notions and wish-fulfilment fantasies us writers indulge in while penning what are all ostensibly semi-autobiographical fictives. As my editor, you should know that.'

'I do, Nick,' Roz replied, nuzzling up to his Dark Fraction. 'But he's hotter than you are.'

Nick sneered, nodded, nodded again, then tried to think of a suitably pithy rejoinder. Then the Dark Fraction revved the bike's engine, clamped the wheel and spun the machine around, burning a flaming hole in the floor of the tunnel. As Roz laughed, Nick watched, deciding whether or not to land her in it after all.

'You know it was *her* idea to pulp my book, not mine,' said Nick, electing to land her in it. '*She's* the one who wanted you dead. I was happy to work out some sort of reality time-share agreement.'

Roz shot him a hateful look. Then the demon biker took a huge swig from the bottle, gargled violently again and pounced forwards, spitting liquid flame in Nick's direction.

The jet of flaming alcohol scorched Nick's mane, blackening his shades so thickly that he could no longer see a bloody thing through them. Yanking the hot spectacles from his face, he turned and fled blindly back down the corridor.

Behind, he heard insane laughter from both Roz and his Dark Fraction. His ears clocked the terrible sound of the motorbike's engine roaring to life once again as both its wheels tore up the tunnel floor and roared towards him.

Nick rubbed his glasses against his sweater, removing what he could of the charred and blackened fuel, then put them back on.

The bike was right behind him.

Where could he run to? He had no idea where he was. Maybe he was destined to stay here for all eternity. Pursued down a supernatural mirror tunnel by a throbbing hot rod while his Dark Fraction and erstwhile literary editor taunted him for all the bad things he'd done in his life. Maybe this, at long last, was Nick's ultimate, permanent Hell.

'*Quick, Nick, through that gap there.*'

Nick turned just in time to dodge a flying bottle of ignited Bourbon. It burst into violent flame beside him as he dived from one side of the tunnel to the other.* Who the hell was speaking?

'*Me, Nick.*'

Liam Neeson?

'*No, Nick. Remember, I sound like Liam Neeson, but I'm in fact Bruford, the psychic dugong.*'

'Bruford! What the hell are you doing here?' Nick yelled as he continued running, dodging another flaming bottle of Bourbon exploding on his other side.

'*I'm in transit, Nick. Currently in the back of a council waste-disposal lorry. I'm passing right by your warehouse. I don't have much time.*'

'What are you doing in a council waste-disposal lorry?'

'*Unfortunately, the swelling of my body failed to go down, Nick. I'm now considered a danger to the public and have been transported to this industrial estate for disposal. Here, the toxic gases building up within me can be safely released or preferably ignited.*'

Hey, Nicky Boy. Are you talking to that damned psychic dugong again?

'*Nick, please ignore the internal voice of your Dark Fraction and leap through that hole of darkness to the left of the next mirror frame but one.*'

'Hear that?' yelled Nick's Dark Fraction to Roz. 'Nicky Boy likes talking to a psychic dugong!'

'A psychic dugong?' tittered Roz as her new demonic boyfriend hurled another bottle Nick's way.

The Bourbon sailed over Nick's head in a flaming arc, exploding right in front of him.

---

* Now recall that this entire sequence is still in slow motion, including that explosion. That just gives you a hint of the intense horror visuals you are currently missing out on because of a catastrophic lapse in editorial judgement. Continue. GM

Nick dived sideways on to his arse, rolling away from the splurg-ing sea of liquid flame. Then the motorbike roared past him, sliding precariously on the burning hot tunnel floor, skidding violently and hurling Roz from her seat.

In seconds, though, she was on her feet, laughing uproariously at her thrilling hell-ride.

'Ignore them, Nick. Just walk away. They're teasing you.'

'Where, Bruford? I've missed my chance. That way is now blocked by flaming Bourbon. I'll never find the hole of darkness now.'

'Relax, Nick. I deliberately referred to the wrong mirrored frame in order to mislead your assailants. The hole of darkness you actually need in order to re-enter this mortal plane is in fact the one directly beside you.'

'Bruford, you bloated genius,' said Nick, leaping into the patch of blackness beside him and smashing his forehead on a dense area of dark matter.

'Other side, Nick.'

Nick nodded, rose from the ground and flung himself at the opposing wall.

Vanishing into it.

CHAPTER NINE

Was he truly back in the warehouse? Disorientated, Nick looked up from where he'd fallen and saw that he'd emerged through a blackened mirror hanging crookedly from the back of an ancient, grimy-looking door. The smell of the room was reassuringly familiar, though, even if the darkness surrounding Nick was heavy with menace. He stood up, lit his *final* match from his trusty box of two matches, and saw, piled before him in neat, even rows, the entire unsold print run of *The Dark Fraction*.

So this was the room he'd been trying to get to when his Dark Fractions had attacked him earlier. And the books themselves explained that reassuring scent. There was no aroma on earth quite like the smell of a freshly printed paperback, even if ultimately it was the smell of dead trees.

Yet now, Nick reflected, these very books faced a second death as they quietly awaited their own destruction.

He reached out and took one from the nearest pile. He marvelled at the novel's gloriously garish cover illustration, depicting a paperback horror author's dark, demonic alter-ego consuming the brain of its own creator from within. Above that, the book title itself, presented in large, ornate lettering, looming over the ghastly spectacle below, itself swamped by Nick's own name in brighter, larger capitals, reigning over the entire dark vision of supernatural self-annihilation like the grand Master of Horror he was.

He flicked through the pages, flipping them close to his nose to inhale more of the glorious 'just published' smell, then glanced at the sincere dedication he'd placed up front.

For Myself

Nick felt himself welling up. Could he *really* destroy his greatest work since his last greatest work? Couldn't he keep just *one* copy? Surely no one would miss a single book? His Dark Fraction was hardly going to be frisking Nick when it had Roz Bloom, leather biker chick, to keep itself busy.

Nick looked around, checking no one was watching him, then tucked the paperback deep inside his jacket pocket. That would show them.

Now, if by any chance Nick *couldn't* destroy these books, he'd at least have some leverage in any reality time-share negotiation.

And maybe, who knew, maybe life in Stalkford *could* be shared between himself, his books, and an army of malevolent Nick Steen doppelgangers?

That's if *Roz* grew up and stopped trying to score points against him for spurning her professional services by engaging in some torrid, ill-starred love affair with Nick's fictional Dark Fraction.

Surely she disapproved of this particular fictional creation of his? Then why the hell was she suddenly so taken with it? Was its fire-belching really that alluring? Nick was beginning to wish he hadn't bothered mourning her presumed death, after all.

Something flickered in the corner of Nick's eye, drawing his attention. He shuddered when he saw what it was, almost completely concealed in the surrounding darkness. (Nick's eyes had adjusted by now, having previously and safely disposed of his *final* match.)

He *was* being watched.

Steeling himself, Nick squeezed himself between the piles of books and edged closer to the dark, imposing figure staring at him from the far side of the room. Though the thing itself wasn't moving, its eyes seemed to follow Nick as he drew closer to it, boring deep into his soul.

Then Nick saw there were *more* figures beside it. *Hundreds* of them.

Identical figures.

'They've *moved*,' whispered Nick.

How they'd got here, he didn't know, unless Clackett had accidentally manufactured even more than they were prepared to admit, but the numerous cut-out promotional headboards of Nick Steen holding his copy of *The Dark Fraction* were no longer confined to the main entrance of the warehouse, but were instead gathered here, as if to stand guard over Nick's condemned novel.

Nick reached for his matchbox again, realising he could get rid of them all, *plus* his books, in one fell swoop. Hell, it would be *easy*.

Then gasped loudly at the cruel trick Fate had in store.

He'd already lit his *final* match.

Now there was no way of igniting the cut-outs, *or* his books. (To be fair, he hadn't figured out an escape plan for himself, either, meaning ultimately his failure to set light to the room was beneficial, in that he wouldn't be flame-grilled as a result.)

Thrown, he took a moment to peruse in detail the cut-out of himself. He'd always been impressed that his physical presence matched the essential *power* of his fiction. How sad it was, then, that *The Dark Fraction* must now go. How crazy it was of Roz to have rejected *this* version of Nick, swapping him for an idealised, leather-clad fantasy she'd never be likely to meet in real life.

Except she *had* met him, Nick realised. His fantasy world was alive and kicking, and threatening to dash the *real* Nick Steen from existence.

263

Nick grabbed hold of himself (not literally). What had he been thinking? How mad he'd been to presume that his Dark Fraction would ever accept life ruled by the chief orchestrator of this entire concept? His Dark Fraction wanted him *dead*.

Nick froze.

The cut-out had moved again.

Was he going crazy? It had been standing right here looking at him half a minute ago, yet now it was several feet closer.

As were the others.

Surely not? Surely Nick had inadvertently stepped back while he was thinking about Roz? But no. He was standing exactly where he'd stood before. He knew that because he had one hand placed on the nearest pile of books in a proud and affectionate manner.

Then the cut-outs stepped towards him *again*.

Nick couldn't believe his eyes.

And again.

Hell, they were *alive*.

Nick watched in horror as their legs suddenly tore free from their backboards, creasing jaggedly at the knees as they moved forwards as one, arms tearing free, too, as they reached out for him with their hands.

Terrified, Nick turned and ran, crashing immediately into a tall pile of his own stacked novels, which teetered and fell in an untidy pile about him.

He scrabbled blindly over the books, legs kicking out awkwardly as he stumbled, sending more of the towering books toppling downwards.

He had to get out of here. *Somehow.*

Sensing the cut-outs closing in, Nick heard the occasional squeak and snap of their corrugated limbs folding forwards and backwards in their urge to capture him. If that happened, they'd crush him, give him horrendous paper cuts by rubbing along his body at the wrong angle. Grimly, he realised he'd never be able to defeat them if they managed to gather themselves about him en masse, as the combined strength of cardboard – particularly three-ply fibreboard with large strength-to-weight ratio born of wavy, fluted corrugation layers sandwiched between a smooth outer facing – would prove insurmountable if placed side by side, thus increasing overall density.

Then Nick remembered. 'Bruford!' he yelled out in panic. 'You've gotta help me, buddy!'

But there was no reply. Dammit, where the hell had the dugong got to? He'd been right here in Nick's mind just minutes ago. So where was he now?

'Bruford, I need your help, dammit!'

'Apologies, Nick, but I currently have problems of my own to attend to.'

'I'm being chased by an army of cardboard Nick Steens, Bruford. Some form of hellish spell cast upon my own image, I suspect by one of my Dark Fractions. Probably the one who's an Elizabethan occult magician from book seven in my proposed series.'

'To repeat, Nick, I'm otherwise engaged. As a matter of fact, I'm starting to lose your telepathic signal entirely, as I'm currently being winched up into the air by an industrial crane, which plans to lower me into some as-yet-to-be-defined mechanical contraption that will theoretically dissolve my swollen mass so effectively that I can soon be fed back into the digestive system of local pigs.'

'Bruford!' screamed Nick, but it was too late. The dugong had once more fallen silent.

'Dammit,' Nick yelled, turning again to see that the cardboard army of Nick Steens were hot on his tail. Scrambling in a total panic, Nick hurled himself towards another wall of piled books, hoping that the collapsing towers might somehow delay his pursuers.

But his pursuers had already caught up with him.

He did his best to tear the first ones apart, bruising and slicing his knuckles annoyingly in the process. As they clamped Nick down, wrapping themselves around him, folding in on him from all sides, leaping on top of each other to increase and press home their combined weight, Nick felt himself giving up.

It was useless, he realised. Though he'd done his best, his Dark Fractions had done better.

Much better.

★

He felt himself being carried from the room, transported inside the cardboard box constructed entirely out of his own selves like a man being carried to his own funeral (this is extremely apt, by the way), until at long last, he felt himself deposited roughly on a hard surface with a heavy bump.

The bastards hadn't even packed bubble wrap round him.

A terrifyingly sharp metal blade plunged through the cardboard, severing a neat line all the way from the vicinity of Nick's head, down to his feet.

As the cardboard flaps were pulled back, blinding light from an overhead bulb prevented Nick from identifying who had cut him free and now stood triumphantly over him.

'Hey, buddy,' said a voice Nick recognised as his own. Shielding his eyes from the light, he realised the blade he'd avoided was, in fact, a scalpel. Then Nick made out a white medical lab coat.

'Hate to break this to you, buddy,' said Doc Steen, M. D., 'but there's nothing more I can do for you. I just need you to sign this.' The medical Dark Fraction handed Nick a piece of paper and pen.

'What is it?' Nick asked, weakly.

'Essentially, it indemnifies me against your death under surgery. Which is guaranteed, sadly, now that you're our prisoner.'

'Balls,' said Nick, pushing the paper away. 'I'm not dead yet.'

'Look, buddy,' said Dr Nick Steen, M. D. 'We're multiplying at the rate of a thousand every hour. As you're no doubt aware, the fictional writer we murdered and put into that prawn masala you ate wrote numerous other versions of us before he died, as did all subsequent manifestations of his memory that you aimed to include as flash-backs in the later novels, meaning those particular memories of the writer are also busy writing more books. It's an uncontrollable outbreak of Dark Nick Steens we can no longer contain, Nick, currently approaching a conservative estimate of eighteen million and counting. So your prospects aren't great.'

This is it, then, thought Nick, resigned to his fate. Maybe death *would* be preferable, after all. It certainly looked like the time-share idea he'd had would be a complete nightmare to organise.

'Where is he?' said a voice, behind them.

As Dr Steen stood back, another face loomed into view, staring down at Nick with a cruel grin.

'Hi, Nick,' said Roz.

CHAPTER TEN

'We're all here,' she said, yanking Nick into a sitting position and twisting his neck so he could get a good view of his surroundings. He saw he'd been deposited in the centre of a vast factory floor filled with ancient, cranking machinery. The plant consisted of several levels, darkly lit in colours of dense orange and blue, with plumes of steam and fiery vapours shooting out from unseen smelting pots and deep, industrial basements.

Yet swamping entirely all this convoluted technical hardware, were Nick's Dark Fractions. Before him stood every conceivable config-uration of dark double his warped imagination had ever dreamed of. He ran his eyes past the terrifying legions massed around him, briefly glimpsing the heart-stitched wrestler again, now wearing the legless old man as a victory belt (his ancient, boneless wrists were tied together at the demon's waist).

Some distance beyond, and clearly the centrepiece of this gigantic industrial operation, was a vast grinding bowl, about fifty-foot high, that turned, via a complex system of pulleys, in slow, relentless circles. From its centre rose an unholy cloud of toxic vapour, which Nick already found himself gagging upon. Whatever was being ground down within it was creating possibly the foulest stench Nick had ever inhaled.

'The pulping mill, Nicky Boy,' said his Dark Fraction, pushing himself through the ranks of doubles and moving Roz aside so that he could assume full control of proceedings. The moustachioed demon pointed up at the giant, twisting pot.

'That's where your books would have ended up. Now it's where *you're* going.' The Dark Fraction glanced over at Roz. 'Right, baby?'

'Right,' Roz replied.

'I don't get you, Roz,' said Nick. 'How come you were all against my book and series proposal, and yet as soon as you encounter some romantic, fantasised ideal of raw masculinity, you're all over it like a Mills & Boon swooner.'

'Because as nasty and cruel as this Dark Fraction is,' said Roz, slipping one arm around the demon's waist, 'he at least remembers our conversations and listens to what I have to say, *when* I say it.'

Nick sighed, yawning deliberately as well. 'Not that old chestnut.'

'Whether you believe it or not, Nick, your work *does* need an editor once in a while.'

'*Once*, perhaps. To re-paragraph things a bit more clearly.'

'Is that so, Nick?' Roz replied, her anger building.

Nick's Dark Fraction winked at him, necking down another flaming Bourbon as Roz finally went off on one. 'Christ, can't you see how formulaic this all is?' she roared. 'Here we are, yet again, in a version of one of your books that includes me being abducted, you being the sole hero and everything ending in some ludicrous confrontation with a massive legion of supernatural creatures in front of some vast melting pot into which someone is inevitably about to be thrown. It's formulaic trash, Nick. All I ever attempt to do is tidy up your writing a bit and try to remove the obvious clichés, plus excise anything that's borderline offensive, which is a huge job, and all that *is* offensive, which is a *massive* job. And what thanks do I get?'

'Fine. *Thank you*, Roz,' said Nick, winking back at his Dark Fraction, pleased they'd found a common bond at last via age-old appreciation of the fiery female. 'But I think you're still fencing, to be honest. I think you're *truly* annoyed with me for having moon-lighted behind your back with a rival publisher and failing to memorise anything about the past successes we once shared. I think you're annoyed that I dedicated this book to myself rather than you, even though I promised you, crossing my heart, that my next book would be the one; would definitely, *absolutely* be dedicated to you, my publisher, Roz Bloom, despite me saying the self-same thing about my last three books, then jokingly implying you'd probably need to pay me a small fee for the privilege.'

'Yes, Nick. That as well.'

'Enough of this crap,' said Nick's Dark Fraction, tossing aside another empty bottle. 'Put him in the pot.'

'No,' Nick yelled as a hundred arms reached in from all directions to seize him, grabbing at his flesh. 'Don't do that. Don't put me in the pot.'

Before Nick knew what was happening, he was dragged from the box and hoisted towards the pot.

'Too late, Nicky Boy,' the doppel-biker jeered (another one nixed by Tony Clackett). 'Should have pulped us when you had the chance. From this moment on, *I'm* the chief orchestrator of this entire narrative concept. From now on, I'll be mixing my internal voice with my own ordinary voice whenever I like, wherever I like, blurring the lines, fracturing the logic, and there's not a goddamned thing you can do about it. Come on, boys. Let's *pulp* him.'

Nick lashed out in vain as he was dragged across the factory floor and deposited on a large, sloping surface that he soon realised was the giant conveyor belt running up to the main pulping machine.

'Oh, Lord! Oh, Jesus Christ!' Nick yelled, then remembered they'd both forsaken him long ago. As had the Devil, so there was no support that end, either.

In vain, he fought and kicked out wildly against his enemies, but was carried ever closer to the rim of the whirling pit. He glimpsed jets of black, humid vapour rising upwards from the interior. And though he'd yet to set eyes upon the horrendous whirling brew within, Nick found himself gagging on the sharp, rancid scent of some poor bastard's disintegrating, waterlogged prose.

'You devils!' Nick screamed. 'You demonic Dark Fractions, you!'

'We're *you*, Nicky Boy,' said a voice to his left, and Nick saw that his double was right beside him on this final walk of death, smiling cruelly at him, tossing a spent cigarette it had lit with its own breath towards Nick's roll-neck sweater, which immediately caught fire.

'Roz! Help! It's cashmere.'

But Roz did nothing to help. Nick tried pleading with her, but was immediately forced to admit that he really *must* have pissed her off, despite him thinking she'd just get over it.

Suddenly remembering he was burning, Nick looked down at his stomach. The bright red coal at the centre of the fag stub his Dark Fraction had flicked was burning a neat, circular hole through his sweater. As the blazing cherry tore through the woollen lining, lodging deep inside Nick's tummy button, he gave out a horrific scream, flailing wildly and violently as his navel began to hiss.

Amidst a frenzy of thrashing, Nick fought like a demon to upend the flaming intruder, managing at long last to repel the white-hot coal by rolling himself back and forth, until he finally saw it bounce free, hotter than ever, and roll from sight along the conveyor belt behind.

But Nick had little time to celebrate this minor victory. Within seconds, he was being dragged up a set of steep stairs and hoisted over the steaming rim of the pulping machine, his head thrust across its edge so that he could finally get a good look at the foul, whirling sludge below.

'That's where you're going, Nicky Boy,' said the Dark Fraction, lighting another cigarette with its breath.

'Bye, Nick,' Roz yelled. 'You know,' she added, her voice softening slightly, 'if you'd listened to me in the first place, none of this would be happening. We'd probably be back in my office, discussing your next vision. Maybe I'd even be making you your favourite cup of Irish coffee.'

As the Dark Fractions began to tip Nick forwards into the pot, he fought back wildly, resisting as hard as he could.

'Maybe so, Roz,' he shouted desperately over his shoulder. 'Except you're right. It *is* too late. But remember this. Though you may enjoy life without me, get what you want in the short term – excitement, cigarettes, regular leatherwear catalogues in the mail – there's only one man living who can fight these demons, and you're casting him into the pot. So when you finally wake up and smell the gravy I'm about to become part of, Roz, when Horseshoe Moustache Boy here inevitably dumps you, maybe you'll realise I wasn't that bad a Nick Steen, after all.'

Then the hands holding him withdrew and he was alone on the brim, staring down into the grey, swirling abyss.

'Not quite, Nicky Boy. Because you have company.'

Nick heard a scream and turned to see that Roz had also been thrust upwards beside him.

'Like you said, buddy. She's the one who *really* wanted us pulped.'

'See what I mean, Roz?' said Nick.

'My God, Nick,' said Roz, attempting in vain to slap Nick's Dark Fraction across the kisser. 'He's ... he's worse than *you*.'

'It's like I told you, Roz. Now you're realising I'm not such a bad Nick Steen, after all.'

'Dammit, you're always right, Nick,' said Roz, tearfully. 'And because of my foolish and reckless change of heart, we now have no way at all of destroying your books. I really shouldn't have let your Dark Fraction sweet-talk me like he did. I guess you're probably happy now, in a way. Given that your books are going to survive, after all.'

'On the contrary, Roz. I wish they were being pulped alongside us.'

'Truly, Nick?'

'Initially I wanted them saved, Roz. But since then I've under-gone some kind of emotional arc that has, ironically, made me realise that the destruction of my books is in fact the only way of destroying these true monsters of my id, all of whom are collect-ively personifications of the negative aspects of my tortured personality, or metaphorical *ego*, if you will. Thus, to find true happiness, I must destroy that which I love the most, which isn't you Roz, incidentally – myself and possibly my family come first, *if* they deign to apologise. But I guess I've found a catharsis of sorts in the slaying of my own demons. Although we're not *quite* there, yet, narratively speaking.'

'No, Nicky Boy, you're *not*. Not by a long shot.'

And with that, the hands of Dr Nick Steen, M. D. and various other Dark Fractions shoved Nick forwards one last time, thrusting him and Roz violently into the steaming chasm.

They fell together, arm in arm, screaming at the top of their voices, down towards the steaming whirlpool far below them, shutting their eyes instinctively as they plunged ever closer to the swirling mael-strom of eviscerating liquid.

Which suddenly and, quite inexplicably, rose. And *rose*. Higher and higher, *towards* them.

'*Shield yourself, Nick. I can no longer contain the swelling.*'

'Bruford?' Nick yelled, incredulous.

'*That's correct, Nick. It's me.*'

Nick opened his eyes, scarcely able to believe what he was seeing. Both he and Roz were plunging towards the moustachioed nose of a vastly swollen Bruford the psychic dugong, who himself was swirl-ing mindlessly in the eddying sludge below and expanding outwards, towards them, at terrifying speed.

Nick's childhood friend was even more immense than before. Fatter and slimier than any other dugong in earthly history.

'It's a dugong, Nick!' yelled Roz. 'A hugely swollen, rancid, half-decayed, dying dugong!'

'A hugely swollen, rancid, half-decayed, dying *psychic* dugong,' replied Nick, correcting her.

'A word of explanation, Nick, while you both fall. Ultimately, the authorities elected to deposit me inside this industrial pulping machine, into which you and Roz are now plunging. Unfortunately, the unknown chemicals used by Clackett's cheap foreign manufacturing plants have reacted with my natural gases in the pulping mix, bloating me to an almost unimaginable size at record speed. And now the swift and sudden shifting of my stalled and unholy metabolism is about to wreak the ultimate havoc, Nick.'

'Nick!' cried Roz. 'I can hear the voice of Liam Neeson.'

'It's Bruford the psychic dugong, Roz. I presume you took in what he just said?'

'About how he got into the pulp machine? Yes, Nick, I heard that. A bit fortuitous, I'd argue. Certainly, if this were one of your books, Nick, I'd have recommended you leave this part out. It's a bit *deus ex machina*, for my liking.'

'Well, that's where you'd be completely wrong, Roz, because were this a book, which it's *not*, you'd have realised that Bruford's appearance in the 'nick of time' was in fact well foreshadowed by his earlier appearances in what, for want of a better word, I'll call "the text", including a moment where he'd specifically mentioned he was being transported via a waste-disposal lorry through this very industrial estate. I guess your inability to communicate with him telepathically means that you missed that crucial piece of information, Roz.'

'I guess you're right, Nick. Meaning that if this were a book, which it isn't, then I simply haven't been paying close enough attention to the details.'

'A bit like failing to remember things that happened in the past, Roz?' Nick asked, wryly.

'Touché, Nick. Yes, something like that.'

'Nick, sorry to interrupt, but I am about to explode.'

Then Bruford exploded. A titanic force of purulent, toxic gas and blubber, blasting Nick and Roz skyward at terrifying speed, rocketing them up into the air with the sheer, primal force of detonating dugong.

Instinctively, Nick reached out and grabbed Roz's hand in his and held on to her for dear life. She might well not understand why Nick's work ultimately didn't require any editing, but no one deserved to die being flung from an exploding psychic dugong they'd only just met.

They hit the far wall at full force, cushioned from the impact by the thick oil and fat in which they were now cocooned. Meanwhile, devastating tremors rocked the entire building as Bruford's internal and external viscera continued to burst asunder, sending the creature's weightless, discarded flesh-sac flying off like a popped balloon.

As Nick and Roz began their slow, inexorable slide down the wall towards what remained of the factory floor, Nick watched the rest of Bruford's innards rain down upon all below through thick, choking clouds of the dugong's internal gases. In the distance, he glimpsed what remained of Bruford's outer skin spiralling to earth like a downed zeppelin. Nick looked away, respectfully, then pointed out what appeared, from this distance, to be numerous fires raging across the factory floor.

'What the hell's happening down there, Nick?' Roz yelled through the fetid slime. Nick turned to her, removing a clump of Bruford's wet moustache strands from her face, so that she could get a better look.

'It's Bruford's toxic internal oils, Roz. They've somehow set fire to everything below us, causing a massive inferno that I presume is now threatening to engulf the entire building.'

'*That's correct, Nick.*'

It was Bruford again. Though from what dimension of reality he was now communicating, Nick hadn't a clue.

'*I'm actually still alive at this moment, Nick. My right eye and forehead are still vaguely intact and currently sliding in the manner of spilled jelly down the opposing conveyor belt, back across the factory floor.*'

'But you'll burn down there, Bruford!' Nick yelled. 'The *fire—*'

'*It was that cigarette stub, Nick. The one that landed in your belly button. A red-hot cherry when it went in, but the thick nest of tummy button hair you always fail to remove, despite polite requests from your family, subsequently enclosed the hot coal, choking it and intensifying the heat within to white-hot levels, until it finally emerged from your stomach, stoked by your unnatural thatch of flaming button fluff, and continued to burn ever more fiercely as it rolled down the conveyor belt into the room behind, where your books were stacked.*'

'Meaning they've now caught fire,' muttered Nick, sadly.

'*I'm afraid so, Nick. But that means your Dark Fractions have also caught fire. And now that I've exploded, too, sending my flammable oils and toxic gases into the mix, there's such an unholy conflagration of flame that anything living in our immediate vicinity will now be utterly destroyed.*'

'Including us?' said Nick, grasping Roz's hand even more tightly in his as they slid ever closer to the approaching inferno.

'*As luck would have it, Nick, the brick wall you and Roz are now sliding down was weaker and more fragile than the others. Consequently, a large hole has been ripped through a lower partition by the sheer force of my ignited fartage. Thankfully, the resultant passageway leads out into the industrial estate's outer grounds.*'

Nick grinned, shaking his head. He could hardly believe it. Despite its nauseating odour, Bruford's flaming death–grunt had saved both their lives.

He and Roz finally reached the floor, sliding across it together in their own fetid pool. As they slapped themselves free of Bruford's goo, Nick spied, through the smoke and flames, the grim vision of his collected Dark Fractions burning to a crisp.

'It's over, Roz,' he said, dragging her with him through the hole in the blasted wall. Then they ran as fast as they could towards the rays of dying sunshine they'd already glimpsed up ahead. 'We've done it, Roz. My Dark Fractions have been defeated.'

'Not *quite*, Nicky Boy,' said a rasping voice. Nick and Roz froze, staring at the black and terrifying thing blocking their path to freedom. Its form still resembled Nick's, yet the thing staggering towards them was now a charred and blackened husk, its horseshoe moustache almost completely gone, smoke rising from still-burning limbs as bright patches of flame licked greedily around its extremities. The figure reached up with one blackened skeletal arm to light a cigarette from its burning armpit.

'Let's go, baby,' it said, indicating the Honda bike behind it, upon which it had evidently managed to evade the fiery devastation on the factory floor. 'Let's ride.'

'What the hell are you doing, Roz?' said Nick. But Roz was already stepping forwards, dazed, to join the Dark Fraction once again. 'Roz!'

'You forgot it, Nick,' growled the Dark Fraction, taking Roz's hand in its own. 'You forgot the *book*.'

'What book?' said Nick. 'What the hell are you talking about?'

Then he remembered. The copy he'd kept back. The one tucked away inside his jacket pocket. *He* was the one who'd inadvertently kept his doppelganger alive.

The Dark Fraction yanked Roz violently towards him and thrust a full bottle of Bourbon close to her throat.

'One hiss of my breath, Nick, and she's *really* hot air. Hand it over.'

Nick's hand hovered near his jacket pocket. Could he really do it? Sacrifice his only remaining copy?

'I'll flame her, buddy. I'm in charge now. The chief orchestrator of this entire concept. Give me the book. Or she *dies*.'

Nick pulled the paperback from his pocket. Examined the gorgeous cover once more. Flipped the aromatic pages under his nostrils. Sampled a final snippet of his dark, visionary prose.

The last copy in the world.

'It *deserves* to live, Nick. It's your masterpiece. Look what it created.'

The burning double grinned at him, exposing a jagged row of blackened, loosening teeth. The demon was right. Nick *had* done a brilliant job. It was one of the most horrific things his mind had ever created.

'Destroy it, Nick,' said Roz, from behind the demon's arm. 'Forget about me. Destroy the book and save yourself.'

Nick looked at her, bravely offering up her own life for his.

An *editor*.

'I can't, Roz. You mean too much to me.' He turned back to the Dark Fraction. 'Here, catch.'

He tossed the book across. Instinctively, his scorched double released Roz from its arms, giggling insanely as it grabbed frantically at the flying book.

With flaming hands.

'And *burn*,' said Nick.

Its laughter turned to hellish shrieking as the pages erupted in flames.

Nick watched as the demon collapsed to the ground, still clutching *The Dark Fraction*. Then, together, Nick's creations slowly burned away to nothing.

'It's over, Roz,' said Nick, as she rushed across to embrace him. '*Really* over.'

'I don't know what came over me, Nick. I'm sorry. Nothing's making much sense.'

'It *is* one of my novels, Roz,' he said, smiling up at her (she was actually a lot taller than Nick).

Laughing, Nick mounted the Honda motorcycle he'd always yearned to own, and found, miraculously, that he could now ride it.

'What about Bruford, Nick?' Roz asked.

'He'll be okay,' Nick replied. 'And by the way, it was Carlo's.'

'Sorry, Nick?' she said, looking confused.

'Carlo's Restaurant. That old Italian place on Gray Street. The place where you first signed me up. And your welcome gift was a fountain pen hewn from cat bone, with blotchy red "massacre effect" ink, inscribed by yourself in mock-Gothic font, with a concealed nude woman beneath the outer casing that lost her skin when you tipped it upside down so she turned into a saucy tissue-fibre skeleton before your very eyes.'

'Oh, Nick,' Roz said, her eyes gleaming. '*Nick.*'

He smiled, helping her up on to the saddle. Then glanced back at the flaming factory.

Thanks, Bruford, old pal.

'My pleasure, Nick. Farewell.'

Sorry there was no lady dugong in the end.

'So am I, Nick. So am I.'

Nick kicked the bike into gear and sped off towards the reddening horizon. Night was approaching fast.

And the dark clouds moved with it.

THE END

FRIGHT BREAK

Welcome, friend, to page 281. You have chosen unwisely *... Now, dim the lights, grab a tissue if you need one, though I'd urge those types not to attend any signings, and enjoy this excised —* but not censored *— passage of pure, unadulterated body horror ...*

They began with my back, tearing a large layer of skin and flesh, approximately nineteen inches (neck to haunch) by twenty-three (shoulder to shoulder), down to my buttocks. I yelled aloud as the cold air brushed my exposed musculature, bracing myself for the assault on my nether regions. Luckily, I still had no feeling in my buttocks, so excruciating pain there was happily averted, but within seconds the Soul Stripper had moved on to the rear of both thighs. It stripped the skin of each down to my heels, making two small incisions around each knee to free the front sides as well, allowing both haunches to be yanked downwards under the knees and slid free over each foot, like flesh-socks. In my delirium, I wondered if they might sell them back to me at a later date so I could keep out the cold, but these monsters were beyond such niceties.

Reeling from the removal of my entire back section, I grimaced as yet more hooks flew downwards from the blackness above, impaling me anew, and immediately I was dragged upwards, to be speared afresh from below by still more hooks shooting from the floor. Suspended between unseen firmaments above and below me, I hung between infinities, half-man, half-flesh-skeleton, as the Stripper went to work on my front side.

I cried aloud in outraged fury as my front thighs were dragged upwards, curling over like scooped ice cream. The Soul Stripper severed them with two swift slices of his knife and flung them backwards, over his shoulder, where the cloud of waiting floaters descended upon them and gorged. I stared in horror as those greedy mites consumed in their entirety my carved-up flanks, then glanced below me in horror as the Soul Stripper lifted up my manhood delicately between two blades and gently clipped it free. I wasn't sure what to expect beneath my natural sheathing system, and was astonished to discover what looked like the neckline of a small diplodocus. Despite my screams, and Type-Face's assurance that this was a fright-ening medical anomaly even he could not explain, I was thankfully unable to dwell too long on my misfortune, as the Soul Stripper had by now moved on to my chest. This was removed far more quickly than I'd been expecting, and I guess I was too distracted by the sight of my own heart beating upwards against the stretched wall of my chest-muscles, as blood pumped visibly through my system via a network of exposed veins and arteries, to object.

The skin from both arms came off much like that on my legs, but this time the Soul Stripper did offer to sell it back to me as gloves. By now, I was too delirious to reply, all the while dreading the ultimate indignity, where the skin of my head would be sliced free and removed, exposing the bald pate of boned skull. No longer would I feel my glorious mane above me. No longer would my hair invigorate, strengthen and testosterise me.

The Soul Stripper went to work on my cranium, forcing both knife blades up my nostrils, slitting sideways to sever my nasal walls and provide the necessary purchase for his fingers. He reached in with both thumbs and peeled my face apart, strip-ping a long vertical line upwards to my forehead and down towards my chin, parting me like a ripe Outspan. When he'd finished loosening each cheek from the attendant bone-plate, he pulled my head upwards by the

hair and tugged me hard. One yank and my
scalp slid free from its skull like the top
half of an over-filled refuse sack, sending
my naked pate crashing back against the hard
surface of the surgeon's table, cracking it
in twain.

Relax. Is everyone alright? I hope not. Heh heh heh. Unpleasant dreams . . .

ADDITIONAL FRIGHT BREAK

Welcome, friend, to page 285 and a second helping of socially unacceptable, visceral body horror that you'd most likely be prevented from selling in physical form on eBay.

Dim the lights, etc.

While the Soul Stripper grabbed my right arm and held it down against the arm of the trolley, the old woman drew out an industrial hole-punch, clamped a handful of my jellied shoulder sinew between her fingernails and forced it underneath the circular plunger blade. I screamed anew as she leaped up and slammed her arse down hard against the handle, sending the bolt piercing through my gathered flesh. I saw a rush of stars, and when said stars finally faded, felt even more excruciating pain. I turned my head to examine my latest wound. No sooner had the old woman removed the hole-punch from me than a fresh cloud of swarming floaters commenced to infest the crater she'd just drilled. Before I could howl in protest, she'd moved on to my left side and was busy carving off a scalloped corner from my shoulder bone, admittedly a less well-known signifier of a remaindered item, but one still in occasional use among cheaper mass-market paperback publishers of predominantly pulp-based material.

Well done, traveller. You have braved the worst. Or have you? Heh heh heh. Now go back to the main story. It's page 68 if you've lost your place, fool. GM

THIRD AND FINAL FRIGHT BREAK

The excised words are as follows:

```
. . . own effluence.
```

Incidentally, while I have your attention: why not buy two copies of this book? One where the spine can be bent backwards (only slightly) and one where the spine can be preserved in its original, unbroken form for display purposes? Or why not purchase three copies or more? Or four? Perhaps you have damp issues in your home, or wish to protect your collection against potential theft? (First editions will command a premium in a year's time.) I would urge you all to think about this seriously. GM

HORROTICA SECTION

Welcome, friend, to this excised passage of spicy horror content. Be warned that if you have turned to this page while reading my book on the tube or train, and someone close by you has also read it, they could well be deducing that you are now choosing to peruse kinky shock-content on your morning commute. If this bothers you, feel free to bookmark this section for private perusal at home, ideally in your bath, bed or shed, and away from any pets. Do NOT *risk becoming tumescent on public transport. GM*

★

We went at it like there was no tomorrow, seeing as technically there was indeed no tomorrow. With my lack of lips, our passionate kissing resembled more the frenzied gnawing of plagued rats. But that only seemed to turn Roz on more, and soon she was clasping me so tightly that her fingers got stuck repeatedly between the tendons of my muscle fibres and I had to help prise her digits free. But my diplodocus bone made up for any delay, rearing upwards, roaring and beating time with Roz's hand as she throbbed me raw (technically raw-er), leaning in close to nuzzle the loosened strands of my exposed vocal cords, causing them to crackle with passion like a telephone dialling tone prior to the sauciest of calls. Then Roz rode me like a butcher's cutting machine, handling and fondling my flayed meat like a professional bone saw.

Then, when my eyeballs finally fell backwards into their sockets, Roz eased her blitzkrieg, reaching in to retrieve them both, sucking them clean and flicking their distended stalks back and forth with her tongue, before showing them every delight her body could proffer, up close and far more *deeply* personal than anything I might have imagined myself (at one point, I even saw the interior of her ear).

This damned *vixen*, I thought as she slotted each eye back into its socket and bade me tend to her village green. Duly I reared my mower, revved its lever dangerously (it was a petrol model), then mowed her straight for ten whole minutes, row after wild row, not stopping once, even when she briefly got something caught in my mechanism (to reassure the concerned, the lawnmower here is a metaphor). As the sun finally came out and her sprinkler hose at last erupted (this is also a metaphor), we collapsed, exhausted, on to a heaped pile

of soggy grass cuttings in the brim-full
garden bin of our love (again, another
metaphor, although I have done it in a
garden bin).

Now go and shower. GM

GARTH MARENGHI'S
ACKNOWLEDGEMENTS

Above all, myself. I dreamt it. Endured it. Suffered it. Wrought it, screaming, into meaning. I sat in a chair for whole days. Hurt my hands. Got a bad back. Fought with floaters. Forwent walking. Overate. But, ultimately, pulled myself through.

To bring you all . . . my TerrorTome.

Volume One (in three parts).

Yes, above all, myself.

Myself.

MATTHEW HOLNESS'
ACKNOWLEDGEMENTS

My agents Matthew Turner and Anthony Mestriner for making it all possible, and for their unfailing support and encouragement throughout. My editor Myfanwy Moore, who saw potential in Garth's writing (despite what he said to her last time), endured my own delays, yet never failed to inspire, cheer and embolden (again, not tautologous as there are subtle nuances in meaning). Harriet Poland, Tom, Dominic, Kate, Alice, Erika, Liam, Lewis, Kwaku and all the team at Hodder for their much-valued assistance.

Joe Avery for another wonderful cover illustration, Hal Shinnie for Garth's photograph, Alisdair Wood for the glorious map of Stalkford and Alice Lowe for advice, inspiration and friendship.

Finally, to my parents for seeing me through the whole thing, and my partner Sarah Dempster, who read it all first and prised me frequently, weeping in despair, from several corners. And for Clara, who I love more than any pulp novel, and who held the camera defensively all the while Garth was snapping at her.

Thank you, all.